KAREN HARPER

BROKEN BONDS

MIRA®

MIRA

ISBN-13: 978-0-7783-1735-7

Recycling programs for this product may not exist in your area.

Broken Bonds

For questions and comments about the quality of this book, please contact us at CustomerService@Harlequin.com.

www.MIRABooks.com

Printed in U.S.A.

Praise for the novels of *New York Times* bestselling author Karen Harper

"Harper, a master of suspense, keeps readers guessing about crime and love until the very end, while detailed descriptions of the Amish community and the Ohio countryside add to the enjoyment of this thrilling tale."

—*Booklist* on *Fall from Pride* (starred review)

"Danger and romance find their way into Ohio Amish country in a lively and endearing first installment of the Amish Home Valley series."

—*Publishers Weekly* on *Fall from Pride*

"Harper's description of Lisa and Mitch fighting the river and braving the elements are so realistic the reader can almost feel the icy winds. A tale guaranteed to bring shivers to the spine, *Down River* will delight Harper's current fans and earn her many more."

—*Booklist* (starred review)

"Haunting suspense, tender romance and an evocative look at the complexities of Amish life—*Dark Angel* is simply riveting!"

—Tess Gerritsen, *New York Times* bestselling author

"A compelling story...intricate and fascinating details of Amish life."

—Tami Hoag, *New York Times* bestselling author, on *Dark Road Home*

"Well-researched and rich in detail... With its tantalizing buildup and well-developed characters, this offering is certain to earn Harper high marks."

—*Publishers Weekly* on *Dark Angel*, winner of the Mary Higgins Clark Award

Also available from
***New York Times* bestselling author Karen Harper**

Cold Creek

FORBIDDEN GROUND
SHATTERED SECRETS

Home Valley Amish

UPON A WINTER'S NIGHT
DARK CROSSINGS (featuring "The Covered Bridge")
FINDING MERCY
RETURN TO GRACE
FALL FROM PRIDE

Novels

DOWN RIVER
DEEP DOWN
THE HIDING PLACE
BELOW THE SURFACE
INFERNO
HURRICANE
DARK ANGEL
DARK HARVEST
DARK ROAD HOME

Visit karenharperauthor.com for more titles

Thanks as ever to my husband, Don, and to
our good friends Dr. Roy and Mary Ann Manning.

BROKEN BONDS

1

Even the look of the place scared her, but she was determined to go in. Three hunt hounds on the rickety porch came to attention, barking and growling, so she stayed in the truck until the front door opened and a thin woman came out. Charlene Lockwood rolled down her window and waved as if they were best of friends and she was just here for what the mountain folk called a "set down." The ramshackle house was a far cry from the Navajo hogans she was used to and yet somehow it was the same situation—hungry, maybe abused kids, in impoverished and often rocky family situations.

With a gruff word, the woman Char assumed was Mrs. Elinor Hanson quieted the beagles. They sat, flicking their tails. Did the dogs mean she'd find Mr. Hanson here, too? It was wild turkey and squirrel hunting season, and she'd heard the bangs of shotguns echo off the rocks when she'd left the other cabin she'd called on today.

Hoping the dogs would stay put, she slowly opened

the truck door and climbed down. She slung her big purse over her shoulder and started uphill from the narrow pull-off on the road. She had to bite back a smile. She'd misheard on the phone when she'd been asked to see this family in Hanson Holler. Char had thought the visit on behalf of the Childhood Education in Appalachia Project was to Handsome Hollow, but this place was a far cry from that.

The old house with its tilted and patched roof sat back in a played-out coal seam under the hunched shoulders of the mountain. No old sofa on the porch this time, but a stovepipe stuck out a window, and there was an outhouse. The cold weather and her nerves made her want to use it, but that would be no way to start here. How was she ever going to make a dent in the real mountain here—the mountain of kids who seldom got to school where they would be given "breakfast, lunch and learnin'," as her last client had called it.

"How do!" Mrs. Hanson called out. "Welcome to the holler."

"How do! Mrs. Hanson. I'm Charlene Lockwood, the county agent visiting the homes of children who would be helped by good attendance in school. Is your daughter, Penny, here today?"

"Right sure is. Need her for chores with the new baby and all. She's afixin' dinner. Make yourself to home, come in and set a spell, get you some squirrel stew."

Char knew not to turn that down, though she'd had her fill of the same with her previous client. It was a chewy, gamey meat that not only stuck to your ribs, but seemed to gnaw at them. But out West near the Navajo reservation, if you were offered mutton and fry bread, you ate it. Here it was squirrel and biscuits. If only things hadn't gone so bad out West. Despite the fact she'd been born in Cold Creek, had two sisters who had welcomed her and given her shelter, even the fact she had found some employment in the four months she'd been back, she still didn't feel at home.

Despite the wood-burning stove, it was chilly in the house, but Char knew it would be rude to keep her coat on. The place looked to be a main room with two small bedrooms out the back. Elinor Hanson bounced her one-year-old son, Franklin, on her lap while Simon, a toddler, played with pots and pans on a blanket spread on the floor. Elinor said Crayton, age four, was out with his pa. Penny, a mere wisp of a blonde girl, aged ten, who looked to be about six, served them at a table while they made small talk.

"My husband Henry's out with his brother Braxton from down the way," Elinor explained. "Brax is eighteen, gonna be a marine if'n he gets his test lettin' him pass high school, whatever test that is."

"Yes, it's called a GED."

"Anyhow, Henry's learnin' him huntin' with bow and arrow, so wants to learn Crayton about huntin', too. Bow huntin' cheaper than buyin' bullets. Dogs don't like it none 'cause he leaves them to home. They spook game when it's with a bow, 'cause you got to get closer than with a gun. Henry, he's between jobs right now. Worked at the gas station, got let go."

Char realized the woman was trying to talk about everything except her truant daughter, so she tried to steer the conversation away from Henry and hunting. "I'm sorry to hear that. But we'd sure like to see Penny in school this winter."

Penny's blue eyes seemed to fill her thin, freckled face, but she kept looking at her mother for answers when Char tried to question her. Even letting Penny take a small gift from her array of them hadn't made the child more talkative. With a shy "Thank you," the girl chose crayons, though Char wasn't sure there was any paper to be had. So far, no one had picked the jump ropes. Char realized one thing they had in the hills was rope of their own. She watched Penny fingering the colorful crayons through the cutout in the front of the box, but she didn't open it.

"Mrs. Hanson, you know a school bus comes up as far as Coyote Rock." Char tried again. "So if someone could get Penny down the road that far, she'd be taken right to school and brought back to the same spot, safe and sound."

Penny looked hopeful. Elinor sighed. "I'll have to ask her pa, but beholden to you for the offer. He don't trust no one works for the gov'ment. Don't like handouts, not our way, don't care what outsiders say."

"I understand that, Mrs. Hanson. And I don't work for the federal government but the State of Ohio. I'm living in Cold Creek now, was born there, too."

"So you din't leave like so many want out?"

"Yes, for a while. I grew up in Michigan, then left

there to go to school and lived out West near an Indian reservation."

"Now that will be somethin' to tell your pa, won't it, Penny? He says the real ones used to live in these parts 'fore the coal mines played out."

It was at least an hour before they rose from the table and headed toward the door with Elinor leading the way and Penny trailing. Char felt she'd built a bridge, but Henry Hanson could be a barrier big as this mountain. Out West, she'd learned the hard way not to buck "the menfolk," though she'd love to challenge them for not valuing their children and wives.

Before they followed Elinor outside, Penny tugged on Char's jacket. "I'd like to go down to school," she whispered. "Wish't you could fetch me."

"I wish I could, too, Penny. I'll be sure to tell the school you'd like to go."

"But if Pa says no…"

Elinor's voice was loud as they joined her on the plank porch. "This view beats all, though, don't it?"

"It's absolutely beautiful," Char agreed as they gazed down the stone gap through the mist toward the foothills that sheltered the small town of Cold Creek below. It was so different from the mesas and canyons in New Mexico, but it was a stunning sight. "And I hope I'll be seeing this view and both of you again soon. Please tell Mr. Hanson about the time the bus will be waiting below, and thank you both for the delicious stew and biscuits." She shook hands with both of them, though she yearned to hug little Penny to her.

Char waved as she climbed into her truck that had survived dusty, corduroy western roads and a long, sad drive back to Ohio when her bold Dads Don't Drink antialcohol campaign had met with stiff opposition from some of the local fathers and tribal elders. It had made her wary of men who browbeat or physically beat their women and children.

Despite being back in her truck, Char jolted when she heard a gun go off nearby. Hadn't Elinor said her husband was out today with a crossbow and not a gun? She gripped the steering wheel and stiffened, waiting for another shot. Nothing. She waved again and carefully headed down the narrow twisting road.

Matt Rowan never drove up into the mountains this far, but he was determined to deliver the cash, groceries and winter coats to Woody McKitrick's house here on Pinecrest Mountain. He had been a big help as a handyman and head groundskeeper in the Lake Azure area. Woody had liked to, as he put it, "talk turkey," and Matt, raised in the "big city" of Cincinnati, had learned a lot about hill country from him. Matt could picture his friend, especially in the coonskin cap he wore in cold weather, looking like old Daniel Boone or Davy Crockett as he went about his work.

The usually sure-footed sixty-year-old had fallen to his death from a cliff above the Lake Azure grounds. With winter coming, Matt wanted to help Woody's family get through the winter. His son had returned from the war in Iraq with problems and didn't hold down a job.

In the Lake Azure community where Matt lived, winter meant some hunting in the hills but mostly ice-skating parties on the lake, alpine and cross-country skiing followed by hot brandy before a roaring fire or soaking in a heated spa in the lodge. Up in the hills, winter meant hardship. And these old coal roads were so hard they were rattling the company truck and his teeth.

He was still rattled anyway from the argument he'd had on the phone yesterday with his senior partner for the Lake Azure community, Royce Flemming. Matt's dad and Royce had been lifelong friends, and Matt was honored to be his junior partner and manager of the upscale community perched on the scenic edge-of-Appalachia town of Cold Creek. When his dad died, he'd felt even closer to Royce, but recently they were at odds over the older man's fast push to drill for oil and gas in the area.

Fracking, they called it, though the actual name was hydraulic fracturing since the process involved forcibly injecting water, sand and chemicals to fracture deep shale, to release the precious products trapped inside. Just in the past few months, drilling here had gone bonkers. There was already a big break between the haves and the have-nots in this area. Now the issue of lucrative fracking contracts going to only a few select people was causing rifts among the locals. Fracking brought in business, but the truck drivers and rig men caused problems in the once-pristine area.

Money talked, but why couldn't Royce see his lucrative new business could hurt the human and natural environment of his big Lake Azure investment? So far, the disagreement hadn't permanently damaged his close relationship with Royce, even when he'd declined the opportunity to invest in Royce's new fracking company earlier this year.

Matt swore under his breath as he made another hairpin turn around the mountain, still heading up. Most of the heights around Cold Creek were foothills, but these inclines were serious stuff. The old 1970s pavement was bumpy and broken. The road was one-lane with pull-offs every couple of hundred yards so cars could pass, but he hoped he wouldn't have to do that. He remembered his dad driving the family up Pike's Peak out West when he was a kid. They got so scared of the drop-offs and the lofty view straight down that they'd turned around at the top and headed right back to civilization.

"Damn!" he muttered when he made another turn and saw a pickup coming at him. It was a rickety affair with the front bumper loose and bouncing—tied on with wire or twine. He could see two men in the cab and a mule sticking its head out of the bed of the pickup as if it were enjoying the view. The rule was that the vehicle heading up was the one to back down to the pull-off, so that was him.

He slowly inched his way backward, using the rearview mirror, his side mirrors and craning around to look out the rear window. He wasn't used to driving this truck. Why hadn't he sent someone on staff up here with this stuff? His bailiwick was his office in the lodge, talking to new owners and investors, and doing community PR. He couldn't fathom how difficult this drive would be in rain or snow.

At least the next pull-off spot was not right on the edge of a cliff. It had a sign that read Falls County School Bus Stop. Tall, scrawny pines and a few oaks had clawed their roots into the rock here and leaned out from the pull-off. He carefully backed into it, making sure his rear wheels were at least six feet from the edge. The other truck passed him with a honk and a wave and a *hee-haw* from the mule. For a moment, he just sat there, breathing hard, his heart pounding.

He reminded himself why he was determined to deliver these gifts to Woody's family personally. The guy had the guts to take a stand against the invasion of fracking in the area. The old man—sixty didn't sound old, but mountain men looked old at that age—had led peaceful protestors with hand-printed signs. They'd insisted the fracturing of the bedrock to suck out oil and gas would break up not only the rock but the families and the town. Matt knew Woody was right. He should have taken a stand, too, but he also saw the good things about fracking, like the money rolling in and, hopefully, less dependency on foreign oil. He was above all a businessman like his dad and Royce, wasn't he?

Sitting on the edge of the pull-off, he was tempted to head back down and send someone else up with the things for Woody's family. But he wanted them to know their family patriarch had not been forgotten, that he meant more than a few nice words at his funeral and a couple of hundred dollars in an envelope. He wanted Woody's widow to know how much the man had meant to him.

"Okay, up we go," he whispered just as another truck appeared, this time heading up. It was another old pickup, but the guy in it was driving too fast. The truck didn't have a front license plate, but then up here, maybe there were no real rules. Matt took a closer look. Was he nuts or was the driver wearing a ski mask? The truck didn't take the turn but headed toward him.

There was nothing he could do but yell and turn his wheels. The truck slowed but bumped into the front of his truck, pushing him back. Matt laid on the horn, held to the steering wheel, tried to get his truck in Drive, but the other truck edged it backward....

The front of Matt's truck tilted upward, throwing him back against the seat. He was going over! His stomach went into free fall though the truck hadn't yet. His back bumper pressed into the trees. The truck stopped, shuddered and hung hundreds of feet over the rocks below.

2

As she made the next sharp turn, Char gasped. A white truck with Lake Azure, Inc. painted on its side was tipped nearly off the cliff, right where the school bus stopped for the kids who lived above. She'd heard a horn honk long and loud a few minutes earlier. Maybe the truck missed the last turn and spun out, since its rear, not its front, was dangling over the edge, propped up by two trees. No other vehicle was nearby to help.

She put her emergency blinkers on and pulled as close to the cliff face as she could. She jumped down from her truck and ran across the road toward the truck. A man was inside!

"What should I do?" she shouted, her voice shrill. It sounded like a stupid question. She had to get the man out of his truck before it crashed over the edge.

The bitter, strong wind ripped at her hair and jacket. What if a blast of air tipped him off? Or maybe even if he moved. She'd swear the two tree trunks that held his truck were shaking as hard as she was.

She could hear the engine was still running. The driver opened an automatic window.

"A guy in a truck shoved me off," he shouted. "Meant to. I don't have any traction. I'm afraid if I shift my weight or open a door to jump out, I'll send it over."

The fact someone had done this on purpose stunned her. What was going on? If her cell phone worked up here, she'd call her brother-in-law, the county sheriff, for help, but she was on her own. It wouldn't help to go back up for help from Elinor and Penny.

"Don't move until I get something you can hang on to if the truck goes. I have some jump ropes I can tie together. Those trees are shaky."

"*I'm* shaky. Hurry!"

She ran to her truck and knotted together the three jump ropes she had, tying square knots because she knew they would hold. But she'd never be able to balance the man's weight if the truck went over the edge.

"I've got ropes here, but I'll have to tie the end to a tree. I don't dare drive close enough to you to tie it to my truck. It would never stretch that far."

She knotted it around the trunk of a pine tree that looked sturdy enough, though that almost took the length of one rope. This wasn't going to work.

A grinding sound, then a crunch reverberated as the truck seemed to jerk once then settled closer to the cliff edge.

"Now or never!" he shouted and opened his door fast.

Desperate, Char wrapped one end of the rope around her wrist and reached toward the man as he lunged at her. A scraping sound bruised the air. The man was tall. She clutched the collar of his leather jacket, scratching his neck. He grabbed her. She held him tight as the earth seemed to break, and the truck disappeared followed by a crunching, crashing sound below.

They were sprawled on the ground, near the edge, clinging to each other. He was big and strong but shaking. He sat up and unwound the tight rope from Char's wrist to free her hand which was going white.

"Sorry—I couldn't help," she told him as they gaped at the patch of sky where the truck had been.

"You did," he said, wiping the back of his hand across his mouth and blinking back tears. "You did. You saved my life, thank God, because someone wants me dead."

Char drove Matthew Rowan down the mountain road toward town. He explained he was not a worker, but part owner and manager of the Lake Azure properties. His hair was cut short, as if he were a military man. It was raven-black, though it was dusted with roadside dust. And he was really good-looking, despite cuts and scrapes and dirt on that solid-jawed face. His jeans, shirt and leather jacket were scraped, a mess, but she, too, looked as if she'd been rolling in the dirt.

"So, you're a Lockwood," he said when she introduced herself. "The third sister, the one who lived out West."

"Everyone knows the Lockwoods because they keep getting their names in the news," she admitted as she carefully, slowly navigated another turn. "Tess years ago when she was kidnapped, and Kate lately with all the chaos at the Adena burial mound."

"At least you know where to find the sheriff's office, since you're related to him," he said, flexing his arms and legs as if checking to see if he could move everything. "A good guy, Gabe McCord. I…I still can't believe someone would do that to me."

"So you don't know why or who pushed your truck? Was he after you specifically, do you think, or just anybody he came across? Like, do you have any enemies?" She realized how upset she was for him. Her sense of right and wrong—and the temper she had to keep under wraps—flared again just as it had when she'd had problems dealing with some of the people out West. She'd also felt angry when she'd returned to Cold Creek and learned about the horrible religious nut con man, who had her cousins in that cult out by the old insane asylum. But Bright Star Monson got her blood boiling in a far different way from this.

"With all those questions, are you sure you're not working for the sheriff?" he asked. She was surprised he could kid her right now, and it calmed her. He turned to face her again, watching her closely, making her blush under his intense scrutiny. "I'd better save all that for him. Listen, I'm not thinking straight. Now that we're down low enough, I've got to call my office, tell them what happened, that I'm okay. My cell phone went down in the truck, so could I borrow yours?"

"Sure—of course," she said, pulling over on a

straight stretch of road and putting the truck in Park. "It's in my purse, behind my seat. It doesn't work farther up in the mountains, but I think we're low enough now."

He reached down and lifted the bag onto her lap. "Heavy."

"That purse is more or less my office. I keep everything in there—my files on home visits, presents for children. Here," she said, handing him the phone, then hefting her bag onto the backseat.

She drove again as he called his office and talked to someone called Jen, explaining what had happened. The woman was upset, and her voice was so loud that Char could hear most of what she said. "Yes, I'm all right," he said. "I'm heading for the sheriff's office to report it."

"But he meant to do it?" the woman shrilled. "To kill you? But who, Matt? I can't believe it. Thank heavens you got out."

"Let's just say a Good Samaritan came along and saved me. I'll explain later."

At that, he turned to look at Char. Tears in his eyes, he pressed his lips tight together and nodded at her. The moment was somehow intimate, as if he had embraced her. Char cleared her throat and turned back to the road.

"Yeah," Matt told Jen, to answer another question. "You'd better call Royce, let him know, though he's due in tomorrow. And check the insurance papers on the truck. No, I'll call you later or be back when I can. Calm down. I'm okay. Right. Bye.

"Thanks," he told Char, ending the call and putting the phone in the storage space between the two seats.

"For the phone and for everything. I appreciate your being much calmer than she is."

She was tempted to ask if Jen was his assistant or—or what. He didn't have a ring on his left hand, but you never knew. And "Good Samaritan" or not, it was none of her business. Then, past the next curve downward, something caught her eye.

"Oh! Look, down there! I think that's your truck in that rocky ravine."

They had looked over the edge from the crash site, but the jutting rocks and trees below had hidden the wreck. He unfastened his seat belt and leaned toward her to look. "You're right," he said, so close his breath fanned the loose strands of hair by her right earlobe. "Can you pull over, so I can look down? I hope that didn't start a fire. Just got it filled up with gas."

She stopped the truck, and they both got out to peer over the rim of rock. He reached for her wrist, then her hand, whether to keep her safe or himself sane, she wasn't sure. When they saw the battered truck below, she gasped, and he swore under his breath. A fire had blackened the foliage around it like an ink spill. A crooked finger of dark smoke pointed upward from the wreck.

"Thank God it didn't hit a house, or start a rock slide," he said, his voice rough. "Maybe the guy who pushed it off was just looking for trouble with anyone, but what if someone wants me gone—down there in that?"

He shuddered and gripped her wrist harder, until

she pulled him gently away from the precipice. “No, it’s not the vehicle I always drive,” he said, as if trying to reassure himself. “My senior partner and his driver sometimes use it, but they’re out of town.”

“Then maybe he was the target. I mean, isn’t he the one helping to finance all the fracking around Cold Creek? Not everyone’s in favor of that.”

“Don’t I know.”

Char tried to remember things he said so that she could tell Gabe if Matt didn’t recall everything later. He did have a scrape on the side of his head, though he seemed clear-minded. “Sorry I didn’t get there sooner,” she murmured, almost to herself, as they climbed back in her truck.

“Glad you didn’t, or you could have been hurt. What a way to meet.”

There was another strange, silent moment between them as she put the truck in gear and they started down again. “There is a Navajo saying, ‘If you save someone’s life, you feel responsible for them.’ But I didn’t really save yours. You got out on your own and—”

“But I had you to give me courage and to hold on to.”

To have and to hold from this day forward. The words to the wedding vows danced through Char’s head, since she’d been helping her sister Kate memorize them for her December wedding.

They both jolted when a black truck drove toward them just where the one-lane road became two near the foot of the mountain. It was fracking rig workers heading up, two in the cab and four in the truck bed.

They tossed beer cans out into the bushes as they roared past. Some folks around here were afraid these people would hurt the natural environment, corrupt the rural way of life. But even before the fracking hit here, Char knew some locals resented the so-called rich folk who built luxury getaway homes or weekend places at Lake Azure. As the face man for that ritzy area, Matt Rowan could have a lot of enemies, and black pickup trucks were thick as thieves around here.

"The guys in the back of that truck are wearing black stocking caps," Matt said, craning around to look back at them. "I'm pretty sure my attacker wore a ski mask, but it could have been almost anyone who nearly sent me over the edge. And I'm going to find out who and why if it's the last thing I do."

Char wished he hadn't put it that way. Back on curves and hilly roads instead of hairpin turns on peaks, she drove them toward town.

"Again, I can't thank you enough," Matt told her as he got out of her truck and hurried around to open her door in the small parking lot next to the sheriff's office on Main Street in Cold Creek.

He was feeling worse—a sudden limp caused by a leg cramp, sore muscles all over, maybe from holding himself so tense as well as his leap for life. He was also mad as hell, but he was trying to control his fury around this woman, not take things out on her.

He figured that Charlene Lockwood was probably midtwenties to his midthirties. She was so petite next to his six-foot height. Slender, almost delicate looking, and yet she seemed as sturdy as they come, despite hands gripping the steering wheel all the way down the mountain. She emanated determination, but seemed strangely vulnerable, which, as bad as he felt, hit him like a sledgehammer. She was a looker in a saucy way with her pert nose, blue eyes and full mouth framed by sun-streaked windblown brown hair. She had a heart-shaped face and, obviously, a big heart. And no ring on her left hand, though he had more important things to worry about right now.

Sheriff McCabe came barreling out the front door of the police station as they started toward it. "Hey, Char," he called. "Thought you were visiting mountain kids truant from school. Listen, Tess and I don't want you to move out, really. Oh, Matt. Things okay out at Lake Azure? You look— Are you okay, Matt? Are you and Char here together?"

"Gabe, someone shoved his truck off a cliff on Pinecrest Mountain where I was visiting a family. I found him just before it went over."

Matt looked at Char. He suddenly felt dizzy. Yeah, that had happened to him. He was not someone else watching it from afar. "I'd better sit down," he said, taking Char's arm because that seemed natural now. "Sheriff, maybe she can come in with me—to tell at least the part she saw. I like to think I would rescue a fair maiden in distress, but it was the other way around."

Matt realized he was staring only at Char, too long,

too close. She stared back at him. The sheriff cleared his throat.

"Let's go inside. You just caught me in time, but what I had to do can wait. How about I talk to you first, Matt, and then interview Char for her perspective on all this after? Do you need a doctor?"

"Not right now. I need answers."

"Let's work on that," the sheriff said as he put his hand on Matt's shoulder and opened the door he'd just exited. "Are you claiming it wasn't an accident, but intentional? Did you get a license plate, a description of the driver?"

Matt shook his head, then looked back to make sure Char had come in, too. She was talking to the receptionist, sinking into a chair.

"It had to be a planned attack," he told the sheriff. "I'm not certain if I was the target or my senior partner, since I was in the company truck he and his driver sometimes use when he's in town and visits his fracking sites. I've never been so shocked or scared in all my life—which I almost lost."

He took a last glance at Char down the hall, just as she looked up at him and their eyes met again. A terrible day, he thought, but something good had come from it, too.

3

Matt turned down Sheriff McCabe's offer of a doctor but did take him up on using the restroom down the hall. He leaned stiff-armed on the basin and stared at himself in the mirror. A mess. But blessed. Blessed to be alive. And, despite the terrible situation, to have met the only woman he'd felt an instant attraction to for a long time. And to have looked like this. Oh, hell, worse than that. Some local lunatic might be out to kill him and he didn't have a clue who.

He washed up with water and the metal dispenser's liquid soap and dried his face and hands with paper towels. If that idiot in the black pickup with the half-hidden face had been after him, why? He must have been followed. Maybe he was being watched.

Matt walked into the sheriff's office and sat down in a chair across the cluttered desk from Sheriff McCord. "You still okay?" the sheriff asked. "Here, I got you some coffee and, sorry if that doughnut's stale, but thought you might need to eat something."

"What about Charlene? Is she okay?"

"As you may know, I'm married to her younger sister, and let me tell you, the Lockwood girls are tough cookies. Char said she was glad she was there for you."

"She's been great, though I can tell she doesn't like driving up there. She lived out West, but not in the mountains, I guess."

"She was a social worker near the Navajo Reservation for several years, an advocate for juveniles and families in the outlying areas. She left recently, still misses it, I think, though she's glad to be back with her sisters and helping kids here. At first, she worked for my wife, Tess, at her day care center. She also helped her other sister, Kate, with her archaeological dig at Mason Mound, sifting soil for ancient Adena bone fragments."

"So, she lives with you and Tess but is moving out?"

Gabe nodded and took a swig of his coffee. "Charlene Lockwood's stubborn as they come. We tried to talk her out of it but she's got a cabin rented, not so far from your area."

Matt sat up straighter. That sounded good. He didn't want to seem too pushy. He owed her dinner at the very least. Probably he owed her his life. If she hadn't arrived and tried to help him, he might not have tried to get out when he did.

"So," Gabe said, pulling out a piece of paper and taking a pen off his desk, "tell me from the beginning what happened today up on Pinecrest, any and every detail. Then, as soon as my deputy runs you home, he and I will find the site of the wreck and take a good look at it. I'll interview Char later."

"Char spotted the wreck. I ought to hire her as a bodyguard— Just kidding," he added when Gabe's eyebrows shot up. "You evidently think she's the one who needs that at her new cabin."

Gabe leveled a long look at him. "With all the outsiders in town, right. She's very idealistic, out to help anyone, especially poor kids."

Maybe he had overstepped, Matt thought. He was a far cry from poor kids, and he hadn't felt idealistic in years. Nose to grindstone, eye on the stock market and building up a big investment in the people and places of Lake Azure. He supposed, especially compared to the locals around here, he was a driven workaholic.

"Okay. Let me tell you what happened from the beginning," he said, and figured he'd start with the fact he was taking things he'd bought for Woody McKitrick's family, things that were now so much ash at the bottom of a ravine where he could have ended up the same way.

Char was disappointed when Gabe called his receptionist in the main office to say that she should go home and he'd get her story tonight. She wanted to see how Matt was doing now, maybe drive him to Lake Azure. But Gabe was going to take Matt and Jace Miller, his deputy, to see the burned wreck of the Lake Azure truck, then he'd see that Matt got home. Matt had insisted on going to the collision and crash site, too.

She headed to Gabe and Tess's big, old, recently renovated house with its newly built preschool child care center addition in front. Char had stayed first with her older sister, Kate, at her fiancé Grant Mason's large home, but the Adena dig team—college students from Ohio State University—were in and out so much it was like an open house.

But now, she'd found an inexpensive three-room rental log house, built as a hunting cabin, ironically located not too far from where Matt must live since it overlooked the Lake Azure area. The place had a great view, not to mention a fireplace, two space heaters, electricity and indoor plumbing. The man who owned it had suffered a heart attack and wouldn't be hunting—or just retreating to his man cave, as his wife had put it—until next year. Char didn't know much about him except that he owned the large racetrack outside of Columbus but had a big holiday home near Lake Azure.

"Tess, I'm home! It's just me. Gabe will be home late again!" she called as she went in the back kitchen door. The fourteen kids at the growing day care would have all left by now.

"Are you all right?" Tess cried, rushing into the kitchen. "Gabe called and said you'd rescued Matt Rowan from a burning truck up on Pinecrest!"

"It wasn't burning until after he got out of it and it went over the cliff."

"Oh, that's terrible! Thank God you were there. You look like you've been through the mill. Take a rest and wash up."

Tess gave Char a hug and helped her take her jacket

off as if she were one of the preschoolers. The two of them had their zeal for protecting kids in common, despite their different personalities and looks. They were the same height at five foot six and both had blue eyes, but Tess had blond, chin-length hair while Char's was brown with natural gold highlights. Tess looked a lot more frail and had been through real-life traumas that made Char's being threatened and forced to leave her dream job out West seem minor. As for character traits, Char figured some people thought she was too outgoing, maybe pushy. She had to admit she was a lot more stubborn than Tess, and mouthier, too, but what was right was right and she intended to say so.

While Char went to the bathroom, Tess fixed them both tea. Char had seen she had the slow cooker going with some sort of dinner in it—hopefully not a third helping of squirrel stew, but she knew better. Since Tess and Gabe's honeymoon in France, her younger sister had been serving French cuisine, which seemed pretty odd around here, though maybe not over at Lake Azure on the other side of town. After a quick change of clothes, Char joined her sister in the large kitchen.

"Char, are you listening? I said, please don't feel you have to move out. Gabe and I don't think that cabin in the woods is such a good idea, especially with the roustabout types pouring in here to work the fracking rigs and drive the water and oil trucks."

"You've both been great, but this is the first year of your marriage and Gabe doesn't need a sister-in-law guest on cozy nights this winter. Besides, the cabin's not really in the woods. I'll drive you up to see it. My cell phone works there, and it's furnished, though I'll take my own bedding and linens. I'm not far off the road and can be down to town in ten minutes—and the view is of Lake Azure, no less."

"All right, all right," Tess said, gripping her mug. "I know not to argue when your mind's made up, but I think you should at least learn to shoot a gun for protection. Gabe could teach you."

"If I lived out West in peace without one, I can do the same here. There are enough people around with guns. I'm having the locks changed on the doors, and the windows have latches. It's almost a luxury cabin, so don't worry."

"You know I do—still. But with Gabe, I'm doing better, really. I knew his job was part of the marriage. It's just I worry about some of my students, especially if they come from broken homes. I'm hardly attracting the Lake Azure kids who have nannies or stay-at-home moms who carpool their kids to school or even send the older ones to private schools."

"And you worry about your older sisters," Char added as she reached out to squeeze Tess's shoulder. Tess still bore the psychological scars of having been abducted as a child. Char's thoughts flew to little Penny up on the mountain with her box of crayons clutched in her hand and her plea to be "fetched" for school.

"You know," Tess said, "we've still got an hour of daylight left, and, like you said, Gabe will be late. How about I pour our tea into insulated cups and we drive up to look at your rental?"

"I don't have a key yet."

"We'll just peek in the windows. Before Gabe called about what happened to you, I was going to drive to the Hear Ye cult gate and ask to see Gracie. She didn't look good when I saw her at the Saturday Harvest Market, and I barely got a word in with her since they guard each other so tight. But maybe we can both try to see her tomorrow and you can show me the cabin now—unless you're too shook up from rescuing a man in distress. Matt's handsome, isn't he?"

"That was the least of my thoughts. He was more dinged up than I looked. And scared, though he hid it well. By the way, the second stop I had today was not *Handsome* Hollow like I told you at breakfast but *Hanson* Hollow, named for the several generations of the Hanson family living there. It's amazing the Appalachian project even has a record of them and their kids since they live way up there."

"Don't try to change the subject. I've seen Matthew Rowan. He gave a sort of PR talk at church after his association paid for the town's Labor Day picnic this year. What did you think of him?"

"I thought a lot of him—but I don't want to think more of him, okay? Stop looking at me that way and never mind matchmaking. If you want to see the cabin, how about you drive? My hands ache from gripping the steering wheel today."

"Which won't stop you one bit from visiting mountain cabins or living in one," Tess said with a sigh as she jumped up to pour their tea into travel cups. "Oh, no, not loves-a-challenge, champion-of-the-poor Charlene Lockwood."

"Sister of the terrific but terrible Tess Lockwood McCabe and Dr. Kathryn, dig-up-those-old-bodies, Lockwood. Well, wish I hadn't put it quite like that. Someone did try to kill Matt Rowan today—if they weren't trying to murder his senior partner who sometimes uses that truck. Matt said he has a driver. Can you imagine? A chauffeur in a truck in Cold Creek? You know, Royce Flemming is not only the money man behind Lake Azure but, the Environmental Expansion Company, alias fracking for dollars."

"Speaking of which, I guess you and Matt Rowan would be like oil and water in your lifestyles and goals, at least. But they say opposites attract."

Char heaved a huge sigh. "I didn't think of any of that, just that he needed help. I liked him, and he kind of ended up helping me, too, because he was so grateful, that's all. I've met enough controlling, overly aggressive men in my day, and if people think that makes a man masculine, they're crazy."

"That's all with him, then? The end? Okay, okay, I'll keep my mouth shut. If I know you, you'll overlook what a hunk—a wealthy one—he is and just try to hit him up for a donation to the Appalachian Children Poverty fund. I'll lock up and let's go."

The sheriff, Deputy Jace Miller and Matt stared at the shattered, burned-out hulk of the Lake Azure pickup. Matt shuddered to think of his incinerated, broken bones inside. The whole area reeked of gasoline and burned leaves and grass. At least the fire had not spread farther than the thirty-foot-wide blackened circle.

"I'll have Jace run you home, and I'll go have a look at the spot you got hit," Gabe said, craning his neck to look up at the rocky ridge of Pinecrest Mountain glaring down at them. "Never know but there might be some trace of the other truck up there. I'll ask around about who the guys with the mule in their truck could have been, too, in case they passed your attacker heading up toward you."

"The pull-off's easy to find," Matt said. "It's marked for a bus stop, but I'm thinking anywhere along the road that...that killer would have found me, he'd have tried to send me over the edge. I must have been followed."

"Or, you told someone where you were going, so you didn't have to be followed close," Jace Miller put in. "I guess you and Gabe covered that."

"Yeah, we did," Matt said. "The people in my office knew where I was going, and I'd sent word to Woody McKitrick's family that I'd stop by during the day, but not when." He shook his head. "I can't believe this. I still can't believe it happened."

"Brad Mason never drove this truck, did he?" Gabe asked. "As your partner Flemming's front man in the area, a lot of people have it in for him, too. He's been worried about his safety. He'll be part of my family when Char's sister Kate marries Brad's brother, Grant Mason, next month."

"I'm pretty sure he drives a red pickup—easy to spot, kind of flashy for around here, even for Lake Azure, where he's bought a small condo. You know, Royce wanted me to take that job, but I turned him down. Maybe some people against the fracking don't know that."

"As for the place your truck went over, I know that spot. That pull-off is near a formation called Coyote Rock, though I don't think it looks much like a coyote. Must have been one spotted up there. Jace, when we get another deputy in, it'll be a lot easier to patrol around here. Could use at least two more deputies, but at least we're getting one soon. Keeping an eye on moonshining, pot patches and meth labs in the hills near town's bad enough, but these mountains are a whole other world, not to mention the fracking."

Matt nodded. "Char and I saw some rig workers heading up Pinecrest in a black pickup, looking pretty happy, tossing beer cans out. New outsiders like that have taken some of the pressure off us Lake Azure people being the intruders."

"It's getting better," Gabe said. "Live and let live—but not kill someone by shoving them off a cliff so it looks like an accident, even suicide."

"Suicide?"

"Sorry to bring that up. When my father was county sheriff, he had a bad case where a guy drove off near Coyote Rock—meant to kill himself, but took his wife's life in the crash, too. Murder-suicide."

A chill shot up Matt's spine as the sheriff started to

pace off the circumference of the burned circle. Matt stood his ground, just staring at the charred wreck. In a way he'd been charred today, too, by meeting Char Lockwood. Crazy thought but she'd heated him up. He'd been burned a couple of years ago, and that made him gun-shy about getting serious with a woman, especially when he kept himself so busy. The women he met in Cold Creek were either married clients, or were locals he just didn't have much in common with—and then there was Ginger Green, who was after him as well as every other man in sight, so she was hardly his type. He wasn't looking for a quick hit, quick goodbye woman.

"Too bad you lost the stuff you'd bought for the McKitricks," Jace was saying. "Bet they could have used it. Gabe, didn't you say that they were on Char's list of families to visit over a truant student?"

"Yeah, that's right," Gabe said, distracted as he wrote in a little notebook.

So, Matt thought, maybe he and Char could go together to visit the McKitricks when he replaced the food and clothes he was going to give them. Not that he wanted to go back up the mountain, but he wasn't going to let this impact his freedom or his duty.

"Hey," Gabe shouted, from across the wreck. "Someone's been here gawking already. Footprints in the ash. I didn't see any on the side where you're standing."

Matt and Jace watched as he approached the truck and glanced inside. "And there's an unburned piece of paper in here with something written on it."

Jace went over to the wreck. Though the burned,

acrid smell was seeping into the pit of Matt's stomach, making him feel sick, curiosity got him. Walking in Jace's footprints, he went over to the wreck and peered in the front passenger-side window, too.

A piece of white paper was lying on the blackened front seat. He could see a drawing of a skull and crossbones, like on an old pirate flag. Under that were big, black printed letters.

YOUR FIRED!

4

"Well, I admit it is kind of quaint looking—in a pioneer way," Tess said as she drove into the narrow, short driveway of the hunting cabin.

For some reason, Char's mind flashed back to driving up to a big, modern hogan on a washboard road for the meeting where the elders and her boss had asked her to leave. But that had been set among yucca, sagebrush and pinyon pines instead of maples, oaks and tall white pines. Even the bedrock here was different; the rocks were gray, beige or black, not the yellow, brown and red rocks she'd grown used to out West.

"And, Ms. Worrywart, the logs have good chinking—insulation," Char assured her as they got out of the day care van. "And, see—there's a carport so I won't have to scrape frost off car windows in the morning."

The sun was setting, gilding the clouds with colors from lavender to pink to fiery orange, which made the view even more beautiful. They peered in all the windows, walking around the small log building.

"I like the stone fireplace and all the wood inside," Tess said. "And there's a leather couch and two upholstered chairs. The front room's a pretty good size, but that bedroom and bath are small."

"Which suits me just fine. It's got a stand-up shower, so I'll miss soaking in the tub, but that's a small price to pay."

"Did they say you could use that pile of firewood?"

"Yes, and they're not charging me for water. The water heater takes up part of the closet space, but does a guy hunting or drinking with his buddies need room for clothes?"

"Did you get the idea his wife ever comes up here?"

"It's a man's world—until now. I did get the idea, though, that his marriage isn't that happy. I feel sorry for her."

"Oh, Char, you can't solve all the world's problems, you know."

"I can try. I'll bet it's great to sit out here on this covered porch on pretty days to see the sun rise or set. Let me show you the view of the valley and lake below. If we could just erase those luxury condos and homes and that big party house down in the valley, it would look really pristine."

"They call it a lodge. It makes the one at the state park where Gabe and I got married seem like a doll's house. It does blend in with the area," she said, pointing, "like the Lake Azure houses do. Wonder which one is Matt Rowan's. What a great view here!"

Char remembered Elinor Hanson saying the same

earlier today. It seemed so long ago she'd been up on the mountain, but only moments ago she'd seen Matt sitting scared to move in his truck and then it going over....

"You okay?" Tess asked. "You kind of flinched. Did you see something below?"

"No. Just the breeze is cold. Winter's coming."

"So then spring can't be far behind, right?" Tess said, throwing her arm over Char's shoulders. They stood leaning together for a moment, looking below at the long lake that gave the area its name. As the clouds passed overhead, the water seemed to change color, one minute azure, the next almost like jade or amethyst. Smoke trailed from chimneys on a few of the shingle or slate roofs of the houses below, though some were hidden under pines. The large Y-shaped lodge with its green velvet grass golf course carved out of the hills looked lonely this late.

Funny, but Char had one of those rare moments when she wished she had a man she loved to share something with and not only a friend or a sister.

"I just thought of something sad," Tess whispered, pulling away and hugging herself.

"About that woman who lives down there? The one who's still trying to get her daughter back from her estranged husband in South America?"

"No. Just that it must have been near here, down that next ridge maybe, where that groundskeeper fell to his death, because they found his body on the golf course a couple of weeks ago—remember?"

Char gasped. "That's the man whose family Matt

was going to visit up on Pinecrest. At least, if he ended up on the golf course, he didn't fall from right here. He must have been over there a little ways to fall straight down, though that doesn't look like a place someone would trip." Again she fought to banish the memory of Matt's truck pitching over the side into nothing but air.

"Gabe said the death was accidental but weird because he was a mountain man, sure-footed, knew the area, all of that. But up on these paths and ridges, anything can happen, so you've got to be really careful. And if this is a hunting cabin, there may be shooters in these woods and—"

"And I'll be careful," Char said, cutting off any more dire warnings. She had to always be on guard to stay the optimist to Tess's worries and levelheaded to their sister Kate's brilliant but scary what-if theorizing. "I'll be away during the day anyway, and people would be crazy to try to hunt anywhere around here at night."

But, Char had to admit, some folks were crazy around here. Starting with someone who would kidnap kids like Tess or push someone's truck over the side with them in it. And maybe, live out alone in a cabin, almost on the edge of a cliff.

"You didn't need to fly in early," Matt told Royce Flemming when he arrived at Matt's door just after dark. He'd just taken a shower and was considering going over to the lodge to get some hot food and try to relax in the spa and sauna.

"I was coming late tomorrow, anyway," Royce said as he stepped in.

Royce and his assistant, Orlando—his jack-of-all-trades including chauffeur and bodyguard—flew in a company plane to Columbus from wherever he was working. Royce kept a car there. Orlando drove while Royce did paperwork in the backseat—always busy. Now he turned to wave to Orlando, who backed the black sedan out of the driveway.

"He wanted to come in to tell you he's glad you're all right, but I told him I'd let you know and he could see you later. He'll be at the lodge in a guest room down the hall from my suite if I need him." When Matt closed the door behind them, Royce gripped his shoulders. "At least you're in one piece." He hugged Matt stiffly, set him back and headed into the living room.

As ever, the seventy-year-old was elegantly put together in his Italian leather jacket over a striped shirt and jeans which actually looked pressed. Royce's silver hair seemed sculpted, and his perpetual tan set off his green eyes. Married and divorced three times—and paying triple alimony—Royce had not always been a successful entrepreneur. He'd made his ever-expanding fortune in upscale housing projects, including Lake Azure and another in the Poconos, and also headed up the Environmental Expansion Company, the EEC, which oversaw the majority of fracking for gas and oil in this area. Though he was a trim, fairly short man, Royce Flemming left huge footprints wherever he went.

As the sun set, they sat at the bar in the living

area with its views of hills and the lake. Matt's three-bedroom house was the medium size for the development and blended beautifully into the natural setting, one of the prerequisites for a Lake Azure home. It was perched on a cul-de-sac that overlooked the lodge and lake with its man-made sand beach, boathouse and dock.

"The usual?" Matt asked. "I could use a stiff one myself after today."

Royce nodded. "Can you believe I'm dating a woman who likes bourbon and branch? But yeah, thanks. Make it my usual—a double."

"Bourbon and branch? Isn't that what evil oilman J. R. Ewing used to drink on *Dallas?*"

"Yeah, that's right. So, Jennifer called from the office and said it was my truck that went over."

Matt heaved a huge sigh and handed Royce his Jim Beam on the rocks. "Yeah, the Azure Lake truck Orlando usually drives when the black car seems a bit too much or you're headed to rough ground."

"I hear you, partner. That's why I liked that truck around here. Believe me, I don't always need Orlando hanging on—or maybe I do now."

They clinked glasses and sat facing each other across the mahogany bar. Moments like this made Matt really miss his father. As close as he felt personally and professionally to this man who had been his dad's best friend and who did not have children of his own, it was never quite the same. He admired Royce tremendously, but there was always an edge to the man that couldn't be smoothed away.

"Okay, I'll just say it," Royce said. "The hillbilly jerk who tried to shove you off might have been after me." It was a statement, not a question, but then Royce always seemed to have all the answers.

"Possibly. But why you, the moneyman, the salvation of this area in people's eyes?"

"In *some* people's eyes. If he was after Brad Mason, my right-hand guy in charge of the fracking contracts, the would-be killer is nearsighted as hell. Brad's always in that fire-engine red, look-at me truck, which is good advertising, though I know he's got fans and haters out there."

"Woody drove the white truck once in a while but he's dead, and you're always driven by Orlando, so that leaves me as the target. But if the guy in that truck wanted me to die, why?"

"Yeah. Matt, you know Woody was a loose cannon. I'm sorry he had that freak accident, but it kept me from firing him for printing up those homemade signs and picketing this place. It shook up the residents here. He should have picketed one of the drilling sites, not here."

"*I* hire and fire here, and I would not have fired him."

"Okay, he was a good worker. I overanalyze everything."

"Me, too, now. Even after hashing all this out with the sheriff, his deputy and Charlene Lockwood, I still can't figure—"

"Lockwood's the woman who just happened to come along in time?"

"What do you mean 'just happened to'?"

"I checked into her. A bleeding heart social worker who could, possibly should, profit from helping you get out of that truck in time. Maybe it was pushed just so far so it wouldn't go over, then here she comes to help. I hear she visits families up in the hills and could no doubt use a hefty reward for her Appalachian project. And, like you said, who has the money around here? I do, you do—and people know that."

"You mean like she set it up?" Matt's voice rose in tone and volume. "Royce, now you're over the edge."

"Calm down. Anything's possible, that's all. You've got to look at all angles."

"She asked for nothing."

"Good. Great. But I wish you'd called me first, not gone to the sheriff. We don't need negative PR or people speculating. The Chillicothe newspaper will pick it up from the police report, or worse yet, good old gossip will get going around here. We've worked damn hard to get along with the townies who think people don't belong even if they've been here for a hundred years. We could have cleaned this up by donating to Ms. Lockwood's cause and doing an investigation ourselves—which I plan to do. We don't need the sheriff breathing down our necks."

Matt slammed his glass down on the bar, spilling some of his drink. "Last time I checked, attempted murder is a criminal offense. Of course I went to the sheriff. He needs to look into it!"

"Okay, didn't mean to take it out on you after all you've been through today. I suppose he had to know, but let's try to keep it from getting tied to bad local feelings about this 'ritzy' area, as I heard one guy uptown put it. And I don't want it tied to the fracking. Hopefully, money talks louder than the environmental do-gooders yakking about the quality of life around here from our drilling." He rolled his eyes. "You know, that crazy Bright Star told his disciples that blasting into the bedrock like that could cause earthquakes, one sign for the end of the world—that is, until I bought out his old property for big bucks. Now he's on my side, and that's what we need, people around here on our side, not trying to shove us off cliffs."

"Royce, we can't sweep what happened today under the PR rug. It might have been some drunk guy, but I think it meant something, and since it was my life on the line, I'm not letting it go. And I mean to thank Char Lockwood and cooperate with the sheriff, too."

"Sure. Sure, I understand. Too late not to. Hey, let's get something to eat at the lodge, then I've got my fracking superintendent meeting me there later to report on how the drilling's going. EEC is helping the down-and-outs here with some very nice drilling rights packages, bringing up the whole area, that's my goal. The locals already owe us big thanks for the influx of jobs and money and revitalizing the stores downtown. Even newcomer Charlene Lockwood must know we're doing great and are making good profits."

Still annoyed that Royce was suspicious of Char's motives, Matt went upstairs to turn out lights. Darkness had descended. As he glimpsed his own reflected image in the large glass window of his loft bedroom before snapping off the light, a thought hit him. If the man in the truck who tried to shove him off the cliff meant for him to die, why did he cover his face? If he just meant to scare him, warn him—set him up somehow, maybe for Charlene Lockwood to come along—he would have covered his face.

No, Royce, wily as he was, had to be wrong about Char. So what if she probably had ties to hill folk, maybe some who owed her favors? Royce just went wild with things his front man and informant, Brad Mason, found out about locals here, so he knew what contracts to offer for what amount where he wanted to drill, including working with that weird cult leader, Bright Star Monson. Talk about a guy with hidden ulterior motives. Royce had said the cult leader was a mind-control guru even he could learn from—which reminded Matt again that, even working for and with a dynamo like Royce, he still needed to be his own man.

He had another unsettling thought. He closed his vertical blinds. If someone was watching or stalking him, they could see right in, and this house was full of large windows.

"Hey," Royce said as Matt hurried down the free-standing staircase and went to the front hall closet to get a jacket. "I'm telling you again, you need a good woman in your life, my man. Now Veronica, this new lady I'm seeing, has a younger sister who's a knockout, and we'd like to fix you up with her."

"The fixing up I need right now is to figure out who almost killed me and why. And to make sure no one tries it again."

"So one thing I haven't mentioned," Gabe told Tess and Char after questioning Char about what she'd seen up on the mountain, followed by a late dinner. "In Matt's burned-out truck, we found a pristine piece of paper that had a crude skull and crossbones on it and read, 'Your fired.'" He spelled it out for them. "I'm sending it to my friend Vic Reingold at the Bureau of Criminal Identification and Investigation to see if we can get prints or DNA off it, but that may take a while."

"Bad spelling, so maybe an uneducated writer," Char observed. "Sad to say, there are plenty of those around here. What do you think it means?"

"Don't know," Gabe said. "Nothing about this whole thing makes sense. Despite the fact he usually has a driver, I'm tempted to theorize the attacker thought it was Royce Flemming in that truck. He's got as many enemies as friends around here, making some folks rich while their neighbor lives in worse poverty, compared to the bonanza next door. It's splitting not only shale rock layers but friends and families when some cash in on the fracking and some don't. Fracking breaks a lot of family bonds. Some have their quiet roads ruined by big semis and their views wrecked by rigs and concrete. Outsiders, blasting, worries about the purity of well water most depend on here."

"Listen, you two," Char said. "Let's try to just forget all that for a while. I'll get the table cleaned up, get things in the dishwasher, then go up to finish my meager packing. You two need time alone without the cares of the world. Go on now. The day care kids will be here all too soon in the morning, and Gabe will be off trying to find the guy or the truck that hit Matt."

Gabe gave her a tight grin. "Thanks, Char. We'll take you up on the clean the kitchen offer, and I'll worry about all that tomorrow. Mrs. McCabe, please come with me. You are under arrest and in my personal care," he said, and took Tess's hand to pull her to her feet.

Char sighed as they left the kitchen. It suddenly seemed very empty. She was glad she wouldn't be intruding on their hospitality and kindness much longer, though they'd never made her feel that way. But as soon as she got the keys to the cabin, she'd be on her own in a beautiful spot. Really, really on her own.

5

"Ah, the keys to the kingdom!" Char exulted to Tess the next morning as her new landlady drove away from Tess's house after giving her the key to the rental cabin.

"But you promised you'd get the locks changed," Tess reminded her as she continued arranging the small beanbag chairs in a circle for the children that were due to be dropped off soon. Gabe had already headed for the office. Char had overheard him tell Tess he was going to interview Royce Flemming as soon as he showed up in town again.

"I said I'd get the locks changed, and I will," Char promised. "I'll get moved in and do my visits with kids closer to town just for today instead of climbing every mountain again, fording every stream, following every rainbow..."

"*The Sound of Music,* my favorite musical. I teach the kids the 'Do-Re-Mi,' song, you know. Oh, here's the first drop-off. No," she said, looking out the window. "I don't know that car. Char, it's Matt Rowan!

Here, you go to the door, and I'll keep straightening up. Don't mind me."

Char almost scolded Tess for her excitement, but her own heartbeat accelerated. She felt herself blushing. Waiting inside the door for him to ring the bell or knock, she fanned her face.

He rang the bell. She counted to five, and before Tess could run in to see what was wrong, opened the door. He was taller than she recalled and looked so good—that is, no dirt, no messed-up hair, no apparent bruises.

"Matt. Come in. How are you doing after—after everything?"

He brought in a blast of crisp, fresh air with him. The first car with day care kids pulled up right behind him, but Char got him inside before the storm of little squealers hit. "Hi, Miss Tess. Where's Miss Char?" she heard as she led Matt down the hall.

"Bad timing, I guess," he said. "Do you help out here?"

"I have but, actually, just if I have free time from my new job. And I'm moving out today."

She indicated they should go into the living room while Tess herded the children into the large play area. "Do you have kids?" Char asked, then felt maybe she'd overstepped by asking about that right away. Might as well ask if he was married. "Tess loves to teach kids, but I prefer standing up for their rights," she rushed on as they sat side by side on the sofa. "I'm not quite as much hands-on as she is." She bent one leg up on the seat and turned toward him. He tilted inward, too, throwing one arm across the back of the sofa, almost touching her shoulder.

"To answer your question, no kids. No wife, either."

"Oh. Well, I'm so glad you are looking good—okay, I mean." She felt like a babbling idiot. Usually, she was in control with women or men.

"I'd be happy to take a load up to your new place. Or I could get a Lake Azure truck—one that's not totaled—to deliver some of your things. Actually, I came to ask something. First of all, I'd like to take you to dinner, and second, I heard from Gabe and Jace that you need to visit the McKitricks up on Pinecrest. I do, too. Yesterday I was taking clothes and food up to the family of Woody McKitrick, our head groundskeeper, who died tragically in a fall." As he shook his head, she realized he was thinking he could have, too.

"I heard. I'm sorry. I knew that would make my visit there harder. Jemmie McKitrick, the six-year-old I'm concerned about, is Woody's grandson. I knew he'd be missing his grandpa and, evidently, the family's major breadwinner. The boy's father was wounded in Iraq and doesn't work, gets minimal checks to support the grandmother, mother and Jemmie."

"Yes, Sam, Woody's son, has post-traumatic stress disorder. Woody said that Sam wants to go out hunting the enemy all the time, and he's disappeared in the middle of the night once in a while. They've had him treated at a VA hospital, but he's still not—not right. So I thought it might work out that, as soon as I replace the things I'd bought for them, which I plan to do today, we could call on them together. At least the money I had to help get them through the winter was in my jacket pocket so that wasn't lost in the fire."

"Sure, we could go together. I'd be trying to help them in a different way, getting Sam and his wife Mandy Lee, to agree that Jemmie should attend school."

"Tomorrow then? We could talk about it tonight at dinner if you'd let me take you."

"That would be great. As for your helping me move things, I've never had my own place since I graduated from college, so I travel light. It won't be furniture or anything like that, but we could put some boxes in your trunk." She knew everything would fit in hers, but she didn't want to turn him down on this—on anything, and that scared her.

"Are you sure you want to live alone? In a cabin, even a nice one? I know the owner and the place. It's kind of isolated."

"I'll be fine. Don't you start sounding like my sister. I lived on the edge of the Navajo Reservation, and now I'll be living on the edge of Appalachia. But thanks for your offer because Tess is busy for a while—obviously." She smiled as the sound of children singing the alphabet floated to them. "And, of course, Gabe's going to be extra busy. He said he's going to interview your partner, Royce Flemming, next time he comes to town. You just winced. What did I say?"

"He's here. And not too happy to have that sort of publicity for Lake Azure."

"I can understand that. Oh, can dinner be a bit late

tonight? When Tess is done today, we're going to visit the Hear Ye cult to see our cousins Lee and Grace Lockwood, and their two kids, who live there."

"Really?" he said, frowning. "I don't know anyone who lives there."

"Anyone who's *crazy* enough to live there, you mean. The entire area is like one big haunted ghost town. We're really worried about all of them. I guess it's an old joke around here, but it sure seems right that the cult has moved onto the old lunatic asylum grounds since their other place was bought with big bucks for fracking—well, I'm sure you know all about that because of Mr. Flemming."

He frowned again.

"Oh, you don't think you're known by the company you keep, do you. I mean that someone would try to hurt you to get to Royce Flemming?" she asked.

"It's crossed my mind. I'll be careful."

She extended her hand to him and he took it, not exactly in a handshake, not really holding hands, but a link, an unspoken bond. The moment passed, and she felt awkward again. She hated to admit it but she was attracted to him, yet felt so vulnerable with him.

"I can wait until you're ready to carry things out," he said. "We can put a load in my car, and I'll follow you up. I've got a lunch meeting, but if you give me your number, I'll call you later, see when you're ready to be picked up for dinner if you think you'll be safe with me— You know what I mean," he added hastily. "Some idiot is loose out there."

But she was starting to think Matt Rowan was a man worth being near even if someone was out to get him.

"I swear, this place always give me the creeps," Tess told Kate and Char as she drove them toward the old asylum gates. When Kate had heard where they were going, she'd insisted on coming, too. "And not just because it's supposed to be haunted," Tess insisted. "Every time I see Brice Monson, I feel I'm looking at an alien, a creature from beyond."

"Bright Star's a mind manipulator of the nth degree," their practical older sister, Kate, put in with a roll of her hazel eyes.

Tess slowed as they passed through the rusted, open iron gates and fence that surrounded the long-deserted Falls County Mental Hospital grounds. The hospital had started life in the 1880s as the Cold Creek Lunatic Asylum. They passed the modern playground area with its swings, slide and jungle gym. The county-owned park was deserted, though with the wind the swings still squeaked back and forth as if someone sat in them. The few dry leaves on the trees seemed to shudder, and little eddies of dead ones on the ground swirled and danced.

The hospital had once been a busy, self-sustaining establishment. Two five-story towers with cupolas stood sentinel over a large main red brick building, a relic from post–Civil War times. Gabe had said the big central structure once had male and female wards and separate dining rooms with patient rooms stacked above, under the copper roof. It was all derelict now. Vandals and ghost hunters broke in at times, especially around Halloween as they had just a few weeks ago.

Empty outbuildings in various stages of decay dotted the acreage, cottages for overflow patients, a small barn and greenhouses that had once helped to feed the patients and staff, even a carriage shop. Two graveyards, one with only numbers on the small tombstones were on the site. Flush with cash from selling the old cult compound site for fracking, Bright Star had hired workers to renovate two of the larger outbuildings and quickly build two wings with more expansion to come.

"They used to do lobotomies here," Kate told them, shaking her head. "You know, primitive brain surgery that turned anxious, paranoid patients into zombies more or less. I swear, Bright Star's doing a version of that himself the way everybody falls in line with his weird ideas. Grace and Lee used to have minds of their own, but no more."

Kate was always the bright one, the scholar, and she'd been like a second mother to Char and Tess when their father had left and their mother had gone to work to support them in Jackson, Michigan. Through scholarships, grants and hard work, she'd earned her doctorate in archaeology, lived abroad and led archaeological digs—and then to Tess's and Char's amazement, had ended up back in little Podunk, Cold Creek, Ohio. And not just because of the ancient Adena Indian mounds here, but because of a man, so let that be a warning. But even here in Cold Creek, if there was any trivia or clue to be had, any theory to be probed, Kate was the one to ask, so maybe later Char would run past her the mystery of who tried to kill Matt on the mountain yesterday.

"Well, Bright Star will have trouble refusing to let Gracie and Lee see the three of us," Tess declared, but her voice shook. "Safety in numbers! If only Lee and Grace would stand up to him, I wonder how far he'd go to keep them here. You're right, Kate. It's like he has some hypnotic hold on them—all of them."

"If their children are being abused in any way, I'd like to get a court order against them," Char said. "He can only hide behind freedom of religion so long if he's hurting those kids."

"I'm sure Gracie—and Lee—would never allow that," Tess insisted.

They got out of the car at the closed gate to the new compound, one almost as ornate as the old Victorian one. The fracking must mean money coming out Bright Star's ears, Char thought. This gate had a star bursting with beams formed from the metalwork.

"Bright Star likes to hit us idiots over the head with symbolism," Kate muttered. "Such humility!"

As usual, a guard stood sentinel at his post. Kate did the talking, asking to see their cousins Lee and Grace Lockwood and their children. The guard, a tall man, apparently unarmed but with a walkie-talkie, moved a few yards away and spoke to someone in it.

"So far, so good," Char whispered. "One for all and all for one."

"You've been reading *The Three Musketeers?*" Kate

whispered. "But don't bet on 'so far so good.' Tess and I have both tangled with the guy."

To Char's relief, the man opened the gate and waved them in. Following him, they went up the new-looking concrete walk toward the main building with its two curved additions shaped like—like embracing arms? Angel wings?

"Gabe told me this was once a cottage for tubercular patients that they used to segregate, but it's been really redone," Tess whispered.

Another man met them at the door, and the guard went back toward his post. This man seemed his clone in their garb, kind of Quaker or Amish—definitely pioneer-looking. No Bright Star so far, but that could be a good sign. The man directed them down the center hall to a small, sparsely furnished room.

Char remembered their first cousin Lee from their childhood—fun, lively, a little shy maybe and handy with all kinds of tools. And Grace—Gracie, Tess still called her—had once been Tess's best friend. They'd all missed Lee and Grace and their two darling kids, Kelsey, age four, and Ethan, two. Char had only glimpsed the children once on a weekend market day since she'd been back. She'd never grasped how Lee and Grace had been caught up in this weird web.

The room where they waited had no windows and was plainly furnished with four straight-backed chairs and a bench. The two torchère lamps reminded Char of the uptilted, soft lights in funeral homes. On the walls were framed quotes from the Bible in beautifully scripted writing. The largest one read:

> You do well to heed a light that shines in a dark place until the day dawns and the morning star rises in your hearts.

"Maybe that's where he took his nickname from," Char whispered, pointing.

"And check out the other Bible quotes framed here," Kate said. "They're about hunting people down. I swear, that's the way he targets people to get them in here, with initial goodwill, then total mind control, so we'd better—"

She stopped in midthought as the hall door opened and Lee and Grace entered. Char was pleased their escort closed the door behind them so the family could have some privacy, but she was disappointed they didn't have the children with them.

Tears prickled behind Char's eyelids. As they exchanged greetings and hugs, Tess started crying. When Char hugged Grace, she realized the sort of cloak she wore over her dress in this chilly place could not hide the fact that she was pregnant—very pregnant. She'd sure seen a lot of that out West under loose skirts and capes.

"Oh, Grace. Another baby!" Char cried. "Congratulations!"

Kate and Tess joined in, congratulating Lee, too, who didn't seem a bit pleased. And Grace was acting so strangely that Char wondered if she was going to faint. She kept darting her eyes toward the scripted, framed star quote on the wall.

"What?" Tess asked. "Are you all right? Dizzy? Want to sit?"

Lee stood back as the sisters fussed over Grace, who looked not only delicate but ill. She had violet shadows under her eyes, and her face was drawn, almost gray. She was too thin despite her bulbous belly.

Finally, Lee answered questions about Kelsey and Ethan—doing well, just fine, yes, very happy here. Grace asked about Kate's engagement to Grant and insisted on seeing her engagement ring, which seemed unusual to Char since she wore no jewelry herself and was dressed so plainly. She exclaimed over the ring but tapped the face of Kate's watch as if it were time for them to go.

"Will you go out to a doctor to have the baby or does a midwife come in?" Kate asked. "I heard they do deliveries here, but we can arrange a doctor for you."

"Yes, I'll have a trained midwife, with lots of good support. I'll be very well taken care of," Grace assured them, but her voice was shaky.

Char wondered if Lee didn't approve—of what?—because he kept glowering at them and had so little to say. She rose from the bench next to Grace and spoke to him. "Do you want a boy or a girl, Lee? With one of each already, do you have a preference?"

"A son. We look forward to a son," he said.

This close to him, Char noted that the pupils of his

eyes were large, as if they'd been dilated for an eye examination. *Could he be drugged?* He seemed almost robotic, zombielike as Kate had said earlier.

After only fifteen minutes together, it was time to say goodbye. Grace gripped Char's hand and darted her eyes toward the wall with the morning star Bible verse again. Did she want them to understand that the name Bright Star was precious, special? Was she drugged, too? Surely not in her advanced state of pregnancy, but Char sensed she dare not ask. Maybe if she came alone later, brought a baby gift here, she could find out more.

They said their goodbyes, promising to be back soon with something for the children and the new baby—a month yet to go, Grace had told them. They all hugged again and when they did, Grace grabbed Char's wrist and whispered what she thought was the word, *watch,* but she quickly stepped back and moved away without another glance.

Then it hit her. Grace had only pretended to admire Kate's new engagement ring but she had tapped her watch. And she had whispered, "watch!" and looked at the wall with the framed quote. Watch for what? Was that a warning?

In the hall, Char noticed another framed quote about a bright and morning star, only in different script—big, bold letters, not fancy, cursive writing. It looked as if it hung opposite the one on the other side of the wall. The glass over the quote reflected in the hall light. On impulse, she stepped forward and lifted the frame from the wall. There was an eyehole behind it, so there must have been one on the other side!

"Hey, put that back," their escort said.

"Oh, I just think it's such beautiful words," Char told him, pretending to stare down at the quote and turning her back on the small hole as if she hadn't seen it. Blessedly, neither of her sisters said a word. "Do you know…" Char asked, giving the quote one more fake, lingering look. "Can I order one of these?" She handed it back to the man as Grace and Lee stood in the doorway staring. "I'll drop by to find out later. And thanks for guiding us in to see our family today."

Tess looked puzzled, and Kate looked livid as they walked out. They were back in the day care van before Tess demanded an explanation. "What was that all about?"

"Good work, Char," Kate said. "But I'm not sure you covered up your discovery like that plaque covered the hole. That sounded pretty heavy-handed about wanting to buy one of that maniac's self-aggrandizing quotes he's ripped off from the Bible to justify his power."

"What? Tell me!" Tess insisted.

"Grace is in some kind of trouble," Char said. "Deeper than just not wanting to have her baby there. There was a peephole in the wall, and she was trying to tell us she—or we—were being watched."

6

Char had hoped to calm down after the visit to the Hear Ye cult by the time Matt picked her up for dinner at the cabin that evening. But just being with him was revving her up in a far different way. It had been a while since she'd got dressed up for a fancy date—and it seemed ages since she'd been with a man so attentive and attractive.

As her mother would have said, Matthew Rowan "cleaned up well." Not that he hadn't looked nice this morning at Tess's, but—well, who knew a suit coat over a shirt and V-necked cable-knit sweater could look so good. Char wasn't one to care about appearances, but to have been picked up in a luxury car, not a truck, which was all she'd been used to for months—years…

Get hold of yourself, Charlene Lockwood, she lectured herself. *You don't care about luxury items. This guy is not Prince Charming. You will not let this turn your head.*

As they walked through the door into La Maison, the

blonde hostess gave Matt a kiss on both cheeks, which jarred Char back to reality. "*Bonjour, mon ami.* Booth or table, Matt?" She had a French accent, no less, and Matt said something to her in French.

The place looked about half-full, probably mostly with Lake Azure residents. A low buzz of conversation mingled with recorded music. Char knew this was one of Tess's favorite places. Since her honeymoon, Tess was into everything French. And this woman knew Matt fairly well, so he was no stranger here.

"A back booth would be great," Matt told the hostess.

They followed her past the bar. Several people sat there, including Brad Mason, the younger brother of Kate's fiancé, Grant. Brad was a slightly shorter version of Grant with dark blond hair, blue eyes and a muscular build. He was talking to another man but was obviously watching the front door over the other guy's shoulder. Char had only met Brad a couple of times at Grant's house, once at the announcement party for their engagement. All she really knew about him was that he used to work at the lumber mill with Grant but now worked for the fracking king, Royce Flemming. So that meant Matt must know him, too.

"Yo, Matt," Brad said, standing to shake his hand. "Glad you're back among the living and—" Brad did a double take as he took her in. "Charlene, future sis-in-law. I heard you were there to save the day—and save Matt."

"He got out of the truck on his own, but I was there."

"So Royce said."

"You're not meeting him here, are you?" Matt asked, taking her arm, rather protectively, she thought. The two men seemed merely cordial, not really friendly, when she assumed their ties to Flemming would make them on the same team at least.

"Met with him earlier today—at length," Brad said. "He's working late at the lodge tonight. Actually, I'm waiting for another local success story, the Fencers, who live down the road from where your family lived, Charlene."

"Sure, I know the Fencer place," she said. "The current owners are probably the third or fourth generation there. It used to be a pretty big farm, but now it's just a few fields. When we were kids, the Fencers didn't have girls for us to play with but we got along well with the boys. So, you're saying they're getting a contract for drilling on their land?"

"That would make sense since they're the closest place to the old Hear Ye cult land that's got so much action there," Matt said.

"Ah, yeah, right," Brad said and took a quick swig of amber liquor from his glass. Not beer, the drink of choice around here, Char thought, but then times were changing. She could see the glass bottoms of numerous wine bottles nestled in a crosshatch pattern of shelves behind the polished wooden bar.

Brad went on, seeming nervous. "Yeah, that old Bright Star cult land above Cold Creek is a really busy place. Getting oil and natural gas out of there galore. Quite a production."

They chatted about Kate and Grant's coming wedding—Brad would be best man and Char and Tess would stand up with Kate. "And the view from the reception in their living room will be a burial mound," Brad said with a shake of his head. "I'm sure the late-night comedians could make something out of that, but I'll skip the one-liners."

He shrugged with a grin that was more of a grimace. They said goodbye, and Char and Matt moved on to their booth in the back corner where the hostess had left their menus. The white linen tablecloth with a single red rosebud in a vase gleamed in the light of a big candle in a glass globe. More forks and goblets were set at each place than Char had seen in a long time.

"Lucky Fencer family, I guess," Matt said, sliding in across from her. "Those leases or sales contracts mean a lot of money."

"I'm pretty sure Mrs. Fencer is the sister of Sam McKitrick, Jemmie's dad. I hope we won't have another Hatfield and McCoy problem when the Fencers get filthy rich and the McKitricks are hurting up in the hills."

"That's one sad thing about the fracking. It's like some winning the lottery and others close to them just watching the riches pour in. But listen," he said, reaching over to take her hand, "let's just get to know each other better this evening. No more talk about fracking, poor kids, how we met. What's important is that we did, and we're going to enjoy our time together."

"Deal," she said, lifting and shaking his big warm

hand. He held on to hers. "And one more thing—no more trying to convince me not to live in the cabin. I'll be fine there."

"At least you're not far away, and I know where to find you."

He smiled. Their gazes held. Her stomach cartwheeled. They still held hands. Suddenly, she didn't care if they were in the best restaurant in the universe or at the Dairy Queen. She was deeply happy to be here with Matt Rowan.

They were sipping wine and eating the delicious, warm French bread when Char saw the Fencer family trail into the restaurant as if they had just entered Disneyland, craning their necks to look around, eyes wide. She knew it was them because, though she hadn't seen him for years, she recognized Joe Fencer. Brad bounced up to greet them. She couldn't believe Joe had four kids already.

For sure she remembered Tess saying that Sara Ann, the mother, was one of the McKitricks. Brad directed them to a distant table, one in Char's line of sight. He was ready to wine and dine them to close the fracking contract on the land of their family heritage.

She didn't say a thing to Matt about all that, since he'd set out rules for the evening, but her mind went again to little Penny Hanson up on the mountain, holding her precious colored crayons. One of the Fencer daughters, maybe nine years old, was obviously in awe of this place. She sat bolt upright in her chair, stroking the white linen tablecloth and nearly jumping out of her skin when the server handed her the large leather-bound menu. Brad was playing host, drinking water now. At least that family lived in town so the kids could all get to the consolidated schools.

"So, you have no one special in your life, besides your family?" Matt asked, salting his salad, as if that were a nonchalant question. "You asked if I have kids. Why are you especially dedicated to children who are hurting, little ones living on the edge?"

"Ha. I knew you'd be the first one to bring up the kids we're not supposed to be talking about. You have a soft heart for them, too. I can tell by your helping out the McKitrick family. It's not only because Woody was your employee and friend, is it?"

"Touché. I owed him for teaching me a lot about the area, about the people outside the realm of Lake Azure. In a way, maybe you can take up where he left off."

"The mountain folk themselves are the teachers. But to answer your question, no—no special man in my life. I had a college romance that I thought would lead to a future, but he had stars in his eyes for a big corporate career in the East—he's in New York City—and that just wasn't me. Okay, I know that look. Yes, you're thinking, there are lots of poor, needy kids in New York, but I prefer, as you put it, living on the edge. Well, the edge of civilization, *not* the kind of edge you almost went over."

"Now we've both broken the taboo conversation rules." He raised his eyebrows and smiled at her as if in a challenge. "But, if you're reading my mind now, I'm in trouble." His smile widened to a boyish grin as he finally looked away and speared a slice of tomato.

Char picked up her wineglass and took a slow sip to calm herself. She didn't even know this man two days ago, and now... But this dinner would surely be it. Just like her college love, she and Matt were so different. Different economic levels, different goals, their futures poles apart.

They both ate chicken *cordon bleu* and *pommes frites.* Ah—so these were what were called French fries in America.

Meanwhile, Matt explained that Royce had been almost like a father to him since his dad had died young. The Lake Azure community kept him busy full-time. He wasn't in on the Environmental Expansion Company.

"You might know," she said, deciding to ignore another one of Matt's conversation caveats for the evening, "they put the words *environmental* and *expansion* in the company name. Don't they realize that—despite the good things the money can do for this area—fracking can also hurt the environment? What about all these new roads and the noise? And I've read it can pollute groundwater. Oops—sorry. Too heavy a topic."

"No, that's all right. There are pros and cons, but if the U.S. can become less dependent on foreign oil, it's a good thing, right? And I do like a woman with her own opinions, honestly. If you were right down the line with things I like or say, I'd think you were just out to please me and had no backbone."

"Good!" she said as their server returned, and they both ordered chocolate crepes for dessert.

It was a frosty night with silver pinpoints of stars stuck on a black velvet dome of sky when Matt drove Char out of town. A bright curve of moon smiled down at them. He took her on a short tour of Lake Azure, pointing out his house and telling her he'd have her to dinner at the lodge soon. All the houses backed up to wooded hills and had treed lots as if the forest embraced them.

"By the way," he told her, "almost all the wood for these buildings came from Grant Mason's lumberyard, so you can tell your sister Kate this place helped pay for her wedding."

The tennis courts, volleyball area, shuffleboard and archery range weren't lighted, but old-fashioned streetlights threw pools of gold along the curved streets. It seemed to her a very romantic place—in the old sense of that word—with several skaters on the lake and people bundled up, roasting marshmallows or hot dogs over a fire on the beach.

"If we just had snow it would look like a Currier and Ives card," she told him.

"We do have sleigh rides next month. I'll take you on one."

So, she thought, with another frisson of excitement, he intended that they would go on, be friends at least.

The way he looked at her and some of the things he said made her believe—and hope—he meant this was the beginning of more. No, that would never work. Not only were they from different worlds, but almost different universes. Without realizing it, she heaved a deep sigh.

"What?" he asked as he drove out toward the highway past the stone sign announcing Lake Azure Community.

"It just seems a sort of haven, that's all. I hope those who live there appreciate it, especially when they drive in past the derelict farmhouses and old town."

"Some know how blessed they are, some don't and won't."

"How about Royce Flemming?"

"He wasn't born with a silver spoon in his mouth, Char. He worked his way up, just like my father."

"At least your father didn't mean to leave you."

"Like your dad did? I got the idea you and your sisters had made up with him."

"We have, but it doesn't quite heal the initial pain of desertion. I was close to my mom, too, and cancer took her."

"We have a lot more to get to know about each other, to share."

As he turned up the curved road toward her cabin, the headlights of the big car slashed through bushes and tree limbs. "By the way," he said, "since I take it you liked the look and feel of Lake Azure, there's a place that needs a house sitter this winter—folks who head to Florida, just in case you change your mind about—"

"You said you wouldn't try to talk me out of staying in the cabin up here. I decided to do it and I will. A woman with her own opinions, right?"

"Right," he said, but he hit the steering wheel with his fist, lightly, just once.

He pulled into the cabin's narrow drive, and they sat there a moment. He switched off his headlights, then turned them on again. She had the feeling he'd say more, maybe try to talk her out of staying here again. But he got out, leaving his headlights on so they could see. She'd left a light on inside the kitchen, but it did little to pierce the hovering blackness here. This place had a different feel from the vast openness of Navajo land at night. Closer, tighter with the hills, even though her location overlooked the open valley far below.

Just to make the point again that she was her own woman, she was tempted to open her car door before he came around, but she let him do it. He took her hand as they headed for the cabin, which now looked so small.

They stood in the beams from the headlights, while she fumbled with the unfamiliar key and new lock. Reluctant to go in, to end this night, she opened the wooden door a crack. It had a glass window that came partway down, lending them wan light from inside, though it was no match for the headlights.

"What's that old but true line?" she asked as he stood close, blocking the wind for her. "I've had a wonderful time—and I mean it."

"Me, too," he said, and lifted a warm hand to tip her chin up. "I want you to understand that tonight was not really payback for what you did. I wanted to do it—for myself, too, as if nothing bad had ever thrown us together in the first place."

Char started to nod as he dipped his head to kiss her. Soft at first, almost friendly, then serious for sure. She felt like a naive teen on her first date, unsteady, curious, needy.

They broke the kiss and stepped apart, still staring at each other, lit by the headlights. She moved her hand to shove the door open and he took a step back to turn away. Without warning, an arrow slammed into the door and stuck there, quivering between them.

7

Matt grabbed her—almost tackled her—and rolled them off the low concrete single step into the wet leaves. He pulled her around the corner of the cabin, where they huddled, kneeling with her pressed between him and the outside wall.

"I—I can't believe that," she whispered. "We could have—could have been hit."

"And I'm the common denominator. Either someone's been following me, looking for another chance at me, or someone's staked out your place, knowing we're together."

They were whispering in each other's ears. "The headlights made us the perfect target," she said. "If we hadn't stepped apart...the arrow came head high, not chest level."

"Either way it could have killed one or both of us."

She was not only scared but furious. Someone had ruined her new place, ruined this beautiful night.

"Stay here," he said. "I'm going to get to the car, turn

it around so the headlights shine into the trees where the arrow must have come from. It's sticking in the wood at an upward angle—like it was shot from the sky. Probably just arced up, then hit."

"Should we call Gabe?"

"Not unless we spot someone. My bet is we'll find no one out there. And it's late. Let's give him a break and call him in the morning. Tonight you can go down to stay in one of the guest rooms at the lodge where—"

"It's my first night here! I'm not running, even if some stupid hunter or even worse wants to scare me off."

"Char, just for the night!"

"I'm not going to leave. I'm going to get that arrow for evidence, tape up the hole and lock my doors."

"Then I'm staying, too."

"What?"

"I'll sleep on the couch, just in case."

"And if it's you the shooter's after? That could have been the second attempt on your life."

"You just hunker down here, and I'll be right back."

He ran low to his car, got in and turned it around, switching on his brights so the headlights probed the trees on the other side of her driveway. She peered around the corner of her cabin. Nothing except shifting shadows of the tree trunks, one against the other. Then glowing eyes, like a cat's—oh, two deer—peered out at them before bounding off. Could some local hunter have been stalking game at night, shot, and the arrow missed and zinged into her door, a freak accident a hunter didn't want to own up to? Elinor Hanson said her husband sometimes hunted with bow and arrow, so others must, too. Lake Azure had an archery range.

Matt finally turned off his headlights and got out of his car. He locked it behind him with a touch of the key. The lights blinked once before the car went dark.

"Did you see the deer?" she asked.

"You mean someone was aiming at those deer and hit your door? If you make me leave, I will, but I think I should stay the night to make sure nothing else happens."

And so, Matt Rowan spent the night of their first date in her cabin. Actually, she was glad to have him on the couch between her and the pierced front door. Except having him so close all night not only comforted her but made her toss and turn in half-waking dreams not of fear but of longing.

At seven in the morning, Char heard Matt talking on the phone about things happening down in Lake Azure, not about their problems. She got dressed, popped into the bathroom, then found him in the living room, pacing and talking on his cell. He tilted it away from his mouth, but kept listening as he whispered to her. "Call Gabe, maybe take the arrow down to him. It's still bagged on the kitchen table. I was online looking at arrows for what must have been a recurve bow. Yeah, Jen," he said into the phone. "I'll be right in. Order me some breakfast from the dining room to be brought to my office, okay?"

"A recurve bow?" she asked when he punched Off.

"A crossbow with a real punch, but luckily it arched upward and caught the door on the downward trajectory—that's what I'm suspecting, anyway. But the arrow we took out of the door doesn't look like ones online. I read that you can unscrew the metal tips and reuse them. I wonder if the shooter makes his own shafts and fletching. Mention that to Gabe when you show him the arrow."

She walked closer. If he'd used the bathroom, she hadn't heard him in there. His clothes were wrinkled but he looked awake and alert. The only way she'd know he'd been here all night was his beard stubble—black, like his hair but flecked with silver.

"So," he said as she plugged in the coffeepot that sat on the wooden counter. "Are we still on to visit the McKitrick family later today?"

"You're willing to go back up on Pinecrest after what happened there—and here?"

He came into the kitchenette, turned her toward him and took her shoulders in a light grip. "I refuse to let someone spook me. As stubborn as you are—"

"Strong-minded."

"Right. You ought to understand that I'm not going to turn tail and run. I want to get to the bottom of this."

"Me, too. We'll go in my truck."

"And I'll bring a gun, just in case."

"You have a gun?"

"And a rifle. Which I never touch, but I've got a license for both weapons. I prefer shooting below par on the golf course. How about three o'clock? And we'll be careful we're not followed."

"I'll pick you up at the lodge?"

"Good. And you know, despite what's happened, it feels right to be with you."

"Me, too—the same."

He bent to kiss her cheek. His beard stubble brushed her skin. "Pinecrest Mountain, here we come again. And watch yourself until then."

"Matt, that archery range down near the tennis courts—does anyone shoot recurve crossbows there?"

"Not that I've seen. Strictly Robin Hood, Boy Scout stuff, but I'll ask Ginger, our instructor. You are heading out right after me, aren't you?"

"As soon as I get my shot of battery acid here," she said, indicating the coffee. "Can I pour you a cup?"

"Sure. To go, please. I have a meeting at eight. You've got my cell number, so call me today if anything seems strange."

He took the coffee she poured into her own travel cup and headed out.

If anything seems strange, he'd said. Oh, yeah, a lot seemed strange. How strong her feelings were for him. Deep concern that someone might be out to kill him—or now, her. And a little bit of mistrust for two thoughts she'd had last night but was trying to ignore. First, that the weird arrow attack gave weight to advice from Matt and her family that she shouldn't stay in the cabin, but surely that could not be a setup or warning from any of them. Worse, that before Matt turned his brights on last night, he'd blinked his headlights as if it were a signal to someone out in the darkness of the trees.

"You weren't home last night at all, were you?" Royce asked, popping his head into Matt's office door, then stepping in. Matt had a suite of offices on the first floor of the lodge, and Royce always stayed upstairs in the guest suite while his assistant, Orlando, took one of the smaller rooms.

"I turned off my phone for a while," Matt told him, looking up from his laptop. Next to it was the tray with the remnants of his hastily eaten breakfast.

"It upset me, considering what happened to you. I was worried. So I had Orlando go over and knock on your door—no dice—no Matt."

"I was with a friend."

"Really? Let me guess. A lady friend?" he asked with a wink.

Matt decided not to play that game. Char and his feelings for her were strictly his business, at least for now. After all, Royce had tried to suggest she had set him up to hit him up. "Royce, how can I help you?"

"You're touchy, but then it is early morning, and you don't look like you've slept. I wanted you to know I have a suggestion for you about a local guy—been a small-time farmer—who would be a good groundskeeper to take Woody's place."

"Woody was head groundskeeper, so he'd need to be good."

"I'll bet he is. Joe Fencer. The family is selling their

land to EEC out on Valley View Road across from the big drill spot, that old religious cult land. Brad said Joe's wife told him on the q.t. she was afraid that he needed something to do and was real conflicted about giving up his family's land. You're the man around here, so how about it?"

Matt hesitated. He'd been looking for someone local who had farm or gardening experience. He decided not to tell Royce he'd seen Brad hosting the Fencers last night when he was with Char. Still hovering at the door, Royce stared at him hard.

"I'll interview him tomorrow, if you want to give me his number."

"Great. Good. Like to tap into local talent, right? I'm learning the wisdom of that myself. See you later for your board dinner meeting, then."

Royce had barely stepped out when Orlando knocked once on the door frame and stepped into the office. Matt put the phone down before he made his next call. He was starting to think his "open door" policy was a mistake today.

"Listen," Orlando told him. "I never got to tell you I'm glad you're unharmed after that freak accident up on the mountain." His dark eyebrows seemed to meet over his aquiline nose as if he were always frowning.

"Thanks. Wish I could say it was an accident, but I don't think so."

"Did you get a good look at the driver? I'm sure the local sheriff's on it, but can I do any sniffing around while I'm out and about for Royce? I'm thinking it could be a local redneck who hates the fracking but hit you instead of Royce since I'm guarding him."

"I only saw the guy's eyes at a distance—through two windshields and my own panic. You'd better leave things to the police. But thanks for being concerned, Orlando."

"Well, sure I am. I know how much you mean to the boss, like the son he never had, he said. He keeps me pretty tight to him, but let me know if I can help—that's all," he said, and went out.

Matt felt good Orlando had made the effort and the offer. Matt knew he thought Royce spent too much time here in the boondocks, as he'd overheard him call Cold Creek—that is, until everyone on Royce's payroll except Matt, who had opted out, starting profiting from the local fracking boom. Matt wondered if Royce had offered Orlando a big piece of that action. But since Matt himself had turned that down, he decided not to ask.

After Char dropped off the arrow at the sheriff's office—Gabe was out on a domestic dispute call—she headed for Grant Mason's home, where Kate was overseeing the dig of an ancient Adena mound, practically outside her fiancé's back door. Kate was always good at thinking her way through things, and Char knew she could use some help.

As usual, there were several trucks and a car parked in the loop of driveway before the large, handsome house. The front door was locked, so rather than ring the bell, Char walked around back.

"Hi, Kaitlyn. Is Kate here?" Char asked Kate's right-hand woman, Kaitlyn Blake. The grad student resembled Kate in coloring, in personality—even in name. Sometimes Char was felt slightly jealous of Kaitlyn since Kate seemed like a big sister to her. But, just like Grant Mason's love, Kaitlyn's friendship had helped Kate get through some recent betrayals and hard times.

"Oh, hi, Char. She's sifting out some debris for teeth and bone fragments. And probably muttering under her breath about how much the undergrads working here have to learn, or about the cave-in, which set things so far back. I'll go get her."

Char sat on a patio chair and watched the busy scene until Kate appeared, looking dusty and sweaty but happy. "We've got a complete female skeleton, the first one!" Kate greeted her, clapping dirt off her hands. "And we've found what I think are the charred remains of a young male, who was probably a slave sacrifice. So, you aren't heading back out to try to face down the person I'd like most to sacrifice—Bright Star Monson?"

"No. I'm going to give that a little time, but I am determined to talk to Grace alone somehow—when we're not being spied on. Kate, I went out with Matt Rowan last night and—"

"Great! That's worth sharing," she said, beaming at her. Big sister Kate had always worried that her two younger sisters wouldn't be happy because of their tough childhood when Tess was taken and then Dad left them.

"Just listen for a minute. Matt and I were standing

outside the door of my cabin..." Char's voice trailed off. Well, she might as well just spit it out.

But before she could continue, Kate spoke. "You moved in. Okay, I didn't think you should, but you're a big girl now."

"Thank you! Anyhow, someone shot an arrow into the door right between us."

"What? On top of his almost going off the cliff? Are you okay? You look all right. I'd hug you if I wasn't a mess. Who was it? Who did it?"

"We don't know or Gabe would probably have him—or her—under arrest. I thought I'd bounce some ideas off you if you have a second."

"Sure. Shoot—I mean talk."

Char explained about Henry Hanson being out hunting with a bow when she visited his family and that he might be angry with her for interfering in his daughter's life. She figured he could be a stalker of people as well as game, maybe an abuser of his wife, at the very least. She mentioned the archery range at Lake Azure and the fact someone could still have been after Matt, not her. She told her they saw two deer shortly after the shot, so it could have been a hunter's arrow that went awry. But she couldn't bring herself to mention how it seemed to her that Matt had blinked his lights as if it might be a signal to someone—nor how he, like her own family, didn't want her to stay in the cabin, wanted her to move down to an empty house at Lake Azure and had really pushed for that after the arrow hit.

"So you went back to Tess's," Kate said when Char

took a breath. "Told Gabe what happened and slept there."

"No, Matt insisted on sleeping on the couch and nothing happened—you know what I mean."

Kate rolled her eyes. "You know, you left out Bright Star's possibly being ticked at all of us, but especially you after you discovered that peephole. The Hear Ye faithful are supposed to be peace-loving folk, but I wouldn't put it past him to have weapons to 'smite' his enemy. You did see those Bible quotes about hunting on the walls of that room, didn't you—could he be hunting people?"

Char's stomach went into free fall. "I saw them but didn't read them, except for the one extolling himself. Hunting quotes—from the Bible?"

"Right. You've heard that the devil can cite scripture for his own purpose, haven't you?"

"Can you recall what the wall plaques said?"

"I looked them up. Just a sec, and I'll get what I printed out. It was a pretty easy search."

While Kate darted inside, Char got up to pace. Too much was happening too fast, and she couldn't just keep running to her sisters. She'd like to run to Matt but could she trust him? At least the way they met could hardly be a setup.

Kate rushed back out with a single sheet of paper. "You know, we found a couple of intact Adena arrows in the tomb," she said as she passed the paper to Char. "That's apropos of nothing, just crazed archaeologist trivia. Check out that first quote from the book of Jeremiah."

Char read aloud.

> "I will send for many hunters and they shall hunt from every mountain and hill, and out of the holes of the rocks."

"Sounds like this terrain around here, doesn't it?" Kate asked. She leaned in, looking over Char's shoulder and pointed at the next one, from Psalms 140. She read it out.

> "Let not a slanderer be established in the earth. Let evil hunt the violent man to overthrow him."

"Creepy, huh? Bright Star probably considers all of us slanderers if we don't support him and his lunatic ways."

"Or if we try to take someone like Grace and Lee away from him."

Char read the last one from Lamentations aloud.

> "They tracked our steps so that we could not walk in our streets. Our end was near, our days were over, for our end had come."

She shook her head. "Kate, I agree he's crazy, but I can't see him—or one of his hunters—whoever that would be—stalking me. They wouldn't even know where to find me."

"I just want you to include him in the mix—and be careful. Most of all, don't even think of returning to see Grace alone."

Both of them jumped when a young man's voice called out. "Kate, we've got a new find!"

"Well, back to the kind of hunting I do," she said. "Listen, you and Matt Rowan have a standing invitation to have dinner here with us. Just give me warning so I can look presentable and get food on the table. And once again, you be careful about more than just wayward arrows. I'll just bet Matt's the kind who could sweep a girl off her feet. And, if anything strange happens at the cabin, you come here or go back to Tess's."

Char hugged Kate despite the fact she looked as if she'd emerged from a coal mine or had taken a fracking job around here. "I'll be careful," she promised. "Can I take these Bible quotes with me?"

"Sure. But don't let them get to you."

Or anyone get to me, Char thought as Kate headed back to her dig.

8

Both Matt and Char were on high alert as they drove up onto Pinecrest Mountain midafternoon. He hunched forward in the passenger seat of her truck, his head turning to check all directions. "You okay?" he asked her more than once.

"With you riding shotgun."

"Sorry if my gun makes you nervous."

"I don't need that to make me nervous. So, are we even going to mention to the McKitricks that their cousins are going to get a big fracking contract? I suppose they'd have to know already."

"Let's see if they bring it up first. You have a specific task here, and so do I."

"Matt, it's never that easy or cut-and-dried with mountain folk. Whenever I think that way—I'll just focus on my job, get in and get out—I get involved in their lives. I'm just hoping they don't have any extra squirrel stew around."

Matt appreciated that she wasn't dwelling on the incident with the arrow. It was in police custody now. Gabe said he'd send Jace to a sporting goods store out on the highway to ask if they knew of locals who did their own fletching, because it looked distinctively made, maybe handmade. Then he planned to send it to the BCI in London, Ohio, to have it tested for DNA and fingerprints. As if—even if they found some—it would be a match to the independent loners around Cold Creek who could fire a crossbow with such precision. Gabe had even wondered if the shooter had meant to miss the two of them, but what would be the message from that?

Although Matt kept an eye on the road above and behind them, he was also watching Char. Unfortunately, they had to pass Coyote Rock, where he'd almost gone off the cliff. As they neared it, she was biting her lower lip, frowning, concentrating. Even so, she looked good to him. She had a natural beauty that would wear well over the years. But why was he thinking like that? And right now?

"I do see the coyote-shaped rock formation," she said. "You know, in Navajo land, their tradition says that coyote is a hero who learned hogan building from the beaver people. All the animals are personified in their legends."

"The humped beaver houses probably resemble hogans, so that's how they made the connection. Around here, like coyotes and wolves, beavers are making a comeback. Royce and I went fishing last year in Cold Creek near where the old Hear Ye sect used to live, and I saw beavers and a small dam they'd made. They were actually changing the course of the creek, forming a pond."

"I don't know why they call it Cold Creek when it's really a river. You know, those beavers are probably near where the Fencers live. I remember from my childhood how much Joe Fencer used to love to trek around the area. He'd show up way down at our place, and Mom would give him lunch sometimes when he must have been no more than nine or ten. Anyway, he helped the search teams who went looking down by the river for Tess when she was kidnapped."

"I'll take that as a character reference on him. I'm probably going to interview him tomorrow about filling Woody's shoes as head Lake Azure groundskeeper."

"But if he's coming into a lot of money..."

"His wife thinks he'll jump at it. She says he'll miss farming his family's homestead and loves to work outside. That's something I hadn't thought of, that even with big bucks rolling in, the people ousted could miss their old place, even if they move way up in the world."

"Like the Fencers could buy a house or condo at Lake Azure? How would your well-educated, well-heeled clientele there take to that?"

"Yet to happen, but it would be interesting. Okay, I'm pretty sure that's the turnoff," he said, pointing.

"If the McKitricks live up here, that's just too far for little Jemmie to make the bus. I wish the consolidated school bus could just come up a little higher, but where would it turn around? Look. Chimney smoke. It must be right here. No dogs this time, so that's unusual."

"Woody said he gave all but one that was Jemmie's pet away when Sam was gone from local hunting for so long—when he was a sniper hunting the Taliban in Afghanistan. Sam lost his temper over that, Woody said, but I can sympathize with Sam. And I can't imagine being a sniper, waiting patiently, taking the right shot..."

She parked and they got out. Matt left his gun under the seat in Char's locked truck. She hefted her purse, big as a small suitcase, and the sack of winter coats while he carried the two other big bags of clothes and groceries for the family. They came to a halt when a man stepped out onto the roofed porch with a rifle, but held sideways, not pointed at them. He had a beard and shaggy, collar-length blond hair and walked with a limp and hunched shoulders. He wore an army camouflage jacket, pants and boots.

"You got business?" his gruff voice demanded.

"Are you Woody's son, Sam?" Matt asked. "I'm his friend and employer, Matt Rowan, from Lake Azure at Cold Creek, and this is my friend Charlene Lockwood."

"Oh, right. Heard of you. Couldn't go to the funeral. Had to keep watch here. Look out where you walk, in case there's a mine. But I think you're okay. I know where most of them's hid."

Matt heard Char give a little gasp. "He doesn't mean old coal mines," she whispered out of the side of her mouth. "Hi. Glad to meet you, Sam," she called out. "When you missed the funeral, you were watching for what?" she asked as they walked closer. You might know, Matt thought, she wasn't going to let him handle this strange man.

"In the woods," Sam said, gesturing in a wide circle with his free hand. "The enemy. Taliban."

Damn, Matt thought. How unstable did his PTSD make him with that gun?

Before Char could ask another question, they heard a boy's high voice from inside the house. "Pa? Pa? You out here?"

Jemmie stepped out onto the roofed porch with a beagle and an older woman at his heels. Matt recognized Woody's widow, Adela.

"Why, Mr. Rowan, you come right in. Wind's cold today," she called to them. "Sam, promise you'll set right here with Jemmie while I talk to our guests. Right nice to have guests. Beholden to you for what you give us of Woody's past salary, we sure are. And this is your assistant?"

"Mrs. McKitrick, this is Charlene Lockwood, a friend of mine." Matt hoped the final say-so on Jemmie's schooling wouldn't rest with Sam but with his mother or grandmother. As the three of them went into the house, he added, "I know Woody had big hopes his only grandson would get to school and learn a trade, so Charlene would like to talk about that. But here, these things are for you along with more money Woody had coming. Sorry they never found his coonskin cap you wanted for Jemmie. It must have come off when he fell and ended up who knows where."

Matt and Char just put their sacks of goods down

when Adela said nothing. She only nodded and pulled out chairs for them around a big pine table with a marred, rough surface. She poured them mugs of coffee that was so strong it looked like tar. Char shot Matt a wide-eyed glance as if to ask, *Is she offended? Won't she take the things?* But then they saw that the old woman's shoulders were heaving. She was crying without a sound, maybe over the old coonskin cap. Finally, as she was still turned away to get biscuits and some sort of berry jam from the counter, Matt saw her wipe her wet face with the palms of her hands.

"Can't thank you all enough," she said, her voice breaking as she set the things on the table. "Help us get through the winter. We have real trouble keeping Sam to home, even at night, though he's not fit to hold a job and Jemmie's too young. We keep the bullets hid, but I'm still afraid he'll hurt someone. Sam's wife, Mandy Lee, she took all this about Sam pretty hard, left for a while, gone down to stay with her brother's kin, Joe Fencer's family. Jemmie missing her something fierce."

Well, that answered that, Matt thought. If Mandy Lee was living with the Fencers right now, despite the fact he hadn't seen her at La Maison last night with them, Adela and Sam must know all about the fracking bonanza. Maybe Mandy Lee's brother, Joe, would help the McKitricks, get Sam more help at a VA hospital or clinic. What a tragedy that old Adela and young Jemmie had to cope with the sick man without Sam's wife around.

"Mrs. McKitrick," Char said, her voice calm and

friendly, "is there any way that Jemmie could get down to the Coyote Rock bus stop to go to school? Like Matt said, I'll bet that's what his granddad would want for him, to get an education. I heard he was going to school and doing very well but not lately."

"Well, see," she said, sinking in the chair across the table from them, "Woody, he used to drop him off at the school bus stop on his way down to work, pick him up later. Sam can't be 'lowed to drive the way he is, or we're feared he'd be goin' off, thinkin' he's in the army again. Mandy Lee, she took the truck, takes me shopping sometimes, 'cause Sam only got him an old beat-up one now and I got the keys hid. And her and me—we had us a tough discussion 'bout not tying him down to his bed or chair. He's so strong, gets angry like all git out. Like I said, we hid all the bullets, so he got him an empty gun."

The whole situation depressed Matt. Just before they left, when Adela wasn't looking, he put the plain envelope with money in it on the table. He had to admire these fiercely bold and independent people, despite the fact their isolation worked against them. And he had to admire Char for what she did among them and, in a way, how much she was like them.

The man was, Char thought as she peeked out her kitchen window, the second most forbidding-looking man she'd seen today. Sam McKitrick won first place, but this guy was a close second. Dressed all in black, he wore his raven hair slicked back, and his dark eyebrows seemed to meld into one over his piercing eyes as he scanned her small yard. Oh, he was kind of a chauffeur, now opening the back door of the vehicle as a silver-haired man got out. They both looked out of place in the driveway of her cabin. Her best guess was that they might be Royce Flemming and his assistant Matt had mentioned, but why would they be here?

She stood back from the window so they wouldn't see her staring out. The older man looked elegant. Whoever they were, what could be their business? It gave her extra empathy for the mountain families she'd visited who must wonder the same thing when she—or with Matt, as earlier this morning—got out of a strange vehicle and approached their house.

She tugged the hem of her sweatshirt down over her jeans and headed for the door just as the three raps resounded. Should she just open the kitchen window to talk to them, to be sure—to be safe? With all that had happened lately, she really couldn't be too careful....

She unlocked and lifted the window over the kitchen sink. "Hello. May I help you?"

The older man spoke. "Charlene Lockwood?"

"Yes."

"Young lady, you are very hard to track down. I'm Royce Flemming, and I'd like to ask your advice about something that affects your work. This is my assistant, Orlando."

Indeed it was the fracking king, Matt's senior partner. She figured they had learned where she was living from him. Or maybe Gabe or Tess. She opened the door.

"May I step in?" Mr. Flemming asked with a smile and a nod. "Orlando's content to admire the lovely view from here—of Lake Azure, my favorite place in these parts."

When she gestured him inside, he stepped past her. He smelled of some sort of tart citrus aftershave or cologne. "Please sit down. May I get you some coffee?"

"No, I'm fine, thanks. I know Winston Richards, who owns this cabin," he said, looking around. "Quite a hunter, but I see they've taken down the bear and stag heads for you."

"I was sorry to hear about his heart attack, but his wife has been very kind to rent it to me."

"He owns and runs trotting horses, which he takes excellent care of, but he forgot to take good care of himself," Flemming said as he sat in the upholstered chair where she indicated. She sat on the couch, facing him.

"You have some questions about my work?" she asked.

"Needless to say, I am overwhelmingly grateful you were up on Pinecrest to help Matt when someone tried to either terrify or kill him."

"I only did what anyone would have. Mr. Flemming, do you have any clue why someone would do that to Matt?"

"I don't. He's very popular, competent and an excellent PR man. And until the local sheriff comes up with something, I'm chalking it up to the rampant moron-factor around here."

She sat up straighter. Granted, there were some eccentrics, some loose cannons around here, but he'd said that with such disdain. Especially for a man who must rub shoulders with his staff at Lake Azure and with the locals he dealt with for fracking.

"The *moron-factor?*" she said, her voice on edge.

"Drunks, rednecks, throwbacks to the pioneer days, et cetera. I don't think the Hear Ye sect's would-be messiah lets his people loose, but the woods are full of crazies. But I—like Matt—am a practical businessman, Charlene, if I may call you that. I have a proposal for you, which Matt does not have to know about." He leaned forward, elbows on his knees, hands clasped. "What could I provide that would most help you with your work to reach the poorly schooled youth of Ohio Appalachia? I'd like to make a contribution, not only because you helped to save Matt, but for your helping to save the next generation of mountain folk. Name your project, damn the price."

She just gaped at him for a moment. Had Matt explained what she did, or did he research that on his own? Raising money for projects—and because of local pride, one had to tread carefully—was something she hoped to spearhead in the future. But she'd been racking her brain to figure out how to best help kids like Penny Hanson and Jemmie McKitrick. Despite his generosity and his ties to Matt, she wasn't sure she liked or trusted this man. Was there some sort of ulterior motive here, and could Matt be involved?

Well, a bird in hand, as they said. She cleared her throat and explained the situation that concerned her most. "There are at least six children up on Pinecrest Mountain—way up—who can't get to school because the bus can't go up that high to get them and find a spot to turn around. Their parents, for various reasons, can't or won't manage transportation. But a van could drive that far and turn around, maybe one with good snow tires even during the winter. And then deliver them back home again, of course."

"I like a woman who knows what she wants and clearly asks for it," he said with a nod. "In thanks to you, I'll get Orlando on that. You'll see I like quick results. And I greatly admire a woman who doesn't ask for something for herself."

"In that vein, let's not tell the beneficiaries who set this up. If the families up on Pinecrest think it's the school or even the state government that wishes them well despite their distrust of outsiders, all the better."

"You're too humble. I imagine it will come out that we're working together on this. I'll let Matt know. I'm sure he's determined to thank you in his own way," he said with a grin as he rose.

He reached out and took her hand. She thought he would shake it, but he held it in his firm grip. He was exactly her height; they looked eye to eye. His hands were small, but just think of the power they must wield.

"I'll let you know," he said, "when our bus is ready and you can liaise with the school district and the families."

"And, it would be helpful," she added as he released her hand and stepped to the door, "if the driver could be someone local who knows the area and needs a job. I hope I can send you a suggestion for a bus driver, someone who hasn't seen the blessings of fracking fall from heaven."

"Ah," he said, tilting his head and narrowing his eyes at her.

Had she overstepped? She couldn't keep the skeptical tone out of her voice about fracking, no matter how generous Royce Flemming was.

"Yes," he said. "Another good suggestion. So, we are partners in this, Charlene. I, for one, am grateful for all you are doing to elevate the level of living here, and, I'm sure, you will come to see that I am doing the same with my fracking company. Good afternoon. I'll be in touch," he called back over his shoulder as he walked toward his car.

I'll be in touch, indeed. He had held her hand so warmly, looked at her so intensely....

She closed the door behind him and glanced out the window. Orlando had been walking around outside. She'd seen him go by the window several times, as if he were circling the cabin. Now he hurried toward his employer and opened the sedan door for him. She watched as they drove away and the car disappeared from view.

Royce Flemming hadn't said a thing about the hole in the door, maybe hadn't seen it, but she felt he was the type to see every detail. He'd said, *I'll be in touch.* Matt had touched her life and her heart, but this man, Matt's friend and mentor, was both loved and hated around here. He surely had the Midas touch when it came to making money. Though he'd asked nothing of her, she wondered if she owed him now. For the best of reasons, had she just made a deal with the devil?

9

As Matt drove into the driveway of the Fencer farm, he noted in the weathered paint over the barn door, Heritage Farm, 1908. As if he'd been watching for him, Joe Fencer opened the front door of the old, but well-kept farmhouse.

"Thanks for the call," Joe shouted over the noise from the huge fracking site across the road. When the work went on at night, how did these people even sleep? Matt wondered.

"I'm really interested in the possibility of the job," Joe told Matt as they shook hands on the porch.

"We can do a formal interview when I show you around the grounds and have you meet some key people," Matt told him as they went inside. "But I thought it might be good to talk to you on your own turf first. It looks like you had gardens, flowers and vegetables, besides your soybeans out back. And I can tell from how neat your bushes look that you're a good hedge trimmer."

"Glad you can tell since we've had so many early frosts, and the flowers and crops are gone," he said with a shake of his head. "Sorry about this chaos inside here. We're packing to move."

"I heard about it from Royce Flemming."

"It was nice of him to suggest me for the job. Brad Mason said he was a nice guy."

"He is. I've known him for years. I'm sad the fracking has caused problems for him around here."

Joe grimaced. Tall and lanky with sandy hair and brown eyes, probably in his midforties, Joe led Matt into a back room that must have been a den or office. Like the front room, half-packed or sealed boxes were stacked in corners, but he'd obviously cleared off the desk and pulled up two chairs.

"I gotta level with you," he told Matt. "Despite the windfall of fracking money, I swear, I almost turned it down. This place has been in my family for generations, and it's hard to let it go. It's what I chose to do after high school, farm with my dad, then when he was gone, go it alone and hope that one of my boys would carry on. The money—it doesn't mean so much to me but it does to the wife. Better life for the kids, got four of them, two girls, two boys."

"I was in the restaurant the other night when you came in. A good-looking bunch—a full house."

"For sure, and we got my sister, Mandy Lee McKittrick, here for a spell."

"I heard. I visited the McKitricks yesterday. Seems we have a lot of people in common."

"So you know about her husband, Sam? The docs at the VA hospital said he was better, but once he got home—well, a short time later he suddenly regressed, so the medical men were wrong."

"Can't he be examined and readmitted?"

"His mother and Mandy Lee tried that, but he seemed to convince the docs he was stable, and they wouldn't keep him."

"Charlene Lockwood remembers you as an outdoorsman, said you were often down by the creek, even when you were young."

"I still love it down there, despite the mess the fracking work is making on the ridge above it. At least when the Hear Ye people were there, it was a lot more quiet. Obviously," he said, "it's so damn noisy now. Forget quiet country living. And I'll miss being able to walk down to Cold Creek to unwind. We're moving to a new place on the other side of town out toward Chillicothe. Sara Ann's real excited about it."

"And the kids?"

"Yeah, it's a lot bigger house. Going to have a playground and trampoline, lots of new stuff, new school. I just hope I can convince them that new stuff isn't what makes someone happy."

"A wise thought, especially in the midst of what some folks around here would kill for."

"Speaking of that, I heard what happened to you up on Pinecrest. Facing death—it really makes you think. Matt, I told both Brad Mason and Royce Flemming that

I could walk away from this bonanza. Not sure either of them believed me, but I think you do."

Matt nodded, and they shared a moment of silence—as silent as it could be with the fracking noise, even here in the back room of the closed-up house. "So, can you come to the lodge for an interview, and we'll talk turkey, as Woody McKitrick used to say?"

Joe nodded, then sighed. He'd been sitting erect, but now his shoulders slumped. "He was a courageous guy. I couldn't believe he had the nerve to lead the antifrackers around here when he worked for Lake Azure since Royce Flemming financed that, too. I saw Woody once picketing with a big sign that read, KILL THE DRILL!" Joe shook his head. "Then he ends up dead. He was an original around here, especially when he wore that coonskin cap. My sister says they never found it."

"No, but then he fell quite a ways."

"It probably snagged in a tree or caught on a ledge. I'll come to the lodge whenever you want. The womenfolk don't understand why I'd want to work outside in all weather with my hands anymore, as if I'd be happy just sitting around toasty warm in the house, watching sports on TV. Your know, the sod on my new place is just rolled out over unworked soil, no trees on our lot, but I'll plant them. It'll be real hard to get a garden of any kind going there, so I promise I'll help beautify your community if I get the chance."

They chatted awhile longer and Joe walked him to the door. Matt heard the voices of women and young children upstairs. Maybe Joe had got them out of their way for this meeting. The light young voices made the high-ceilinged, bare rooms of the old farmhouse seem at once friendlier, and sadder to be deserted. Unless the rig workers wanted an office here, the house and barn would be torn down and the land would soon be under concrete and drilling rigs, water retention ponds and trucks.

"The noise is amazing this close." Matt stated the obvious as Joe walked him to his car and they shook hands again.

"At least that hellish light is gone."

"You mean night-work lights?"

"No, not those. When they first hit gas, they flared a fifty-foot-tall flame out the top of that big drilling framework, kind of like a beacon day and night screaming, 'Look what we've done!' It erased the night, crept into the house even with the curtains closed."

He shook his head and stayed standing there as if watching the work site as Matt got in his car, honked and drove away. In his rearview mirror, he could see Joe standing in his front yard still glaring across the road.

Despite how pleased Matt was that Royce had put him onto Joe Fencer as an excellent replacement for Woody, he left feeling depressed.

"Oh, forgot to tell you something," Tess told Char as she opened the mail during the day care nap time. They were drinking coffee while Tess's friend and helper Lindell Kelton took charge of the sleeping kids for a half hour, a task Char had helped with when she first came back to Cold Creek. "Sara Ann Fencer phoned to say she'd like to put her two boys in day care here three times a week. At least that's something good they're doing with the fracking money. Some folks went crazy when they got it."

"Money talks—and walks. I saw them in La Maison the other night, meeting with Brad Mason."

"Hmm. He may be Grant's brother, but I wouldn't trust him. Anyhow, I told Sara Ann that will be fine. I don't want to take on too many new ones right now, though, so that I wear myself down, especially now." She looked at Char as if waiting for her to say something.

"Tess, you don't think that large area of fracking down Valley View could work its way down to our old homestead, do you? Wouldn't that be something, since we don't own it anymore?"

"Yes, but I wanted to tell you something else," Tess said, almost pouting. "I was going to wait until you, Kate and I were together, but I just can't. Gabe and I are making up for lost time."

"Wait—Tess, do you mean…"

"Yes. Yes! I'm even getting morning sickness. Isn't that great?"

"Well, I wouldn't put it that way but—yes!" she cried, before remembering it was nap time and they were making too much noise. "Yes, that's wonderful!" They hugged and held tight, rocking each other.

Tess started to cry. "Mom would have been so happy, but having you and Kate here helps a lot. We're going to call Dad this weekend. That will make him feel older, to be a grandfather."

As least, Char thought, even with Tess's childhood abduction, her little sister was obvious ready for this. She evidently considered Cold Creek a safe place now, but Char wasn't so sure.

After leaving the Fencer farm, Matt drove around the big fracking site on the old Hear Ye cult grounds. The continual clash of sounds, human and mechanical, grew louder as he approached. He saw the tall iron framework in the shape of an obelisk Joe had mentioned. From it, thin guy lines spreading out like tentacles attached it to the earth. Near that, a maze of massive pipes three times as tall as the trucks snaked around each other. Since the crew worked day and night shifts, tall pole lights studded the area. More than once Royce had said that work did shut down for a while on Sundays—his "gesture" on the Sabbath in an area where most people still went to church.

Though he'd taken an early tour of the site before it was really up and running—and had to admit, he'd boycotted it since—now he noted new, huge, round silos for storage and numerous wellheads cluttering the ground near a series of metal trailers. Big, noisy tanker trucks, some with their diesel engines running, surrounded the site, and men in hard hats hurried here and there. And in the midst of it all was an artificial lake, nearly as big as a football field. The main fracking lagoon had been dug from the earth and lined with gray polyethylene.

As a tanker drove up behind him, he went past the site, turned around and drove back. If he remembered right, the massive lagoon held recycled water that had been treated and collected to be forcibly injected into the deep shale beneath the surface. From this angle, the water looked golden brown. Matt knew the polluted flowback from the drilling had to be stored in steel tanks before being taken away to be treated and returned. Remembering Woody's claim that such sites could taint local wells and springwater, he decided to walk down to Cold Creek to take a look for any signs the water was being polluted. Joe had said there were paths near here. If the beavers were still building, maybe he'd bring Char down to see them.

He parked and found a path down to the river everyone called a creek. Had it been smaller when the pioneers in these parts had named it, or did Cold Creek just sound better than Cold River?

He saw a cluster of beaver dams but didn't get too close as they were busily building. The noise from the fracking site didn't seem to faze them, so there was one sign the environment wasn't being seriously damaged. He jumped and hunkered down when he heard what sounded like a gunshot nearby. For sure, way down here, off the road, that wasn't a truck backfiring. Considering his recent record for getting in harm's way, he stayed put a moment, scanning the ground beneath the leafless trees. It reminded him of his search Thursday morning for a spot where someone could have shot that arrow into Char's door.

As he moved out of his hiding place, he saw there was a dead beaver over on the creek bank. People trapped, not shot, beavers, and it wasn't hunting season for them. He didn't want to risk hanging around here, walking out in the open to check it. He knew vultures would make short work of it.

He headed out of the valley, staying hidden in the trees, but he saw something strange. He approached what looked like a black metal ladder attached to a tree. It was a tree stand for hunting with a seat about fifteen feet off the ground overlooking where deer could come to drink or the beavers worked and lived. But someone shooting from here would be shooting down so the bullet would seem to come from the sky.

"Damn!" he muttered. "Like that arrow."

With a last glance up at the hunter's stand with its empty seat and shooting rail so someone could steady a gun or crossbow, he ran up the path he'd come down. He needed to talk to Char.

Matt saw Char pulling into her driveway ahead of him. He honked once and parked behind her.

"What?" she said as she got out. "Are you okay?"

"I went to see the Fencers. I'm probably going to hire Joe to take Woody's place, as if anyone could. You—Have you been crying?"

"Happy tears. Tess just told me she and Gabe are going to have a baby."

"That's great. But listen, after I talked to Joe, I went down to the river—creek—near his house."

"I used to know that area well. I can't tell you how many frogs we caught. Dad taught us to fish there, though I haven't done it since."

He took her arm and steered her away from the cabin, back into the area where they'd seen the deer Wednesday evening. "What?" she asked again.

"I spotted a hunting stand attached to a tree there with a seat and bar to steady a rifle or crossbow. High up, so—"

"I get it. We should have thought of that, looked up into the trees, not just down for footprints. So we're going to look now? It makes sense that, since this is a hunting cabin, there could be something like that nearby—or more than one."

"Which someone could use to watch your place."

"But why? Some voyeur, Peeping Tom out here in the cold dead of night? I close all my curtains at night, so you can't think—"

They both saw it at the same time, a metal ladder attached to a tree, with not only a seat above, but a kind of camouflaged tent around it, gray-brown so it blended with the tree trunk.

"The arrow could have been shot into your door from there," Matt said. "Here, don't want to have these drop out." He handed over his keys and wallet. Reaching for the lower rung about three feet off the ground, he climbed up.

"Be careful."

"That's our motto lately, partner. I just want to check the trajectory, see if there's anything left up here."

She craned her neck to see while he stuck his head into the small canvas cover, then lifted a side flap to get better light inside.

"Anything?"

"Not that I can see, but the view of your door and most of that side of the cabin is clear from here. There's a wadded-up package of—of, get this—Red Man Chewing Tobacco."

"It should change its name to American Indian or Native American."

"Char, let's take up that cause later, okay?" he said as he carefully came back down with it.

"You know," Matt went on. "Maybe Gabe can at least get prints off this—if he eliminates mine—or even DNA." He took his keys and wallet back, then carefully nestled the wadded tobacco package next to the low step by her back door. "Let's look around more."

"I can call Mrs. Richards to ask if her husband used chewing tobacco or put up that tree stand."

"That would eliminate him, but who knows who else could have used it, besides our crossbow shooter."

They hurt their necks looking up, turning this way and that around trees until Char spotted another tree stand, perched almost on the edge of the ridge high above Lake Azure. "Bingo!" she called to him, and he hurried over. "Are you going up again? Or I can this time."

"Can-do Char. I'll go." He handed her his keys and wallet again and climbed up. This one didn't have a canopy. "Nothing but a great view—not of your cabin this time but the other direction, clear to the lodge below. I wonder how close that would all seem with high-powered binocs. Coming down."

Again, she handed him his things, and they started along what seemed to be a path back toward the cabin. "Oh, I see a raccoon!" she cried and jumped behind him.

"Or maybe not so can-do Char," he said, trying to lighten their mutual mood. "No, it's..." He approached the fur in the leaves and squatted to study it.

"Is it dead?"

"No, it's—it's a coonskin cap," he said, his voice breaking as he picked it up and examined it. "Woody's name's inside—and, damn it, this is a long way from the place where he had to have fallen."

10

Char could see that Matt was really upset. She stepped closer not only to look at the coonskin cap but to put her hand on his arm. "How did his cap end up over here? Maybe it blew here in the wind?"

"It's snagged on the wrong side of this tree to have blown here. The wind up here comes from the northwest," he said.

"So..."

"So he must have lost it here. But he fell way over there, at least twenty-five or thirty yards. There was an autopsy—no heart attack or anything that would have made him stagger on without it, then trip and fall. If he'd been able, he would not have left it behind."

"And if he was hurt, he would have headed back toward the road, not farther from help. Why was he even up here? It isn't Lake Azure land."

"A home owner had complained about pinecones falling and knocking on his roof, jamming up the eavestroughs, so Woody came up to cut some of the limbs back. He drove a golf cart up here, which he often used to get around. It was found down in your cabin's driveway."

Matt bent over to look closer at the spot where the cap had been. "I'm just wondering if he could have fallen and hit his head, kind of lost it—his sense of direction."

"Should we go look at the pine trees where he wanted to cut cones off?" she asked. "Maybe there's something there."

"The sheriff searched the area."

"But didn't see this cap here?"

"Wasn't looking way over here, I guess," he said with a deep sigh. "And it was kind of buried. You know, Char, as different as Woody and I were from each other, we really got along. Ever had someone like that? I mean, Royce is like that for me, too, but Woody was different, so down to earth, no pun intended."

He got to his feet and put his arm around her shoulders. "Yes," she told him, leaning close. "I had someone like that. Maria Whitehorse. A lot older than me, a great-grandmother to one of the kids I worked with out West. The Navajo have a matriarchal family system, you know—power to the women. But she told me, however much that was their heritage, it sometimes robbed the men of power they felt they should have, so some took it out in the wrong ways—drinking, fighting, dominating their wives and kids. It's the opposite culture pattern to most families in Appalachia, where the man's in charge. Anyway, she understood what I was trying to do, even warned me about my ill-fated 'Dads Don't Drink' campaign that turned some against me. Her strong advice was that I should leave so that some of the disgruntled young bucks who liked to drink didn't harm me."

"In other words, she kept you safe. Jumping in with both feet to do what you thought was right—that does sound like you."

"Maria burned all the signs I was putting up in town and using to picket a bar just off reservation land."

Still holding the fur cap close to his chest, he shook his head. "Your story reminds me of Woody again. He made enemies organizing a picket line with 'KILL THE DRILL!' signs."

"So are you thinking— I mean, did Gabe consider..."

"That he might have met with foul play? Yeah. But there was no evidence, no witnesses."

"Let's go look at that spot where he was cutting the pine tree boughs."

"Okay, but like I said, it's been searched and it's not where he fell."

Holding hands, they carefully walked the ridge to the cluster of white pines. Their crowns were loaded with cones; some lay on the ground, but no branches looked cut off, even near the edge of the steep hill.

"Like I told you, Gabe looked in this area and where he fell," Matt said. "And whatever happened to him, he obviously didn't get the boughs cut. If I hire Joe Fencer, he can cut them off—and I'll bodyguard him the way Orlando does Royce."

"Okay, then. Let's walk back."

Still holding hands, they headed away from the area where Woody must have stumbled and fallen. Her cabin was in sight.

"Look," she said. "A sort of deer path, partly hidden by more leaves."

He squatted to look at the ground she pointed out. I was about twelve feet back from the edge. "You know, from this angle, it looks like—"

"Something was dragged," she finished for him. "Or someone."

"But, as I said, it's really far from where he fell. Maybe deer have been sleeping here and it looks like drag marks. Or a bear killed a deer and dragged it."

"Could your friend have crawled along here?" she asked, squinting at the half-hidden site. She followed in Matt's footsteps along the strange path that perhaps wasn't a path at all. "Maybe we should call Gabe."

"But look," he said, holding out an arm to stop her. "The drag marks, or whatever they are, stop right here, and we're still a long ways from where he went off."

"You said Woody had enemies—"

"Yeah," he interrupted, "but I don't want this pointing to Royce, who would never do or allow anything like that. Some locals were upset by Woody's stand on fracking. We can't just start making accusations."

"Matt, I didn't even mention Royce. What if whoever

hurt him got tired of dragging him and picked him up here to take him way over there and shove him off?"

"Only if he'd been unconscious could someone else control him. He was a strong guy. He did have head injuries, broken bones, but with that fall, none of that was suspicious. Besides, if you're tired of dragging someone, it takes more strength to pick him up and carry him. But you're right. Let's get the sheriff in on this—the cap, these possible drag marks. See if your phone works in this spot, because mine doesn't."

"It's in my purse. You tried to call from this area already? Mine works in the cabin."

"I've been up here a lot, even when I first came to Cold Creek. I took photos of the progress on the buildings below. I love the view—especially of the lake."

"Let's head back. We also need to tell Gabe you found tree stands and that tobacco package."

They hiked back, staying off the drag marks, if that's what they were. Char wondered if any of this would make Gabe open a new investigation. She could tell Matt was torn between loyalty to Woody and to Royce. Back at the cabin, she got her phone from her purse, which she'd left in her truck. She dialed the number of the police station. But before she put the call through, she jumped as Matt shouted. "Char, the tobacco package isn't here! I put it in this corner where it couldn't blow away, and there's not much wind, anyway. At least I have his cap."

She spun toward him. "Are you sure?" she started to ask. But the empty tobacco packet was nowhere in sight.

After Matt and Gabe walked along the ridge for a good half hour, they came back into the cabin, looking chilled and dejected.

"It would have helped if we'd found a rock with blood on it," Gabe was saying. "We can try to investigate the tobacco, have Jace ask around in a couple of area stores who buys it. It's a real stretch that someone was watching you or Char, but I agree it didn't blow away. The coonskin cap placement is significant, but I can't bank much on whether those are drag marks or not—human drag marks."

Char poured them both coffee as they took off their coats and slumped in chairs across from each other at the small kitchen table. She wanted to help. "I can go over that path inch by inch tomorrow, see if anything else fell or—"

"Char," Gabe said. "Matt and I agree that, just in case there was a crime committed up here, a possible homicide, not to mention that arrow in your door—"

"And the disappearance of that package," Matt said. "I looked all over for it in case it blew away, which it didn't—"

Gabe interrupted. "You should take up Matt's offer to move down to Lake Azure to house-sit that empty place, at least for a while."

"What? I'm not leaving. That's the story of my life—

find some place I want to be and—out! Besides, I just paid for three months' rent."

"Just until we get some answers," Gabe said. "Those tree stands may not be suspicious—I'm going to check with your landlady to be sure they're not new—but someone could be using them to watch the cabin for some reason."

"Gabe," she said, hands on her hips, "I haven't been here long enough to make enemies. I'm helping people, working *with* them, not against them."

"Think it over," Gabe said, finishing his coffee fast and getting up. "At least for a night or two until we get some answers here. That arrow in the door was too close for comfort, a warning, at least. I've got to get going. Matt, I know you want to return that cap to Woody's widow. I've marked the spot and examined it, but I'd better take it back with me for a better once-over."

"The thing is it's for his grandson."

"I'll get it back to you soon. Meanwhile, I'll leave you two to arrange Char's *temporary* stay down in the valley. Char," he said, throwing an arm around her stiff shoulders, "it's for your own good. Tess said she told you about the baby. We want her to have two willing and able aunts in town when he—or she—is born. Okay?"

"Maybe. Probably. Gabe, that reminds me about Grace out there with that crazy Bright Star. She'll have her baby in about a month, and we've got to get her out of there, for the birth at least."

"You let Matt get you settled down below, and I'll go with you and Tess—not in uniform, just as a family member—to see Grace and Lee. One last try to talk some sense into them. We'll find some place where Bright Star and his cronies can't spy on us with that peephole I hear you discovered."

He hugged her, shook Matt's hand and headed out. Matt closed the door behind him.

"It sounds like you're his acting deputy now," she said, standing her ground across the table from him. "Am I under arrest?"

"I'd like that, but you wouldn't be staying in a vacant house down in Lake Azure then, but with me. Come on, Char, pack some things, let's lock up and I'll follow you down before it gets dark. We'll have dinner at the lodge and think this all through again—everything. I need you to help me figure it all out."

"I spent last night here with no problems. No more arrows, no nothing. I had a good night's sleep."

He rolled his eyes. "That was then, this is now. Two nights out of the three you've been here, weird things happened."

"I suppose I don't have a choice," she admitted. His words, *That was then, this is now,* and especially, *I need you,* in whatever context he'd said them, snagged in her heart and head. Her theory was that people always had choices. Still, being near Matt again sounded not only safer but sweeter than a night alone in this cabin without him.

"This place is big—beautiful," Char whispered as Matt let her into the empty house of a retired Dr. and

Mrs. Manning, who lived in South Florida in the winter months.

"It's three bedrooms. The layout's similar to mine, although none of the houses are completely alike."

"You're sure they won't mind?" she asked as Matt set her suitcase down and started turning on lights in the great room. It had a U-shaped beige leather couch with lots of throw pillows. Several tall windows reached to the ceiling, but there were vertical blinds hung from halfway up, which were closed. A lovely oil painting of the Mannings hung over the raw stone hearth. He had silver hair and a round face; she had dark hair and sparkling brown eyes.

"They prefer having someone in here, though we have good security. The community's never been gated, but there's a guard who makes the rounds at night, and the groundskeepers are aware during the day. We have had a few problems in here over the six years. I have an interview with Joe Fencer coming up for Woody's job, by the way, so we may soon have another good pair of eyes here. I'll show you the guest bedroom and bath."

"Anyway," she said, following him as he carried her suitcase down the hall, "I probably won't be here long enough to qualify as an actual house sitter, though my sisters will both rest easier to know I'm here."

"Then I like both of your sisters," he said, clicking on the bathroom light from the hall, then the bedroom light next door. "Almost as much as I like you, however stubborn you can be."

He put her suitcase on the double bed. The room was

tastefully done in neutral hues with splashes of color from bright pillows, pictures and lamps, much like the great room. It had a TV, an easy chair and a desk where she could put her laptop, so she didn't spill out into the rest of the house. She didn't want to leave a footprint here, or get in food—anything like that. Surely, she wouldn't be here long.

Matt smiled at her. "I actually thought I'd have to carry you here, kicking and screaming. I'll wait in the great room, give you some time to get settled, then we'll go eat at the lodge."

"I'll take you out this time."

"Char, I have dining privileges there. We're together, but it won't be a date, if you don't want it to be."

"I didn't say I didn't want it to be."

His face lit up at that. "Okay. Maybe when I bring you back here tonight, we won't have someone watching, won't have an arrow shot at us kissing, like on some old-fashioned Valentine's Day card."

She laughed out loud. The mental snapshot of that compared to what had really happened was too funny. She could just picture a frilly card with a man and woman kissing in front of a big red heart, stuck through by Cupid's arrow.

But the truth was, she felt as if she'd been shot through with need for this man she hardly knew. Not quite love at first sight, but it made her believe in that. If he'd grabbed her and kissed her right now, she wasn't sure what she'd do.

There was an awkward moment between them, as

if he'd read her thoughts. "How about fifteen minutes and we'll head out?" he said. "Casual clothes are fine for the lodge, though a few like to dress up."

His eyes went over every inch of her. Like an idiot, she backed up a step. Her thighs hit the corner of the bed, and she sat down on the edge of it, bouncing once. She felt his look as if he'd touched her.

He nodded, looking serious, went out and closed the door behind him. But to her, a big door to who knew where had just opened in her life.

11

The dinner with Matt at the lodge was far different from their date at the French restaurant. Although they had a quiet table in an alcove of the dining room facing the large fireplace, people knew him and many came by to say hello.

Char soon discovered Matt was an everyman—problem solver, font of information, enforcer, friend. She loved people, but she was introduced to so many her head spun. And, despite herself, she secretly resented having to share Matt's attention.

"There you are, Matt," a cute redhead said as she walked by, evidently looking for someone she didn't see. She was dressed as if she were ready to go skiing with tight pants and a sweater with deer and pine trees on it. "I got your note. What do you want to know about the arrows I make?"

"Ginger, this is my friend, Charlene Lockwood. Char, Ginger is our archery instructor and sports director, except for the golf course."

"You all are right about that," she said in an exaggerated drawl that Char quickly realized was not a put-on. "But soon as I get *your* job," she added, smiling and punching his shoulder, "I'll manage the golf course, too." She winked at Char. "Just teasing now."

"Char's house-sitting for the Mannings for a while," Matt explained.

"Lovely people. Well, Matt, anyway, bring me the arrow, and I'll try to answer your questions. Is it one I made?"

"I don't have the arrow, but I'll bring you a drawing of it. You aren't meeting Royce for dinner, are you? He said he was coming here tonight."

"Water over the dam, that man. Sad to say, I was just a fill-in-the-blank after his last divorce. His Majesty's in here somewhere, though. He gave Orlando the evening off, so I'm stuck with him for a drink uptown. Doesn't talk much and I do, so that may work out. See you later, then. Nice to meet you, Charlene."

When she sauntered off, Matt apologized. "Sorry about all the intrusions. If you want, tomorrow I can just bring food from here to your place or mine."

"That would be fine. By the way, my sister Kate invited both of us to dinner sometime soon, if you'd like to go. You should see the archaeological dig she's supervising—dirty but fascinating.

"So Ginger makes her own arrows?"

"Shoots her own pheasants and wild turkeys, uses those tail feathers, and, I think, buys some."

"Matt, sorry for sounding paranoid, but she wouldn't

shoot at us, would she? You don't have to answer this, but could she have a personal interest in you, then she sees us together..."

"No! You heard who's had a relationship with her here. She aimed pretty high, though, like she said, it didn't last."

"Aiming high—a good way to talk about an expert archer. So she and Royce—"

"Did I hear my name?" a familiar voice behind Char asked. Royce walked up to their table, on his way out of the dining room. His shadow, Orlando, walked on by with a nod instead of stopping, too. Maybe that's who Ginger had been looking for. Then Char saw Brad Mason. He stopped a moment at their table. She remembered that he'd moved into Lake Azure now, so he could be around anytime.

"We have to stop meeting at restaurants," Brad said with a smile. It seemed to Char he'd had a bit too much to drink. "Good to see you both again—together." He winked and headed away.

"Good evening, Matt, Charlene," Royce said.

"You two have met?" Matt asked.

"Today, at her cabin. We're also partners of a sort," Royce said, putting his hand on Matt's shoulder. When Matt looked confused and frowned at her, Royce continued. "I made Charlene an offer to help with her work for the mountain kids, and she suggested the donation of a van to deliver them to school each day—and a local driver."

"And when were you going to mention that?" Matt asked her.

"Royce said he'd tell you, so I assumed he had. I hope to have a suggestion for the driver soon."

"Orlando will drive the new van in from Columbus," Royce said. "We're in business. Matt, I just hadn't had time to tell you yet, and I did promise her I'd fill you in. I'm glad to see you busy tonight with so many residents stopping by, but don't let that—or me—keep you from your lovely dinner partner."

He smiled at Char, squeezed Matt's shoulder and moved away.

"I would have told you right away, but we've been interrupted a lot, and he did say he'd tell you."

He leaned forward over the empty dessert plates and coffee. "Char, the man has been great to me over the years, before and after my dad died, but once you are in bed with him so to speak—"

"You don't have to put it that way! And if you care for him, trust him..."

"My gratitude to and affection for him doesn't mean I completely trust him. And be warned he's a ladies' man."

"I got that idea from Ginger."

"Let's just say her, three wives and countless others."

"Get real. He would never be interested in me that way, and he's old enough to be my father." She almost accused Matt of sounding jealous. And as much as that annoyed her, she liked it, too. As for Royce Flemming, her deal with him was going to make a big difference in some young lives—and that didn't include hers.

The next morning, Saturday, Char decided to go to the holiday market on the town square, despite the fact that Tess had called to say she was too queasy to go with her. Ah, Char wondered, was there always a price to pay for something good?

Matt had been in a silent huff last night when he took her home. He had not come in or kissed her. She'd been surprised how much she wanted to be kissed again. Ever since that arrow had hit her cabin, he was being too possessive and overly protective. And he was riled she hadn't immediately blurted out to him that she'd made a deal with Royce. He should just be happy the new bus would help Jemmie McKitrick. Matt had said they could still go up on Pinecrest together when he took Woody's cap to the boy, but that might be just because he didn't trust her out on her own again. After all, he was the one who'd been in danger on the mountain. So despite the magnetism between them, there was friction, too.

She drove to the gas station, for once not the old, familiar one uptown, but the new one near Lake Azure. She was here for two reasons. She needed gas, but Tess had mentioned that Gabe had ordered Matt's burned-out vehicle to be hauled here. Though it was a total wreck, Gabe was going to go over it again, looking for signs of scraped paint from the other truck or fingerprints from someone who could have tossed that weird note into the front seat. She was curious to take a look at the wreck up close.

She noticed the gas was more expensive here than uptown, but why not? People at Lake Azure probably didn't blink an eye over prices. But wasn't all the local fracking supposed to keep oil and gas prices down?

After she filled the tank and moved her truck, she walked around back. Matt's truck sat forlorn, so broken with its black, charred, crumpled metal. She could still smell gasoline and smoke. A web of neon-bright police tape surrounded it so she could only look through the driver's-side door which had once read Lake Azure, Inc. She shuddered. At least something good had come out of this. She'd met Matt; now if they could just get along and stay safe.

She turned to walk away and saw a man watching her, someone she didn't know. She went on the alert.

"Miz Lockwood?" he said. He was thin, with beard stubble, dressed in worn jeans and a plaid flannel shirt that surely couldn't keep him warm in this weather. "Henry Hanson, ma'am. Come here to ask for a job, but they don't need no help. The Mrs.—Elinor—said you wanted to have words 'bout Penny, 'bout her missing school. I seen you were here."

"Oh, yes," she said, but, not wanting to be back here alone with him—had he been following her?—she walked to the front of the station near her truck. He walked that way, too. "But how did you track me down here, know it was me, Mr. Hanson?"

"Penny said you got you a state sticker on the back

of your black '06 Dodge Ram truck, license with letters and number 400. Penny, she's smart, I'll say that, but we need her to home. Can't get her down to school no more. I mean, I got a truck, but gas costs, and without my job at the other gas station, it just don't work out."

Yes, thank you Lord, for a clear sign about this, Char offered up a quick prayer. He'd said he come here to the gas station to get a job, and she could provide that. But should she? Was this too much of a coincidence? On the other hand, didn't this prove something good could come out of a wreck?

"Mr. Hanson, if you had a steady job and a way to get Penny down to school and back safely, what would you say then?"

"Well, when pigs fly— But sure, if'n Elinor can manage the young'uns alone."

"I take it you have a valid driver's license and experience driving up on the mountain, even in the winter."

"Well, yes, ma'am," he said, cocking his head and squinting at her.

She hesitated for one more moment. Elinor had said this man knew how to hunt with a bow and arrow. It still seemed strange that he'd found her here, especially behind the station near Matt's wreck. And he could hold it against her that she wanted Penny in school rather than 'to home.' So, just to be sure, she decided to quiz this guy so she could report to Matt and maybe even Gabe.

"I know this sounds like a crazy question, Mr. Hanson, but when you use the bow and arrow, like Elinor said you're skilled at, where do you get your arrows?"

"I done taught a few friends to shoot. The job—you need arch-ry lessons?"

"No. I'm just interested in arrows. My sister has excavated a few prehistoric ones from the Mason Mound—arrows made by the Adena." Darn, she knew she was making a mess of this, way in over her head now. This man might be uneducated but he had street sense—well, mountain sense.

"Promise not to tell what I done, 'cause it's not quite on the up-and-up?"

He was going to confess to something. Her heart pounded.

"Who should I not tell?"

"You're sister-in-law to the sheriff, ain't you?"

Of course, that could be another reason this man didn't like her. She was related to and working for the law, the government.

"Oh, all right," he said when she hesitated. "If somethin's thrown out, it's not stealing. Not proud of Dumpster diving, heading out at night to get things others don't want, food back of the grocery, stuff out behind the Walmart on the highway. For the arrows—I get them out of the trash can by the arch'ry range at Lake Azure, fix 'em up a bit, good to go."

Char didn't know whether to laugh or cry. This man raided trash cans to feed his family—and took Ginger's arrows to hunt for meat—and she was afraid he was a would-be murderer? At least this time she'd tell Matt right away what she'd decided to do.

"If you can drive a van, I might have a job for you

driving it as a school bus. Of course, you'd need to have a driver's license and have a background check, be tested on some driving laws by the sheriff or his deputy, but I think we could make that happen pretty fast."

The smile of relief he gave her made her feel she could trust him with the van, with the kids—with her life.

Matt took his crude sketch of the arrow and went to find Ginger. He wished he'd asked the sheriff for a photo, but then he'd have to admit to Gabe and Ginger he was doing some serious detective work on his own. Ginger Green—Royce once kidded her she was named for her red hair and green eyes—was hardly a suspect, despite the fact she was a skilled archer. It's just he was hell-bent to find out if she could have made the arrow that had just missed him and Char.

He'd racked his brain over who would want to kill him on the mountain and if it could be linked to the arrow attack. He kept coming back to the fact it had to be tied to negative feelings about Royce's fracking company. Maybe one of the locals thought he was partners in that, too. Surely, people were past pent-up passions over the "rich folk" invading the little town of Cold Creek. With the local PR he'd done, he supposed he was the poster boy for that, however much charity work he'd done in the area.

And no way did he believe the arrow was to hit or scare Char. He was the common denominator—that is, if the two totally different incidents were related.

He was really annoyed at Royce for suggesting Char had "just happened" to come along to help save him, and that she'd try to ask for something in return. Yet the sly fox had offered her carte blanche and, typical Char, she'd asked for something to help the mountain folk. He shouldn't have been angry with her over that. He had to admit he'd acted like a jerk last night, but the woman got to him in all kinds of ways.

Ginger's car was parked behind the lodge. It was midmorning and chilly, so he didn't expect her to be giving a lesson on the archery range. He figured she must be in her office, a small wood-shingled building between the range and the tennis, volleyball and shuffleboard courts. He was ready to knock on the door when he heard sounds from inside. Panting. Moaning. Was someone in distress?

Just before he pounded on the door, he realized what the sound was. Man, had it been that long since he'd heard the sounds of sex? "You idiot," he muttered, meaning himself, not Ginger or whoever was with her. But she was on duty this morning, so he could nail her for that. Besides, this was midmorning, and anyone could walk in on them.

Yeah, he'd talk to her all right, but he didn't want her to get so upset she wouldn't answer his questions about the arrow.

He walked to the range and waited behind one of the large, straw-stuffed bull's-eye targets. Since residents could come here to use the range or courts, Ginger was really over the line with this. He rolled his eyes as he saw Orlando leave the office, straightening his shirt collar and jacket. The guy always looked neatly attired. He emulated the way Royce dressed, only for less money. Royce paid Orlando well, but Matt always sensed Orlando felt he was worth more, though the guy kept a tight rein on his opinions and emotions.

But Royce had said Orlando had an Italian temper. The only time Matt had ever seen that was years ago when he'd made the mistake of using his first name, Gordon. "Don't call me that!" he'd shouted. "No one's supposed to even know that, so the boss shouldn't have told you! I hated my mother and sisters calling me that, and the kids at school in Orlando mocked me with it, like 'He's off his gourd.' Then they always called me Gordo."

Though surprised at the outburst, Matt had stood his ground. "So is Orlando even your real last name or did you just take the name of the place you grew up and—"

"None of your or anybody else's damn business. Sorry, but that just gets to me. Don't tell Royce I blew up, okay?"

Matt hadn't. It was the only emotion he'd seen from the usually stoic, dedicated man. It was hard to even imagine him with a woman and—well, he'd better not go there. But Ginger was coming down in the world if she'd set her sights for Royce and moved on to Orlando. He didn't like to think about it like this—but she'd aimed high and missed.

The Christmas trees and array of homemade crafts at the holiday market on the town square had the opposite effect Char was expecting: it didn't cheer her up but made her sad. Ornaments and hand-sewn tree skirts, fresh pine door wreaths, carved wooden manger scenes, scented candles and baked goods of all kinds made her miss her mother, especially family times around the table at holiday time. If the invitation to Kate and Grant's still held and if Matt was willing, it would be nice to go there soon for dinner. Tess had asked her for Thanksgiving Day next week, and that wasn't good, because the way she was doing with her pregnancy, Char would probably have to fix the meal. The mere delicious smell of it might make Tess spend her time on the sofa or in the bathroom, anyway.

But what made Char sad but also angry was seeing the long tables staffed by the Hear Ye people. She knew she wouldn't find Grace there, as pregnant as she was, but she did see Lee amid the others. Maybe she could find a way to talk to him alone.

Even from here, she could see the Hear Ye workers displayed framed Bible verses—probably ones Bright Star was distorting for his own ends. Sewing baskets, holiday aprons, jars of apple butter and jam, baked bread—it all reminded her of pioneer days, and that's just how those people looked.

She hovered next to a big oak tree that kept its leaves all winter. They rattled in the wind. She stood there, watching the cult faithful, agonizing about how to talk to Lee here, or Grace in private there, maybe get her out of that place to have the baby. But she'd probably never leave if she couldn't take her children with her. The vibes between Grace and Lee had seemed stiff—almost frozen, but if they knew they were being watched…

Her knees nearly buckled when a voice behind her interrupted her thoughts. "I think you're one to always see the hole in the doughnut or in the wall. Because of a hole in your life, perhaps?"

She gasped and spun around, though she knew who she would see. Brice "Bright Star" Monson stood there, his pale eyes as piercing as laser beams. He was thin with pale hair, pale skin; his clothes were reminiscent of both Daniel Boone and Buddha. Thank God, she was in the midst of a busy scene with other people, or she would have been afraid. He'd obviously been told she'd spotted his peephole and made a subtle point about it, because he couldn't mean the arrow hole in her door.

But maybe that arrow hole could be a sort of symbolic peephole, a retaliation for finding the one in his wall earlier that day. Maybe Kate was right that she was looking under the wrong rocks to learn who was behind that arrow.

12

Char had heard talk of Bright Star Monson's charisma, but the man repulsed her. Her mind raced to decide how to respond. "I see your people are selling framed calligraphy quotations here," she said. "Are they about hunting, like the ones hung in that interview room with the peephole?"

"Do not be so swift to judge. I have had the honor of meeting both of your sisters, but I had hoped you would be more reasonable. I believe you are what the world calls a social worker. That is what I do, too, only with deeper intent. That room is where I sometimes place those who are distraught or sad so they can be observed and then cared for, that is all."

"I find it hard to believe anyone under your care could be distraught or sad." She tried to stay calm, but the sarcasm was clear. "And cared for, how? I worry about my relatives who are there. The children. Grace being so far along in pregnancy, especially. She needs a doctor for the delivery."

"Grace is full of grace and very well cared for, as are all the children there. Let the little children come unto me."

"The Lord said that. Do you make a practice of stepping into his shoes? And am I welcome to visit to see how you care for the children?"

"Of course. Come to the gate in the light."

That too sounded biblical. Was it? "My sister noticed the quotes about hunting on the walls of that room. How could that give comfort to someone who is sad or upset?"

"Those give comfort to me. Some hunt game or even other people. I am a hunter of souls."

He smiled. He had yellow teeth. Weird, but something about the moment he looked at her, then turned and moved away reminded her of a wolf she'd faced on a rocky outcrop near a hogan one morning, a gaunt, hungry-looking gray wolf with sick eyes.

Char watched the man walk away and shuddered. He was heading for Brad Mason. She hadn't noticed he was here, but he waved at her before he huddled with Bright Star. Grant's younger brother seemed to be everywhere. She'd overheard someone call him "The Fracking Enforcer," which didn't seem the right nickname for someone who just sealed deals for drilling property. That's why Brad knew Bright Star, of course: he'd no doubt arranged the lucrative sale of the old cult site to Royce's company.

Since Bright Star wasn't headed back to the cult's

sales tables, she seized the opportunity. Lee was still there, down on the far end where she hoped to have a word with him.

Matt punched in Char's cell number. When she picked up, he heard a buzz of voices behind her "Hello? This is Charlene Lockwood."

"You don't have caller ID, huh? It's Matt. I hear noise. Where are you?"

"At the holiday market uptown. You won't believe who I just talked to."

"Don't keep me guessing."

"Bright Star Monson. He came up to me, knew who I was, so I'll just bet he was looking through that peephole I told you about. He gives me the creeps, but I'm still going to talk to my cousin Lee who's here today with the cult members. Anything new?"

"You're new in my life, and I like that. Sorry I was in a bad mood last night. I talked to Ginger about the arrow, but she says she's sold lots, so she doesn't know for sure who had them."

"Henry Hanson admitted to me he took some she threw away, fixed them, used them. I'm hoping he's going to drive the mountain school van and make sure his daughter gets to school, so that will help Jemmie and some others, too."

"Great, but were you up on the mountain again? You shouldn't go up there alone."

"Matt, you're the one who nearly got killed up there, not me."

"Calm down. As a matter of fact, I wanted to see if you still want to head up to see the McKitricks this afternoon with me. Where did you see Hanson?"

"He was at the gas station near Lake Azure. His daughter had described my truck and license number to him. She's a sharp little cookie."

"You've heard what they say in police work, haven't you? There's no such thing as coincidence."

"I hear you. I thought of that. What time do you want to go up Pinecrest again?"

"The earlier the better, because the weather forecast says significant snow is coming."

"I'll talk to Lee right now and meet you at the lodge. I can drive up the mountain, so—"

"Royce not only sprang for a school van but a new company truck is here already. When you fall off a horse, you get back on, remember?"

"So you want to drive?"

"Right. And Char, be careful talking to Lee. I don't care if he is your cousin. He's also under the spell of that guru."

"I'll be careful," she promised and hung up.

I'll be careful. He'd told that to Royce just an hour ago when he decided to drive the new truck up the mountain. Royce had said, "Famous last words, so you better mean it."

"Oh, hi, Char," Lee said as she stood before him at the long table of homemade goods. She picked up a hand-dipped dark green candle and, talking low, pretended to study it. "It's going to snow, you know," he added.

"He tries to snow everyone he talks to, doesn't he? Did you see me talking to your leader?"

"I did. He's something, isn't he? Such wisdom." He said those words loudly, so she figured the man standing down the table a short way might be listening. Did these people all spy on each other?

"Lee," she said in a quiet voice, "Bright Star's initials are B.S., so don't forget that. How is Grace doing—really?"

"Nervous about the birth, of course. She had a bit of trouble last time."

"She needs a hospital, a doctor, maybe a specialist."

"I've been assured the midwife is very good."

"B.S. said she's full of grace, and Kate told me he said she had been chosen. Chosen for what? What's going on?" When the cult member down the way glanced at them, she raised her voice. "I'd love to have two of these green candles, please. No one hand dips candles anymore. It's kind of like the Colonial days."

Lee took two candles from the table and pulled a sheet of newspaper from under the table to wrap them. *Bright Star allowed outside news in the cult?*

"It's going to snow soon and quite a lot, I think," Lee repeated, his voice loud, too. "The sky looks heavy with it. I hope you'll get to see the creek near your old house before it freezes—Cold Creek will soon be ice creek, you know," he said and forced a laugh.

She laughed, too, but she was crying inside. Her kin

were living in a nightmare world with a wolf in charge who wore sheep's—or shepherd's—clothing. But why refer to seeing the creek near her old house, near where Matt had said he'd looked around below the cliff with all the fracking?

"Lee, if I take a look at the creek, you mean to see the beaver there, don't you?" she asked quietly, just to keep him talking.

"Yes, that's where you'll see the water," he whispered as he put the candles in a plain brown sack, making a lot of crinkling noises. "Maybe you'll have to go ice fishing, chip through the ice. Here," he added in a loud voice, "since you asked for a receipt, I'll write one out for you."

He scribbled something on the corner of a page of newspaper and tore it off. She paid him. He put the piece of newspaper in the sack with the candles and handed it to her. She knew there must be some sort of message on that paper, hopefully something about Grace or about meeting with him again.

She walked off the square and way down the street to her car without glancing in the sack. She had the strangest feeling she was being watched. A quick glance back before she got in the driver's seat showed several people coming her way, but no one really watching and no cult members in sight. In her car, she locked the doors and dug out the piece of newspaper.

"Poison water," the scribbling read. "Bright Star—

Big bucks." She looked carefully at the printing. Did it look like that found on the note in Matt's burned-out truck?

"Poison water?" Char asked Matt again as he drove them up the mountain in the new, dark blue Lake Azure truck. "I realize Bright Star got a lot of money from selling the old cult site for fracking to EEC, but what's with the poison water?"

"Could he mean cult members are drugged through holy water they drink or something like that? It's beyond me how that lunatic can keep so many people in line. I remember my dad talking about that Jim Jones religious cult from back in the '70s. He used drugs and probably drugged his followers. He claimed to be God and ended up coercing about nine hundred of his flock to kill themselves with cyanide-laced grape juice—men, women, children."

"I wish you hadn't said that. I've got to get Grace out of there, and since Lee is warning me about—something—maybe he can grab his kids and leave, too. But you don't think his printing on the newspaper is the same as that found in your truck?"

"Hard to tell. We can give it to Gabe and have him check it out. We don't want to jump to conclusions, and why would Bright Star send Lee or anyone else to knock me off the mountain? I'd say he's in tight with Royce after that huge purchase and wouldn't want to cross him by hurting me."

"Yeah. Lee's note suggests Royce and Bright Star

owe each other. I've got to visit the Hear Ye cult again, though it's the last place I want to go. But the other thing Lee was trying to say was something about the water near the old cult land, the area you were at the other day. He said he hoped I'd get to see the creek there before it freezes, and he made a joke about ice fishing—like fishing for answers?"

"Since he's so familiar with it there, it makes me wonder who that hunting stand I saw could belong to. Maybe the cult? Do they hunt for food?"

"Tess said they do. Back to the past, back to the old days. You can tell that from the way they dress. Anyway, I'll take you up on your earlier offer to see those beaver dams and the water there. He could mean there's some runoff from the fracking."

"They try to be really careful with that. The wastewater, which can be toxic, is shipped out in tanker trucks to be cleaned and then recycled. If the snow we're expecting is not too heavy, maybe we can check out Cold Creek soon—together."

"I do like the sound of that," she told him. "Let's just hope right now we can get Sam's permission for Jemmie to take the van down to school starting next week. Royce left a message for me that Orlando went to Columbus to get the van. Monday can be the first day it's used, but you might know there will be snow on the ground by then. Maybe not an easy start for Henry Hanson as the new driver. Matt, why do you keep looking in the rearview mirror? Is someone behind us?"

"I glimpsed a truck a couple of curves back."

"Does it look like the one that hit you?"

"It's black, but can't tell. So many look alike. I can only see it creeping up the mountain on curves when I look down and back. Okay, here's the McKitrick turn-off. And here's hoping we find Sam at home for you to talk to and Jemmie for me. We need to get Sam on board for this and not just get his wife's permission. The guy could still be volatile if someone crosses him."

The old coonskin cap lay on the console between them. Gabe had returned it after checking it for any evidence, but it had been out in the elements too long to be useful. She saw Matt had cleaned it up, brushed it to get the dirt off. A strange heirloom, but maybe not up here on the mountain.

They got out, and Jemmie, with his dog at his heels, came out to greet them. Adela followed, drying her hands on a towel. There was no sign of Sam at first, but he suddenly limped, almost slouching, from the line of trees—with a weapon in his hands again. No, it was a pair of binoculars. They all met on the front porch.

"Guess what?" Jemmie blurted. "Dad's got glasses that can see in the dark, and he showed me how cool that is last night!"

"Very cool," Matt said. "Night vision goggles?"

"Right," Sam said, holding them up. "You never know who's out there."

"That's for sure," Matt said.

Char looked at the binoculars Sam handed to his son. On them she read, Nemesis, but she couldn't get the other word. She saw Adela crying as she reached out and touched the coonskin cap.

"You found it," she whispered. "The sheriff had it?"

"No," Matt told her, putting a hand on her thin shoulder. "Char and I found it up on the hill quite a ways from where Woody was working, far from where he fell."

Sam snorted as if to dismiss that, so Char wondered if he, too, suspected foul play. And had he gotten along with his father, a hardworking man who, Matt had said, could not accept that his able-bodied son Sam was too sick to hold a job because of emotional problems?

"Sam, I hope you don't mind, but Woody told me more than once that this hat was for Jemmie," Matt said. "I want to give him this, and Charlene has another gift, if you'll agree."

Sam stood up straighter. He and Matt looked eye to eye, with Adela and Char hovering and Jemmie looking on.

"Sure," Sam said. "I care for my boy, more'n my pa did for me."

Adela began to cry again. Matt got down on one knee to Jemmie's height and put the cap on his head. "Now you know that your grandpa loved you, thought the world of you," Matt told him. "And he wanted you to have his favorite cap but also to get good schooling. There's a special bus Miss Charlene here has arranged to pick you up right down on the road and to bring you back from school, so I hope that's okay with you and your parents."

"Mandy Lee flew the coop," Sam said as Char held

her breath. "But us chickens say 'Let's give it a try,' don't we, Ma?"

"Oh, yes. That would be real good," Adela said, her voice breaking as Matt got to his feet.

"And I'll escort him that far, be sure there's no scouts or insurgents around," Sam promised, looking as if he believed every word of that. "Damn IEDs can blow a man to bits." Though it was broad daylight, he took the night vision binoculars from his son and headed out into the trees, crouching again as if he would spring at someone.

As soon as he disappeared, Jemmie hugged Matt. Char was so happy she could have hugged him, too. "This cap will be kind of like Grandpa's with me," the boy said. "I don't want to forget him, how he was like a dad to me when Pa was gone, but don't tell Pa I said so, okay, Mr. Matt?"

Char blinked back tears. Matt had handled this just right. He was hugging Jemmie, patting the boy on the back. Her heart went out to them both in different ways. A man who was good with children.... For the first time, she admitted, as fast as this was happening, she was falling in love.

On the way back down the mountain, tiny pellets of snow began to pepper their windshield. Matt turned on the wipers, which made a *thwack, thwack* sound. All Char had said so far was, "Thank you, thank you," but he figured she was just keeping quiet because the road was getting a little slippery. Plus, she'd had tears in her eyes and had been sniffling ever since he'd given Jemmie the cap.

"I think that went well," he told her. "Despite the fact Sam's delusional. He's still got PTSD, for sure. I hope he sticks to his guns—his decision, I mean, to let Jemmie get back in school."

"Yes, thanks to you," she said, "that went great."

He breathed easier when they passed Coyote Rock and met no other vehicles on the way down. But on one of the lower turns, he looked in his rearview mirror and saw a truck behind them again.

"At the bottom, I'm going to pull off into that road we saw the drunk fracking guys come out of," he said. "I want to see who goes by us in that truck. I think it's the same one that followed us up."

"That's all we need. This morning I felt I was being watched even when I left the holiday market, but I figured it was either my own nerves or Bright Star still watching. Remember how we used to say certain teachers had eyes in the back of their heads? Well, that's how I feel about him."

"Don't forget Henry Hanson, who just happened to find you at the gas station earlier."

Matt backed the truck into the small access road, pulling in far enough behind some pine trees that they would be difficult to spot by someone driving past. He turned on the intermittent speed of the wipers to keep the snow off the windshield.

Peering through the shifting flakes, they waited. The truck drove past and they saw Orlando at the wheel.

13

"Would you rather wait in my office or at home—I mean, at the Mannings'?" Matt asked Char. "I'm going to talk to Royce about Orlando tailing us right now."

"I'll wait inside here," she told him.

He got out of the new truck in front of the lodge, slammed his door and came around to open hers. He was trying to control his temper and not doing very well. Royce had mentioned something about finding out who had shoved him off the cliff, but by having him stalked?

"Maybe you should blame Orlando," Char said as she got out into the increasingly heavy snow. "Royce thought he would be in Columbus, picking up the new school van, so maybe he didn't know—"

"He knew," Matt insisted, steering her toward the lodge. "I've never seen Orlando be anything but a good soldier. Orlando wouldn't do that on his own. He follows orders from Royce."

"Matt, look!" she cried as she caught sight of a tan

van with Falls County Schools stenciled on the side. "That must be the new van. Wow, that was fast! I'll just peek inside, then come in. I'll find your office and wait there."

"Ask for Jen, my secretary," he said, and strode up the paved walk. At least someone had put salt down on it, but it would have to be shoveled soon and the plow would be needed from the maintenance garage to keep the streets and driveways clear. Woody would have been on that already. Since Joe Fencer was due for his interview in—he glanced at his watch—twenty minutes, he'd have to have it out with Royce fast. Sure, he'd watched over Matt for years. Royce's finances had built and backed this community, which supported Matt's management job. Matt owed him a lot, but putting someone on his tail without asking permission was way over the line.

Jen, who worked for them both when Royce was here, was not at her desk. Matt walked down the hall. He opened his office door, clicked on the light and tossed his jacket and gloves in a chair, then backtracked to the hall with Royce's office. The door was ajar, and he could hear his voice inside. One thing Royce had never adapted to was speaking quietly when he was talking long-distance, as if he had to shout to be heard. And he had an open-door management policy Matt had emulated.

"Make sure they stay off our backs on that," Royce was saying. "Of course it's under control. Yeah, got the adjoining property, that is, across the road. Always onward and upward, you know that."

Still furious, Matt decided to make his point, make a scene. He knocked once on the door and swept it open. Royce was still talking on the phone. "Wish I could close that road, but that's going a bit too far."

"You've already gone too far!" Matt said, and stalked into the room.

"Call you back, Myron. Right," Royce said, and stabbed his finger at the phone. Appearing completely calm, he looked up at Matt. "What are you talking about? And what's worth interrupting me? I just got word we're going to have a group of radical greeniacs called Green Tree on our backs, picketing like that ragtag bunch Woody organized. So I may have to stay here for a while long—"

"You forgot to mention you were siccing your bodyguard on me! Anything else I should know?"

"Sit down and calm down. Yes, I asked Orlando to keep an eye on you, especially up on Pinecrest, since you were nearly killed there."

"Even little kids are told when the babysitter's coming."

"And, since you were with Charlene, don't you want her kept safe, too?"

"You could have asked, Royce."

"I know what you would have said. 'Thanks but no thanks.' I promised your father on his deathbed I would take care of you, and I meant it."

"That was years ago. Call Orlando off. Thanks for caring, but that's not the way."

"Oh, when you see Charlene, tell her the van's sitting out front."

"Nice try to remind me how helpful you can be. She saw the van. She's thrilled. Keep Orlando off her back, too. As a matter of fact, let him just stick to you—and Ginger."

"You know about that?" Royce asked, steepling his fingers in front of his mouth. "I figured he could use a little R & R. And speaking of leveling with each other, Ginger told Orlando you're trying to trace an arrow that was shot into Charlene's door when you were standing there, so don't you think you should have shared that? You know," Royce went on, still completely unshaken by Matt's tirade, "Orlando is totally loyal to me, and I need that—from him, and from you. I can't apologize for wanting to protect you. I hope you feel the same about me, no matter what happens."

Matt forced a nod but didn't trust himself to say anything else. The nod meant to him that he'd said his piece, not that he agreed with everything Royce said anymore. He turned and walked out.

"Matt, would you quit pacing and sit down," Char said. "Are you worried about the snow closing the roads?"

They were at the Mannings' house that evening. He'd brought pizza and beer from the lodge. It was snowing like crazy outside, but he was still revved, still upset.

"I'm still mad Orlando was stalking me—us. At Royce's royal command, of course."

"You've been walking from window to window. If Orlando's out there looking in, he's going to be frozen. Okay, everything's ready."

He sat across the table from her in the bright kitchen. She'd laid out dishes and even poured the beer into tall glasses, though he was used to drinking it straight from the bottle. The small table, her so close made everything seem—well, cozy.

"I usually don't get this way," he said, "but it's like a betrayal—not to have Royce consult with me, at least."

"He went about it the wrong way, but at least he cares. If you'd ever had a father who deserted you—I mean, I know your dad died fairly young—but you'd be grateful. Family and good friends are important."

"So your advice is to cut him some slack?"

"Yes, but I have to admit when the ones we care for deeply let us down, it's doubly hard, like breaking something special that's bound us together. I still can't believe the terrible choices my cousin Lee made to take his wife and kids to live in that Hear Ye dictatorship. And can I even trust him since he's under Bright Star's thumb?"

"If you ever want someone to go back to the cult with you, I'm willing. And I still think we should follow up on Lee's hint to check out the water below the old cult grounds. The snow and ice will make it hard, though. Maybe tomorrow if the snow lets up. If Lee means it's being poisoned from fracking runoff, I'd need to have

Royce take a look at that before a new antifracking group in town called Green Tree sets up protests."

"Green Tree? I think Kate said that's headed up by Grant's ex-wife out of Cleveland. Her hanging around is all Kate needs about a month before her wedding. But—you don't think Lee could be baiting a trap to get us there, then someone takes shots at us from that high tree stand you saw? They could claim it was a hunting accident. Maybe Bright Star wants to get rid of me, set me up somehow. There's a big time-factor, cause-and-effect thing there. Just a few hours after I found that peephole and made a big deal of it, an arrow whacks into my door. Bright Star pretends to be caring and concerned, but he's dangerous, and his robots will do anything he says."

"Which is why you have to be careful about trusting Lee or even poor Grace. But they can't trap us near the creek—unless someone's camping out there in this blowing snow—because they'd have no idea when we'd show up. We won't park on the road above, but walk in a different way, be sure we're not followed. Talking about trust, I swear, if I didn't know Orlando wasn't in the area when I got shoved off the road, I'd put him on the person-of-interest list. But I know Royce would never have ordered *that.* Orlando has never really liked me, especially since I turned down an interest in EEC. I suppose he thinks I was disloyal to Royce."

"Matt, you're not eating. How about time-out?" she said. "We both need to relax or we're going to go off the deep end—well, you know what I mean."

"Okay, okay. I just wish we could figure out if someone is out there in the dark watching me—us."

"Oh, that reminds me. I'd never seen night vision goggles, so I looked up Nemesis, the brand name of the pair Sam had. Would you believe they sell for over a thousand dollars? Where is he getting money like that?"

Matt shrugged. "Wounded veteran pension? Maybe he took them when he left the army."

"I checked. They don't use that kind. And the word *nemesis*—it sounds like a warning."

"Thanks for checking all that out, but you're clutching at straws with that guy. Sam's a sick man."

"Who seems to have money for something like that when his family's hurting for groceries and winter coats. Big bucks, as Lee put it, talking about Bright Star in that note. Oh, I know, it doesn't make sense."

"It doesn't, but what does right now? Except us."

She smiled at that. He sighed. They clinked their glasses together.

"And there are other good things," she told him, a slice of pizza halfway to her mouth. "You hired Joe Fencer."

"Right. And he's out with the guys clearing our roads already."

"You built a bond with Jemmie and honored your friend Woody's wishes that his grandson got his coonskin cap. And you got Sam to agree to his son's schooling."

He could feel himself start to relax. She had a bit of spinach from the pizza on her front tooth. Despite his distress over Royce and at least one attempt on his life, when she licked the spinach off, he found it incredibly appealing. If it took that little to make him want her, he was in trouble here, too.

"Mmm, good pizza and good to see you smile," she said. "And I never had a beer called Tuborg."

"Danish," he told her and took a piece of the pizza—veggie on her half, pepperoni on his. "Not the brand they imbibe out in Navajo land?"

"Definitely not."

"The grounds staff is going to get the sleigh out early with this snow. Want to take its maiden voyage with me after we eat? I can have them bring it around."

"You don't have a horse or stables on the grounds, do you?"

He shook his head with his mouth full of pizza and took a minute to swallow. "We rent horses from the farm just to the north, but stables are on the drawing board for the very near future. You like to ride?"

"I learned to out West. But like to? It seemed I always got on a horse that had its own idea about everything, always wanted to go its own way."

"You should have named it Royce. Tell you what. I'll give the crew a call and see if they can get the sleigh and the horse here tonight."

"You don't drive it, do you?"

"No, we pay the farmer's son, and he doesn't mind a little canoodling in the backseat, either."

She burst into laughter. "Canoodling? Where did you hear that?"

"It's hills talk. A sleigh ride in the snow is very romantic—if you're with the right person. And I am."

She actually blushed. Charlene full-steam-ahead-take-charge Lockwood blushed. For him. It was as revealing as if she'd taken off all her clothes.

Char loved the sleigh. Shiny dark green with fancy runners, it looked old-fashioned, elegant yet sturdy. It had an elevated perch for the driver and seats in the front and back, so it could carry at least eight. The horse was a big Belgian, and the deepening snow let them slide smoothly down the roads and lanes the snowplow hadn't scraped clean yet. Where the plow had already been, near the lodge and the road around the lake, the farmer's son, Brady, took them over the grass. The teenage boy was polite and discreet and dressed for the weather in a fur cap with huge earflaps.

They had a blanket over their knees but huddled shoulder to shoulder and thigh to thigh for warmth against the sharp wind. Snow swirled around them in big, lacy flakes, as if they were in a shaken snow globe. And with this man, and the things that had happened near him, her world had been shaken.

"Here with you like this," she told him as her breath made small, puffy clouds in the cold air between them, "it seems like smooth sledding with everything."

His arm around her shoulders tightened. "Don't I wish."

"I know. Me, too. Just dreaming."

"Wait a sec," he said. "If we're dreaming, let's make

dreams come true." He kissed her gently, then harder. The mere touch of his lips warmed her more than this blanket could. She tipped her head to open her mouth to his. His warm tongue intruded, tasted her, but she tasted him, too. Pepperoni, the bite of oregano—and the lure of Matt Rowan. Beneath the blanket, his free hand moved to her waist under her short down-filled coat, skimmed lower to caress her hip, then squeeze her thigh as they deepened the kiss, breathing in unison, lost in the swirling wonderland of each other.

"I think," he said, finally coming up for a breath of air, "we're canoodling. But I don't mind missing any of the scenery. Let's go back and get warm. How about my place? We can build a fire, and I'd rather not do that at the Mannings'."

"All right," she whispered, feeling she was ready for the kind of fire he built in her.

"Hey, Brady," he called. "Drop us at my place on Oak Lane, okay?"

They were swiftly, smoothly turned in the other direction. Matt's home was up on a slight rise at the end of a cul-de-sac, set in thick but now-leafless trees. The wood-and-stone houses were widely spaced, similar in style, yet distinct. Two houses on the street were already decorated with colorful Christmas lights. Old-fashioned lamps on poles threw small gold pools of light into the snow, and windows with electric candles peered at them through the flakes. They swung around into Matt's front yard, since the street and driveway had been plowed. No doubt, they did the boss's place first, she thought.

With all the snow, perhaps she'd have to stay all night. Her stomach did a little flip-flop. Maybe that was exactly what Matt had planned.

Brady stopped the horse and called back to them. "You sure left a bright light on out in back, Mr. Rowan."

Matt sat up and craned to see where Brady pointed. Through aligned front and back windows in the dark house they could see a big golden glow in the backyard.

"I didn't," Matt cried, throwing the blanket off himself and jumping out. "The house—something's burning!"

Char fumbled for her purse, long lost on the floor of the sleigh, while Matt ran around his house through the snow. She found her phone. She knew dialing 9-1-1 meant the call would go through Gabe's night receptionist to a volunteer fire department. But as she jumped from the sleigh, her phone fell into the snow.

"I can call, ma'am," Brady said, jumping down, too. "Dad got me a phone."

"Yes, good. Thanks!" she cried, even as she dug hers out and ran after Matt. His house was not on fire, thank God, but a large bonfire blazed in the backyard under a picnic table, which was also aflame. The heat had melted a big ring of snow. For one moment, the scene reminded her of the wreck of his burning truck with the fire-blackened grass and leaves.

"I've got a fire extinguisher in the house," Matt shouted. "But it will burn itself out."

"Brady's calling 9-1-1."

"Have him cancel it. Nothing Gabe can do here till

morning, so why should we roust him or the volunteer firemen out of warm beds?"

Char only hoped it wasn't too late to learn who was tormenting Matt and why. She turned back to tell Brady not to bring the volunteers out tonight, but in the flickering light, she saw a piece of paper stuck on the wooden wall of the house by the back door—stuck there with an arrow pierced through it. It bore a crudely sketched skull and crossbones. In bold letters, wavering in the backyard blaze, were the familiar words,

YOUR FIRED!

14

It was too late to stop the Falls County Volunteer Fire Department from arriving and bringing out the neighbors. But, at Matt's request, Char went inside to call Gabe's home phone number. He and his deputy, Jace, were both out on calls, but the dispatcher put her through to Gabe. He said not to touch things and he'd be there as soon as he could.

"I'll have to bag that note," Gabe told Char as she stood in Matt's kitchen, watching the firemen put out the last remnants of the blaze. She saw that, besides the picnic table, it had been fed by firewood someone had taken from Matt's own woodpile out back. "Char, were you at his house when it started?"

"Not exactly. We ate at the Mannings', then took a sleigh ride. The fire was really going when we got here. Gabe, Royce Flemming's assistant, Orlando, followed us up on Pinecrest today on Royce's orders. Matt was mad because he wasn't asked or told. It's been quite a day."

"Don't lose the note Lee printed for you that you told Tess about. I'll compare the handwriting and get a specialist, if I have to."

"Lee wouldn't do all this—the truck wreck, the arrows."

"You and Tess have been telling me Bright Star has complete sway over his people. You don't really know Lee anymore—can't trust him. That's what I've told Tess."

"But I think Lee's note might have been accusing Bright Star of something. Lee had to hide it from the guy next to him, who would probably rat on him. That's why I've got to get to Grace again—to make sure she and the kids are safe."

"Char, do me—and Tess—a huge favor. Don't involve her in that. If she finds out you're heading there again, she'll insist on going. I've got to worry about her pregnancy now, more than Grace's."

"Okay. I'm just feeling desperate and so is Matt."

"At least the two 'Your Fired' notes have to be from the same person, but why? When we get the why, we'll get the who. Take care of yourself. At least the arrow wasn't aimed at the two of you this time."

But it was Jace Miller who arrived a few minutes later to take the arrow and note and survey the scene, since Gabe was still busy on a call. Jace only stayed about fifteen minutes and told them Gabe would be there to get their statements in the morning. "We're stretched pretty thin, and there's a full moon, which brings out the worst around here," Jace told them on his way back to his cruiser.

Char fumbled around the kitchen to fix coffee for the six firefighters and Matt, who were still standing around the debris and ashes outside. She located enough mugs and cups and carried them out on a tray.

"You got a good wife there, Mr. Rowan," one of the men said.

"A good woman, for sure," Matt replied.

It had taken little time for the fire to be put out, though the fire chief—who owned the bakery uptown—interviewed Matt before leaving. Finally, though in circumstances they did not want or plan, Matt and Char were alone in his house.

"I'm tempted to go out right now to follow foot tracks so more snow doesn't bury them by morning," Matt said as he leaned stiff-armed on the granite countertop by the sink, glaring out a back window. "But that might be just what some idiot wants—me out there in the dark alone. Ten to one footsteps go up into the trees and toward the ridge, even up to the level of your cabin."

Though she felt defrosted by now, Char shivered. She figured from their location that directly above Matt's property was where they'd seen the drag marks that could have been from Woody's body being dragged, then carried to be thrown off the cliff.

"I'm going to talk to Orlando in the morning if I can find him. I don't trust the guy. I want to tell him to steer clear of me," Matt said.

"You said before he doesn't like you, but why? If

he's so loyal to Royce, you'd think he'd like anyone Royce likes."

"Yeah. You'd think a lot of things."

"Well, I've been thinking that I've been with you when both arrows hit, even probably when that first note was left in your burned-out truck."

He turned to face her. "Char, you're obviously not the one who's being 'fired' or fired at. But you have lit a fire in me. Sorry our sleigh ride mood got ruined tonight. I'm so frustrated I could chew nails, but I'll settle for some more of your good coffee made in my kitchen. I don't want to sleep tonight or get too distracted."

She nodded and got up to fix more coffee. It felt funny to be in a strange kitchen yet to feel at home.

"I'll stay on patrol in case that 'Your Fired' warning means someone might try to burn the house. How about you sleep in the guest room or on the couch in the front room or my den? Once again, I don't want you alone tonight. I'll keep guard, get you home first thing in the morning. I'd rather not leave the house right now, and I can't have you going out alone. I'm starting to see why Royce has a bodyguard, and he's so much more powerful, wealthy—and unpopular—than I am, more of a target, it's ridiculous. Everything seems ridiculous, except us."

She went to him, hugged him. He clamped her full length to him, holding her so tight she could barely breathe. She was amazed how strong a man could feel, even one who was afraid. Despite all that had happened, she felt safe in his arms and yet scared, too, for him, for both of them.

In the morning, Matt dropped Char at the Mannings' place, then went back to his house where Gabe was following footsteps up the hill. Before leaving Matt's home, Char had seen that the fire had melted snow for quite a distance, so Gabe had to start tracking pretty far out. At the Mannings', she changed clothes, got her warmest things on, grabbed Lee's note to her, then drove back to Matt's. She handed Gabe Lee's note when he came into the house from his search of the grounds.

"I'm going to drive up to Char's rental cabin," Gabe told them. "I need to see if I can trace the tracks from that height since I lost the trail on the rocks. They disappeared below the ridge as if the single person had simply flown away.

"Oh, great," Char said when Gabe drove off in his squad car. "Now we just have to sit around and wait to get answers."

"It's Sunday but how about we go check out how the beavers are doing? I think you're dressed for that. I'm going to drive around town first to be sure we're not followed. Once I saw that tree stand, I took off fast and I meant to do more there, including check the water in the creek. With all that brownish water in the retention lagoon above, I think leakage from it would be easy to spot. Let's go out to my truck through the garage door. Since we were followed in that new Lake Azure truck, we'll change vehicles. Oh, wait, the snow shovel's in the basement and we might need it to break the ice or dig something out."

She waited in his truck and nearly screamed when a man suddenly came in through the open garage door and knocked on her window. Orlando! Although Matt had wanted to talk to him, that's all they needed right now. She was tempted to just lock her door and sit there. She couldn't open the window since Matt had the truck key. While she vacillated, Orlando spoke in a loud voice. "Royce heard what happened last night. Is Matt all right?"

He must have realized Matt was coming soon since she was sitting here. And since he was hardly whispering, he wasn't just sneaking around. She opened the door a crack.

Orlando bent down, pulled it farther open and looked in. He was clean-cut but his olive skin showed the outline of a dark beard. Even in the cold, he was bareheaded with his raven hair swept straight back. His piercing eyes were brown, his nose prominent, though his lips were thin. But those heavy brows that looked linked when he frowned made him seem angry.

"Yes, Matt's fine," she told him. "Once again, the sheriff's on it. As you may have heard, Matt wasn't real happy that Royce had you follow us yesterday."

"I take orders from him, not Matt. And it was for his own good, always is, so—"

Matt came into the garage with the snow shovel. "Orlando! What are you doing here? I was going to look you up later," he said, putting the shovel down and coming closer. "Didn't Royce tell you to bodyguard him and not me?"

Char held her breath as the two men glared at each other. "We'll be late for brunch with Kate and Grant," she said, when they'd discussed nothing of the kind. It suddenly seemed a good idea to go there, change vehicles with them and not go in this truck since Orlando had seen it. And it seemed an even better idea to try to distract these two guys.

"Oh, yeah, you're right," Matt said, then turned to Orlando again. "Thank Royce for his continued concern." He walked around to the driver's side of the truck.

Orlando didn't budge. "Why didn't you take him up on going in on the fracking?" he asked. "Very lucrative. More cheap oil and gas is good for the country. That hurt him."

The two men stared at each other over the top of the truck. Char gripped her hands in her lap as Matt responded. "I trust him, of course—his judgment. It just wasn't for me, with all the possible fracking fallout when I need to be a community liaison around here. Maybe he'll let you in on it."

If Orlando said anything else, Char didn't hear it as Matt got in and slammed the door. Orlando stalked out to Royce's black sedan, parked in the curve of the cul-de-sac.

Matt started the truck and muttered to her. "Good move to make him think we're going to visit your sister."

"I think we should. Park there and either borrow one of their vehicles or else have them drive us to the creek, drop us off and come back later."

"Big sis won't like that idea, will she?"

"No. She'll probably want to come along and look for Indian artifacts. Just kidding." She craned around to scan the street behind them. "He's gone. Let's go."

They found Grant and Kate sitting in Grant's kitchen at the table, huddled over the Sunday paper and drawings of ancient burials and bodies. After they explained everything, Kate said, "I can take you in the Ohio State van the latest group of archaeology undergrads left here."

"Kate, it's one thing to be looking for old arrows and bones in our backyard," Grant said. "But you don't need to get involved with looking at water samples. Out of your element."

"Yes, but I have contacts at OSU who can test the water if there's a problem with runoff."

"Actually," Matt said, "I have a friend who can do that."

Grant shook his head. "I imagine that's one of the first things Ms. Lacey Fencer and Green Tree will do, too, if they're showing up like Matt says. Picketing and protesting are their specialties. Green Tree rattles trees, and then we'll see what falls out about fracking. No offense to Royce Flemming, Matt."

"I'm sure he's doing everything by the book. If

there's any toxic runoff, he'd take care of it right away—if he's aware of it."

"Is Lacey Fencer related to the Fencers, Joe and his family, who live on our old road?" Char asked. "Matt just hired him as head groundskeeper at Lake Azure."

"Cousins, I think, like us to Lee," Kate said. "Man, that's a weird note he slipped you, Char, so I can see why you guys want to check the creek water there. But do you know Lacey is Grant's ex-wife?"

"Lacey always has a cause," Grant added. "Thank God, it's not me anymore, but the environment. Okay, how about you two hiding in the backseat of our car and we'll drive you there, then we'll go see how Tess is doing. Kate's been driving me nuts about that, and a phone call won't do. In case your cell doesn't work in the river valley, we can come back at a set time to pick you up. That way this Orlando guy can't follow you, and there will be no telltale truck sitting around for the fracking site workers to get suspicious."

"I think," Matt said, with a smile, "the four of us could conquer the world." As they all stood, he put his arm around Char's shoulders. Kate, big sis that she was, surveyed them for a moment with narrowed eyes. Then, as if she'd decided Matt had passed muster, she nodded and smiled, too.

"Sounds good," Kate said. "Let's just hope the best laid plans of mice and men don't go astray."

15

In the valley, which Cold Creek had cut into the rock over the ages, it was bitterly cold. The sharp breeze sifted little snow showers on them from oak limbs and fir needles. The briar bushes rattled, and the wind sighed through the bare branches and swaying pines.

Matt had left the snow shovel behind, but he had his gun in his coat pocket, and that bothered Char, but she was glad she had come along. When they crunched through the eight inches of snow to where the beaver dam diverted some of the water to a pond, she wished she'd brought her sunglasses for the blinding light off the expanse of snow and ice.

"I see the beavers have made their own hole in the edge of the ice," Matt told her, "but I'll get a tree limb to make ours. Glad we brought a jar, though it will hardly do for a complete test sample of water. But I feel like a traitor."

"To Royce?"

"Yeah, like I'm going behind his back, but then he

went behind mine, even if his intentions were good. I'm sure he'd want to know if something's going wrong from fracking runoff. Unless I have something to really warn him about, I don't plan to shake him up with any of this. No offense, but your cousin Lee doesn't seem like a reliable source to me."

"Unless he wants to get back at Bright Star, so he's telling the truth, even if it endangers him."

"Get back at him for what? Lee must know his guru and Royce both owe each other big-time, so why get Royce in trouble? Bright Star got bigger, better land and a lot of money for selling the original Hear Ye property. Royce got a prime fracking spot. Besides, as for Royce being shook up, he is already from someone trying to scare or murder me. He has a calm demeanor, but I can tell he's upset in his own way—which, unfortunately, included him putting Orlando on my tail."

At that, Matt looked behind them and all around again. But for the cawing of black crows glaring at human intruders from their perches, it was silent. The lack of noise from the usually loud fracking site overhead on this Sunday morning was almost eerie.

They both ducked and jumped when a small tree crashed to the ground across the creek. "Over there," Matt said, pointing. "Those two beavers must have gnawed through the trunk until it fell. I wish they'd shouted, 'Timber!'"

She smiled. It didn't take much to spook either of them lately.

"I want to check that tree stand I saw the other day somewhere around here," he said. "Since we came in another way, I'm not sure exactly where it is. And with all this snow, things look different. Come on. Look, deer tracks. It will be hunting season on them soon. The way things have been for me lately, I sympathize."

Char followed in his deep footprints along the creek, coming closer to the section of frozen river that lay below the fracking site. "You know," she told him as the cold air bit into her lungs, "I can see the river's not frozen solid clear across but only close to the edges. No way we're walking out on it."

"We'll get a sample near the edge. I'm sure the tree stand was right along here," Matt said, craning his neck to look around. "Why would someone take it down now with deer season coming?"

"Maybe it was there temporarily just to observe or photograph the beavers—everything's a big guess lately. Look," she cried, pointing farther down the creek. "There's a small lean-to or shelter way back under the trees before the hill starts. It looks almost like an outhouse. Do you think hunters would build one down here? Or maybe it's like a blind, hiding hunters so they can shoot game that comes to drink, or even pick off beavers."

"I did hear a shot when I was down here and saw a dead beaver," he said. "But people trap beavers for their pelts, not their meat, and it's not trapping season yet."

To her surprise, he stepped in front of her and drew his gun, but would that be any match for a hunting rifle?

"Matt, there could be a peephole in the wall of that place. What if someone's in there now?"

They approached it from the rear, near the ridge, moving carefully from tree to tree. They heard nothing from the windowless, shedlike structure, made with wooden planks, only the whistling wind, bird cries and their own rapid breathing.

"Get down. Stay here," Matt whispered and rushed behind the structure. He edged around it, knocked once, then, standing to the side, yanked open the wooden door and, after a moment, peered in.

When nothing happened, she called out. "What is it?"

"Not sure. A slanted table. Not much else. Come take a look."

She joined him at the door and looked in. It was dim inside; her eyes adjusted slowly after the outer brightness.

"A place where hunters cut up their meat?" she asked. "But what are those metal things? To keep the carcass from sliding off?"

He stepped inside; she followed. Four metal rings were embedded in the slanted wooden table which took up most of the room, two rings on one side, two on the other. The tilted table turned out to be an old door. On the floor at their feet were several wadded-up, thin pieces of cloth and, of all things, a garden watering can.

"Water to wash off the blood after the meat is butchered?" she asked. "So that's why it's slanted. What do you think?"

"I think chains or handcuffs or anklets fit in these metal rings," he told her, his voice shaky. "See the scuff marks on the metal? I think it's a waterboarding table to torture someone."

She gasped. "What? Like the U.S. got in trouble for, questioning terrorists? But that can't be… Who?" she cried, then an answer came to her. "It is right under the old Hear Ye commune site. But surely they don't torture— At least, not like this."

"I doubt if Bright Star does any of the dirty work himself. You don't think brutal corporal punishment could be one way he keeps his little zombies in line? Why don't they rebel or run away?"

"Maybe this is for ones who try that," she said, her voice shaking as hard as she was. "Or, he threatens their spouses or children. I feel sick to my stomach. Should we get Gabe down here to see this?"

"For sure. But even if the Hear Ye bunch were asked about it, they'd deny it was theirs, that Bright Star had anything to do with it."

"You're right. Matt, I have to help the Lockwood kids, even if their parents aren't rebelling."

"Like you said, maybe he threatens the kids—terrifies or hurts the kids to keep the parents in line."

"And maybe this is not even his. Maybe somebody else uses it to get even with someone. No one would hear screams with the usual drilling and truck noise just above here."

"That's for sure. Maybe Lee sent us here not to find poison water but this. Gabe said Bright Star speaks in riddles. Maybe Lee does, too. Or what about Sam?"

"Sam? Down here, so far from Pinecrest?" she said. "I get the connection with the torture table and the Taliban he's obsessed with, but they say he has no way to get around. And wouldn't he build something like this near his place, so he could question enemies he caught, not way down here where he has no connection?"

"Yeah, you're right. Still, since we're here, we'll get a water sample. But right now, I'm going to take some pictures of this horrible place for Gabe, just in case it disappears like that Red Man tobacco pouch. Here, hold this gun."

He shot a series of photos. She moved off to the side, holding his gun tentatively, pointing it down. In the light of his phone camera, she saw something carved into the wall behind the table, writing that had not been obvious in the dim shack.

"Matt, look! Back here. Do you suppose a prisoner carved something? I can't read it. Can we use your phone for a light?"

"I've got a flashlight app," he said, and walked past her to shine it on the wall. When he did, they saw traces of gold or gilt paint had once highlighted the words but had worn away or been scrubbed out.

"We've got the goods on that sadistic, phony cult leader now," Matt said as they studied the writing.

The Lord threw Jonah into the sea for disobedience.

"That supports your waterboarding theory," she whispered.

"I'll bet one of Bright Star's lackeys slipped up about destroying this hut when they moved, so I pity whoever that is if Gabe can bring charges against that maniac. Let's take some water from the creek and get out of here."

At Grant's house, they all sat in front of the fireplace and listened as Matt explained to Gabe on the phone what they'd found. "Okay, hang on a sec," he told Gabe. "Yeah, I'll forward them to you." He got up from the sofa and moved away into the kitchen. "We were just going to get a water sample. You know, because of that cryptic note Lee Lockwood handed Char. But I guess we should keep the possible water problem quiet for now. I have a friend who can get it tested. We don't need a panic around here over tainted water when it's probably not even true."

Matt came back in and told them, "I'm going to send him the photos from my cell right now. He's coming over and I'm going back with him, to show him where it is."

"I'm going with you," Char said. "I saw it all, too. I should be there."

Grant put his arm around Kate. "She's as stubborn as you are, my love," he told her.

"A Lockwood trait," Kate said, and kissed his cheek.

"That's for sure," Grant said. "Kate's lecturing on her Adena mound finds at Penn State this week, and that's quite a drive. I told her to shut down the dig for a few days and take Kaitlyn with her since I can't get away, but no, she has to keep things going here and head out on her own in this weather tomorrow."

"Grant," Kate said, "I've trekked all over Europe and driven on the wrong side of the road, as we say, in the Highlands of Scotland, so I can get to the next state and back with no problems. All right," she added, jumping up. "The least I can do is fill you two up with more hot chocolate and sandwiches before you head out again. Not only is Tess still going to feel nauseous but she'll be so ticked off to be missing all this. I'm glad I was in on this much before I leave." She headed to the kitchen.

"One other thought in all this," Char said, talking privately to Grant while Matt was working with his phone and Kate was in the kitchen. "Speaking of family ties—I know your brother Brad works for Royce and is close to him. And, like Matt said, we need to keep this quiet right now."

Grant narrowed his eyes. Char hoped he wasn't going to take offense about her not trusting his brother, but, like Orlando, Brad seemed loyal to Royce. She felt bad vibes about Brad Mason, though she couldn't exactly explain why.

Grant cleared his throat. "Brad's had some setbacks in life, but he's doing well, riding high right now, using his people skills working for Royce Flemming and EEC. But you're right. He'd tell Royce right away. What worries me is, if he finds out later that we're in collusion, he'll probably take it real personally with his big bro. The two of us are still patching up our relationship, but Kate and I will keep this info privileged right now. I appreciate your asking me straight out instead of asking Kate to tell me."

Grant left to help Kate in the kitchen as Matt came and sat next to Char. She spoke in a quiet voice. "Are you sure you want to wait to have the water tested before you tell Royce there could be a problem? I asked Grant to keep it from Brad, but he was uneasy with that."

"It needs to be our secret for now. I'll move as fast as I can. My friend in Columbus is a state geologist. I'll ask him for a personal favor. I know he'll keep it quiet, too. Then, if anything looks strange, we'll have it done again—officially."

He'd said *we,* but she wasn't sure if that included her.

Matt wished Char had not come along with him and Gabe, but he knew anything that could help to spring her family from Bright Star's hold was important to her, and a cult torture chamber would sure make headlines. It was probably just his nerves, but again he felt they were being watched. He found himself looking ahead, back—especially up on the ridge—as much as Gabe did.

The shack was just as they'd left it. "Not a place for cutting up meat," Gabe observed when he looked inside. "If it was for butchering game, there would be blood-stains on the table and floor and these rags would be a mess. And, yeah, that quote is pure Bright Star," he added as he swung his flashlight beam over the words. "You know, I saw a place where someone had been waterboarded when I was serving in the Middle East. It was pretty crude, too, but similar."

"I checked on the carved words," Char said. "They aren't a straight biblical quote, but it would link someone being waterboarded to Jonah being almost drowned for disobedience before he was swallowed by the whale. And, I swear, Bright Star sees himself as God or the Messiah—he's that messed up."

"Either delusional or deceptive, but dangerous either way," Matt put in. "But, if Bright Star's behind this, the belly of the whale is that prison cult, and people don't get out after three days and three nights."

Despite feeling warm from their hike, Matt shivered and not from the cold. If this sort of thing was going on inside the cult, Char and her sisters would be even more panicked to get their family members out.

"So, will you go question Bright Star about this?" Char asked Gabe.

"Yes, and he'll probably deny it and give me some mumbo jumbo."

"Could I go along?"

Gabe looked at her instead of frowning at the bizarre scene. "Not if I'm on official business."

"I told her I'd go with her," Matt said. "Even if you were out of uniform in a civilian car, he'd see you as the enemy."

"Anyone who bucks him is his enemy," Gabe said. "I never thought this kind of thing was in his bag of tricks. He's usually into mind control, but this has to tie to him and his wackos. I'm going to look around outside. The photos you sent me were good, Matt. Wish I could put you on salary," he added as he stepped outside and they followed. "I need a second deputy with the local growth and influx of outsiders around here."

"I can talk to Royce Flemming about lobbying for one, maybe even helping to pay for it."

Gabe turned back to face Matt. He stopped abruptly, and Char bumped into his back. "Thanks for the offer, but your boss has made that suggestion already—twice."

"I didn't know that. And?"

"And, no offense, but I turned him down. Conflict of interest, even if he got me a retired or off-duty cop. Royce's money talks. A lot of the new problems around here stem from the fracking teams or tensions between the locals who've had the windfall of fracking money and those who haven't. There's a lot more being shattered around here besides shale. And now we're going to have more upheaval with the Green Tree people protesting to rile everyone up. I feel like I couldn't protect Woody McKitrick and now I'll have to keep an eye on Lacey Fencer and her crew—but I'll find the extra help I need."

"But you do think Woody was killed?" Matt asked. He'd come to that conclusion, and it both angered and scared him.

"In my gut, especially since you two found his cap and the drag marks, even as far as they were from where he fell. But I can't prove it—yet—not with his catastrophic injuries from the fall."

Matt nodded and watched Gabe walk around the structure in a tight circle, then farther out, staring at the ground, just as he had in his backyard after the fire last night. Char took Matt's arm and stood close; he clamped her elbow tight to his ribs. He wasn't sure if it was a good or a bad sign that he could read her thoughts. *Catastrophic injuries from the fall. Matt, that could have been you going off the cliff near Coyote Rock.*

They both jumped when Gabe cried out from behind the shack. "Oh, no!"

"What?" Matt yelled and started around the corner toward him.

"Stay back! Don't come closer in case this area is another crime scene!" Gabe shouted. "Get me a tree branch or something to clear away the snow, will you? Just throw it to me."

Matt searched under nearby trees and found a broken limb. Char stood nearby, squinting in the brightness to see what Gabe was standing over as Matt yanked the branch free. It was long enough he could almost hand it to him, but he heaved it at his feet. "What is it?" Matt demanded.

"Just a sec." Gabe retrieved the branch and brushed snow away with it. "Oh, damn. Under the snow, leaves and some soil—a shallow grave with a brown-haired person buried in it!"

Char gave a little scream. "Lee has brown hair!" she cried. "Could Bright Star have found out about the note he wrote me and had him tortured until he confessed—then had him killed?"

16

Matt threw an arm around Char's shoulders to prop her up. Eager to see what Gabe had uncovered but scared to move, she leaned against him. "No, wait!" Gabe shouted. "I— Sorry. It's a dead beaver buried here. More than one. Shot, I think, five of them. Covered like that, the head on this first one, it looked like human hair."

Char nearly collapsed in Matt's arms. Gabe was not the only one who had jumped to conclusions. Thank God, it wasn't a human—not Lee or anyone else. But why so many beavers shot and buried when their fur was valuable?

"Just some lunatic taking potshots?" Matt asked, still hugging her. "Can we come closer?"

"No, don't. It's still a crime scene. It's not trapping season and there's a big fine for off-season kills. Maybe someone was just drunk or gun happy. Or upset with how the beaver dams are changing the pond here, messing with the way things were."

"Or," Matt said quietly to Char, "shooting animals to protest the fracking above."

"That's a terrible thought," she whispered. "But it's nothing next to someone trying to hurt or kill you to warn Royce. How militant is that Green Tree group that's supposed to be coming here?"

Gabe overheard that as he headed toward them. "They've been around here before protesting Grant's lumber mill cutting trees but they weren't violent. Still, when I researched them, I learned they've been known to follow some of the more aggressive tactics like the better-known Greenpeace uses. I hope we don't have to deal with protests like stopping supply trucks or sabotaging equipment. Look, guys, I need to order a necropsy for at least one of these carcasses—an animal autopsy. It may take a while, but I've got to know if it was the gunshot that killed them or something else."

"Like something in the water?" Matt asked.

"Fracking's still in its infancy here in Ohio," Gabe said. "There have been problems. That's a guess right now, but could be. It will take a while for me to get the necropsy results back, so keep me updated on possible water contamination from your sample. Okay? You can probably get results faster than I can."

Char's head snapped up just as if someone had slapped her out of a daze. "You two are actually thinking contaminated water killed these beavers? I mean, Matt said he saw one dead on the creek bank the other day, but why would someone shoot them then—and bury them?"

Gabe shrugged. "I hope not to hide that they died of contamination—or were suffering from it so they were put out of their misery. We'll have to keep an eye out here for sick or newly dead animals. Lots of game would drink from the water here, but since the beavers live in it, maybe they'd be hit harder first. It's all a guess. But with the usual noise from up above, no one would hear a shot—or five."

"Sorry to say this," Matt said, "but I'm hoping it's just some sadistic nutcase. Besides, if the water was tainted from fracking runoff above this site, we'd see dead fish and frogs, turtles, too."

"This time of year they hang out on the bottom and barely move," Gabe said. "They might not float, or being lower means they've got purer water. But would a poacher or someone out just for the fun of picking off beavers bother to bury them?"

"The Hear Ye people used to hunt down here—maybe they still do," Char said. "Maybe they shot these, then someone came along—like Matt earlier. They didn't want to be caught, so they buried them. Matt, you said you heard a shot when you were down here and there is, or was, a tree stand you saw where the shooter could hide. And it's apparently gone now, so maybe he tried to cover up using that, too, since trapping beaver is off-season."

"Char, I know you don't trust the Hear Ye robots," Gabe said, his voice stern. "Neither do I, but don't you think, if it was Bright Star's hunters, they'd actually eat beaver? They've obviously even left their pelts here.

Now I'm going to call someone to come and collect one of the beavers. These look like fresh kills, and it's been cold enough they haven't rotted and don't stink—yet. Then I'm going to visit someone who is rotten and stinks to high heaven, the illustrious Bright Star Monson."

"I know what you're thinking," Matt told her quietly as the two of them trudged through the snow out of the valley. "But let Gabe do his thing first, and don't you go near that old lunatic asylum unless I'm with you."

When Matt drove his truck back home with Char holding the precious Cold Creek water sample, he saw the Green Tree protestors were out in full force along the highway at the entrance to the Lake Azure community. What really ticked him off was one sign among the usual KILL THE DRILL placards. It read, FLEMMING IS FRACKENSTEIN.

Matt pulled in past the landscaped entry, sorry for the first time he'd talked Royce out of making this a gated community. At the time he'd been worried it sent the wrong, elitist message to the locals, but lately they could use the extra security. He stopped the truck, pulled over onto the berm. "Stay here and hold tight to that sample," he told Char. "I'm going to tell them to keep off the property and see if I can get them to move to the EEC office in Columbus or the largest fracking site here instead."

"You mean the old Hear Ye cult grounds? All we need is them hearing about dead beavers."

"Yeah, well, they don't belong here. They're standing on private property. This investment of Royce's is separate from the fracking. I've tried to make certain of that."

He slammed the truck door louder than he'd meant to and strode back toward the highway. What a hell of a day—a week, except for finding Char.

"Good afternoon," he called to them, seven protestors to be exact, four women and three men. They got even more animated when they saw him coming. Several vehicles passing on the road honked as if in sympathy—or to protest the protest.

"I'm Matthew Rowan, general manager of the Lake Azure community. Can I ask who's your spokesperson? The private citizens who live here have nothing to do with fracking."

"That's a good one," a burly man said. "Royce Flemming, CEO of EEC, lives here and is here!"

"He lives in Columbus but is visiting here. You need to take your protest to his corporate offices in Columbus or to a fracking site. This is private property."

"He needs to know how citizens feel about their environment—especially in a natural, beautiful place like this!" one woman insisted. When she yelled nearly in his face, the strong scent of her clove chewing gum wafted toward him. "And I'm Lacey Fencer, the spokesperson here."

"Lacey, glad to meet you," Matt said, thrusting out his hand. She ignored the gesture. "I know and admire your cousin Joe Fencer. I just hired him here as a groundskeeper. You see, we do care about keeping the environment beautiful."

"He's my second cousin, but he just sold out to the enemy," she insisted. Compared to the others here, she was really made up, green eyeshadow and crimson lips. Everyone wore coats of synthetic material, no leather or even faux fur, of course. Their signs were all professionally printed, except for the burly guy's attacking Royce, which was lettered in block print with some sort of big marker pen. Matt noticed that the burly guy must be chewing tobacco, because he turned away and spit a stream of the brown stuff into the snow. If this bunch wasn't new to town, he would have asked him if he was chewing Red Man.

Matt fought to keep his temper. "With that huge fracking site across the road from your cousin's place, I don't blame him for selling, do you?" Matt asked Lacey. "He was devastated to leave his family farm but he did it for his kids' future and to keep his family happy. It was a tough, honest choice and should be accepted and honored, not to mention that fracking keeps our country from being so dependent on the evils of foreign oil."

"Never mind all that smart, smooth talk," Lacey said, even louder now, her voice strident. That got her some fist pumps and backup noise from her buddies.

And Grant Mason was married to this woman once? She was night and day from Kate Lockwood. He admired Lacey for taking a stand to protect the environment, and this area had once been her home, but he wished he could toss them all out in the street. Instead, exhausted and on edge, he spoke in a controlled voice. "Please be sure you keep off the private property here. We like to keep our grass under this snow and our foliage unharmed by intrusion from outsiders—including the pollution of spit from chewing tobacco. If you break the law, I'll call the sheriff. And be careful of the big timber semis on the road from the nearby mill."

He heard Lacey gasp as he turned away and strode back toward his truck. Char, thank heavens, had waited there without getting involved for once. As he turned his back on them, he recalled that Grant had told him just today he had confronted Lacey and her crew when they were picketing his lumber mill last year. And Matt recalled a TV show he'd seen on how some protest groups would go to extremes to draw attention to their causes. He hoped this Green Tree bunch wouldn't try something crazy like harming animals on their own to draw attention to the evils of drilling. Or could they have done that already?

When he got closer to the truck, he saw Ginger Green standing beside it, talking to Char through the passenger-side window. She had a quiver of arrows on her back and a recurve bow in her hand.

"Hey," he called to her. "You aren't headed for the protestors, are you?"

"Been there, done that. It really frosts me they have my last name in their title, the rabid greeniacs. I'd like to put an arrow or two through their signs, but I restrained myself. You know what one of them—that Fencer woman in charge—said to me?"

"Tell me," he said, standing by Char's open window, too.

Ginger pouted, her free hand on her hip. "She said the chaos around here from the fracking reminded her of reruns of that old TV show, *The Beverly Hillbillies,* where Jed Clampett struck oil on his poor Appalachian property and moved to Hollywood and made a fool of himself. I told her the Green Tree protestors have been polluting the air around here with their chanting. Sorry, boss, but I just came down through the woods from the archery range to tell them to knock it off."

"They've been standing on our property, so I'll get Sheriff McCabe or his deputy to give them a warning."

"You know," Ginger said with a little grin when she'd looked so angry a moment ago, "I must admit I do like to see Royce riled, since he 'done me wrong.' You all know what I mean. I swear, I'd like to sic Orlando on those loudmouths—and I just may do that."

"You keep Orlando and Royce out of this," Matt told her. "I'll handle it."

She hit his shoulder lightly with her fist and strode back into the fringe of pine trees, from which she must have emerged. He'd never noticed it before, but her quiver was covered with sleek fur, and he stared after her, wondering if that could be beaver. And the fletching on her arrows—hell, they looked pretty much like the ones that had whacked into Char's cabin door and the back of his house. But what annoyed him more than anything was the fact that the bottle of creek water Char held on her lap could prove that those picketers were right.

After Matt dropped off Char, he headed home and put the jar of creek water on his kitchen counter. He fixed himself a sandwich and a beer and stared at the jar, held it up to the light, trying to decide how to get it safely to his friend in Columbus tomorrow. He'd gone to college with the guy, knew he'd do this for him, keep it quiet until they could get a better sample. The water looked clear to him. Wouldn't it have the golden highlights of the water in the fracking lagoon if it was deadly?

He jumped when his front doorbell rang. All he needed was Royce or Orlando right now. He put the jar in the cupboard and went to see who it was. Joe Fencer. He'd insisted on working this weekend because of the snow—and, Matt figured—because he just couldn't stand to be in his old farmhouse he was soon leaving for good.

"Hey, Joe, come on in."

"Thanks. For a few minutes. Just wanted to apologize about my cousin leading those protestors out there."

"Not your fault."

Joe came in, wiping the snow off his feet on Matt's sisal rug. "I tried to talk to them. For all the good it did, me. You know, I never thought about a groundskeeper job being dangerous before."

"Before facing the Green Tree zealots out on the road? What did they do?"

"I mean, considering what happened to Woody. Then Ms. Green—I mean, she seemed real friendly, said to call her Ginger—read me the riot act of stats that ground maintenance workers have a high percentage of fatalities, like 160 nationally a couple of years ago, she said. And get this—falls are a common cause of accidental death. Made me think of Woody again."

"Well, that's a lousy welcome from our sports director," Matt said. "Sometimes I wonder whose side she's on. Here, let me take your coat. Come on into the kitchen. I forgot to turn up the heat when I came in. Want coffee or a beer?"

"Coffee would be great. I'm not quite ready to go home. The family's packing. Actually, I'm going to drive to the new place with some boxes I've got in my truck, spend the night there. Sara Ann and Mandy Lee will probably yak half the night, anyway."

"Won't Mandy Lee be going back to her family up on Pinecrest soon? I'm sure her son, Jemmie, needs her, and old Adela could sure use help."

"Mandy Lee's husband—you've seen Sam, right?—is acting so strange. I think she's actually scared of him. He's there for a while then just disappears."

"Yeah, watching for terrorists."

"Sometimes I think, in his own way, he's turned into one."

Matt started the coffeemaker on his counter. "Your new place is on the road to Chillicothe, right? Listen, I need a big favor. If you're going to be that far, can you take a package to a friend of mine in Columbus tomorrow morning—just come in here late, however long it takes for you to wait for test results on a sample. Keep a record of your trip and I'll pay you mileage out of my pocket—not the community money."

"Yeah, sure. Glad to. Like a medical sample to a doctor's office?"

"I'm going to level with you, Joe, because I want you to agree to what I'm asking—understand what it is. I think you and I see eye to eye on this, that the country and some people get the benefits of fracking, but we need to keep an eye on its possible excesses. It's a sample of creek water from near the Hear Ye fracking site and your heritage farm—that needs to be tested for possible runoff pollution. This has nothing to do with the Green Tree protest and is not to be shared with anyone other than me. No one right now."

Joe's eyes widened. He sat up straighter. "I get it," he said. "I'll do it. Like I said, I'm torn, too."

"Which is partly why I'm trusting you with this. Deal?" he asked and extended his hand over the corner of the table.

"Deal," Joe said, shaking his hand. "Say, you didn't think of this earlier and tell someone, did you? I mean before you almost got shoved off Pinecrest Mountain?"

"No. Good theory, though. I still haven't figured out why that happened—or what really happened to Woody McKitrick, so be careful around here. Maybe Ginger's warning was legit. If you ever go up on the ridge above the golf course, let me know, and I'll go with you."

Joe nodded. "You bet I'll keep this little errand quiet,

even from my family, 'cause this is big. I mean, if word got out what you're thinking, you'd really get hounded by the Green Tree folks and others. It could be huge for Mr. Flemming. It could put you in danger again."

17

Though she was exhausted, Char hardly slept. She yawned and turned over once again, twisting the bedcovers. Today was Monday. She'd only known Matt five days, but she felt as if she was having withdrawal symptoms when she wasn't with him. And she was so worried about her family in the grasp of Bright Star. Who knew what he was capable of?

Thanksgiving was this Thursday, only three days away. Since Kate would barely be back from Pennsylvania and the mere smell of food sent Tess running to the bathroom, nothing had been decided about where they would celebrate the holiday as a family. Char intended to ask Matt if she could pay to have her family dine at the lodge, but there might be no places left this late. And, except for Tess's pregnancy, could they feel really thankful considering all that had happened? Well, she had found Matt—if they had any sort of future.

She got up early while it was still dark, forced herself to get ready and eat breakfast from food she'd brought from the cabin. Then she just paced around the first floor of the large home—large to her, at least. As much as she had looked forward to being in the little hunting cabin up on the cliff, she guessed she could get used to a large place like this or Matt's.

She made herself sit down at the kitchen table to review her notes about the house visit she'd make this morning up on Pinecrest. Bethany Antrim, age seven, had not been to school yet this year, evidently because she lived so far up and her mother was an invalid. Bethany would be the third child Henry Hanson could pick up in the new school van, and there were at least three other families Char hoped to call on. She had to concentrate on that this morning, helping the mountain kids, as much as she'd like to help the ones she was related to. Little Kelsey and Ethan were just as trapped as the impoverished Appalachian children. Lee and Grace had decided to join the Hear Ye sect, but the kids had no say in that.

When daylight finally filtered through the trees, Char got her things together to head out. She jumped as her phone rang. She'd been hoping Matt would call, even though he hadn't wanted her to go up on Pinecrest alone, and she was going, anyway.

"This is Char."

"Char, it's Gabe. Deputy Miller and I called on Bright Star last night, and I have some things to tell you. I'm almost to Lake Azure, so stay put, okay?"

"I'll wait for you. Did he admit that his people killed those beavers and had that waterboarding place?"

"Actually, that wasn't our most important topic. He denied knowing anything about it, despite the quote carved in the wall. He said maybe someone from his group did it but for a place to meditate and pray, that the table was a makeshift altar and he'd ask around."

"Meditate and pray? But—"

"Just sit tight. I'll be right there."

Her stomach cramped. What else could Gabe be alluding to as more important? She waited, pacing again. If he had something else on Bright Star, now would be the time to try to get her relatives out of that horrible place. She looked out the front windows and saw the sheriff's car pull in. Gabe got out and came up the walk.

She pulled the front door open. "Let's sit down," he said, giving her a pat on the shoulder, then going past her into the living room. She closed the door and followed him in. He put his hat on the end table but left his leather jacket on. He sat on the sofa, leaning forward, elbows on his knees, looking at his hands instead of her.

"Is Tess okay?"

"Yes, if you call puking off and on okay. She's still happy as can be. The doctor says it should pass after her first trimester. Her friend Lindell's running most of the activities today."

"I could help out again. I have to make several house calls and set things up with the school district, but—"

"Char, please sit down."

She sat beside him on the sofa, turning to face him. "Something about Bright Star," she said. "It's bad—right?"

"Let me tell you a couple things. First of all, I made another jump-the-gun mistake about the dead beavers. They weren't shot with a rifle but with arrows."

"Oh, no! Then—"

"The carcass I have still had the metal-tipped arrow point in it, although the shaft was pulled out. My deputy and I went back down there. The other beavers didn't have the arrow points in them—but no bullets."

"Gabe, you have to check that arrow point against the others—you know, like a ballistics test. Well, I don't mean to tell you your business, but we have to let Matt know."

"I just talked to him. There's more. Actually, I was called to the Hear Ye compound before I went on my own. The Falls County coroner asked me to meet him there last night. Char, I'm sorry, but this is a next of kin call, and I hate to make those."

He turned toward her, finally looked at her.

"A next of kin call?"

"Six cult members were sickened on Friday by botulism from home-canned peaches that obviously went bad. They've had a doctor out there as well as the coroner. Several kids and two adults got severely sick. One died. Char, it was Lee. He got violently ill and died nine hours later. They claim they had no idea it would be fatal. As I said, the others pulled through—three are still in the Chillicothe Regional Medical Center. Tess is devastated, Kate's en route to Pennsylvania, and—Char, did you hear me? What you said yesterday when I thought we had a human corpse buried in the snow was almost prophetic. Lee is dead. I'm so sorry."

"I—can't believe it, but I feared it. You saw his body?"

"Yes, before the coroner took him."

She sat still, rigid as his words sank in. Then she put her head in her hands but didn't cry, just breathed in huge gasps. He slid over to sit beside her, put his arm around her shoulders.

"Gabe, that maniac killed Lee or had him killed. You know he did."

"We don't know that. We can't prove that—yet."

"I swear, the others were a cover—expendable if they died, too. I have to get to Grace, get her out of there."

"That's partly why I'm here. Bright Star's been very cooperative."

"Oh, I'll just bet," she said. She broke into tears and jumped up to pace, flinging gestures. "After all, he gets away with everything. He told Kate once that Grace was a chosen one, but I think poor Lee was chosen to die, especially since he tried to tell me something to help expose that monster! The cult member next to us at the market must have guessed he told me something."

"Listen to me!" Gabe said, getting up and swinging her around to face him, then holding her by both upper arms. "I have permission to attend what the sect calls a resurrection ceremony this afternoon. Tess and Kate are obviously not available—I wouldn't let Tess go if she could—but if you want to go, I'll take you, if you can control yourself from attacking that bastard or getting in the way of my investigation."

Char wiped tears off her cheeks. She pulled away from him and fumbled for a tissue in her jeans pocket and blew her nose. "Yes, good. I prayed for a way to see Grace and Lee but not like this. It—it isn't their kids that got sick, is it?"

"No. I checked that, have the names."

"You'd think the kids that got sick would have been worse off than a big man, having smaller bodies."

"I know. They must have eaten less of the peaches."

"An autopsy?"

"Bright Star has allowed it despite the fact he said it dishonors the body. The coroner would have done it anyway, did it at seven this morning. No signs of homicide. He confirmed the botulism—it's a deadly toxin with a long name. He declared the cause of death as accidental from food poisoning."

"Maybe Lee was force-fed the poison peaches and waterboarded to death!"

"Char, I'm not taking you with me if you pull anything—say anything like that. I repeat, you're not to get involved or screw up my investigation of Bright Star and this incident. Agree with me, or you don't go."

"Yes. Yes, I'll play the part of meek family mourner. But this so-called resurrection service is today—already?"

"The cult buries its dead before the next sunset, something like Jewish or old biblical beliefs, I guess."

Still blinking back tears, she nodded. "I'll be back

here by three, if you can pick me up. I—I have to help a little girl up on the mountain, even if my own kin is past saving."

"You're going up the mountain today? Without Matt? He said he's busy and doesn't want you to go alone."

"The living need help, not the dead."

"Don't start sounding like Bright Star. Be careful then. I'll pick you up here at three-thirty. I won't be in uniform, and we won't go in my sheriff vehicle. The service is at four, followed by the burial at sunset. Like other churches, they have permission to bury their dead in a new graveyard nearby, the third one on the old lunatic asylum grounds."

"More burials of people who have somehow lost their minds," she said as he took his hat off the table. "Thank you, Gabe. I'll be ready and I'll be careful."

"Good. Sorry to be the bearer of that news. Tess is trying to get hold of Kate to tell her, but she must have turned her phone off while she drives. No reason for her to come back until after her lecture anyway, especially if he's buried this fast."

Char watched him drive away. Somehow, she was going to get Grace and her kids out of Bright Star's version of an insane asylum.

After she returned from the mountain, Char dressed in an all-black pantsuit and her only good coat, a camel-colored one with a belt.

Gabe drove them toward the starburst iron gates of the Hear Ye commune. "That's great news about another mountain kid getting to go to school," he told her. "Something good today, anyhow."

"Thank heavens Bethany's mother wanted her to get to school, even if it meant she was often alone during the day. She's only forty but she has real breathing problems with COPD. I talked to a neighbor who said she'd look in on Mrs. Antrim, even though the term 'neighbor' means about four miles away. I just wish Grace would think about her own kids and sacrifice for them—by getting out of here, especially before these people get their hands on her new baby. Tess said she doesn't even think families get to stay together here. It may take a village to raise a child, but children need the family structure, too."

"Right. For sure," he said as he parked his civilian car. They were both on edge. Char was holding back her tears; Gabe was stoic and hadn't said much on the drive, even while she'd rattled on.

She hadn't seen Matt but had talked to him on the phone, and they were planning on eating out tonight. He said he'd sent the water sample to his friend in Columbus but he didn't tell her how—she knew for sure not with Orlando. Funny, but she had the feeling Matt thought their cell phones might be hacked since the moment she'd started to tell him she was desperate to help Grace, he'd cut her off and said to tell him in person. That was fine with her because she knew if she told him, he'd try to stop her from— Well, from whatever she could manage to do.

As the guard opened the gate and gestured for them

to enter, it was clear they were expected. "I almost had to tie Tess down to keep her from coming along," Gabe whispered as they were allowed to go up the curved walk alone.

"Bet they tie people down here who don't cooperate—and waterboard them."

"I said, don't start, Char. Not here, not now. It's in Bright Star's power to let us in or kick us out."

"I know." She sighed and bit her lower lip.

Inside, they were escorted down a long hall and into a large, unfurnished, low-ceilinged room draped in muted, shimmering silver-and-pale-yellow swags of cloth. *The colors of starlight?* she wondered. Another man ushered them toward a plain wooden coffin with a split, hinged lid. It was bare, unfinished pine and, she figured, was probably made here on the grounds. The lower part of it was closed, and the upper third open so only Lee's shoulders and face were visible. It was him, but it didn't look like him, slack-faced and white with his hair—beaver-brown hair—combed too flat. Of course, he was clothed in cult garb, so this whole thing looked like a pioneer funeral. No flowers, only more draped cloth, and a podium near the head of the coffin.

"The battle behind him and now peaceful in eternal repose," a soft voice behind them said, as their escort was replaced by Bright Star himself. A low murmur swept through the crowd of forty or so adults behind them, standing in neat rows. Was that sibilant sound of whispers due to the presence of outsiders, including the sheriff, or because their master had just entered?

"Sad when he was so young and healthy," Char said, staring into Bright Star's pale eyes, though that gave her the shivers.

"A tragic accident from our view, but planned from above."

She almost said, *I'll bet!* but she'd promised Gabe and Matt she'd control herself. And then, over Gabe's shoulder, she saw Grace.

"Excuse me," Char said, and moved away to hug her. It wasn't easy with her bulbous belly. Though she was not even thirty, Grace looked older, a pale ghost, not a woman blooming with child. "I'm so sorry, Grace."

"Me, too—for everything."

"Will the children be here?"

"Best not. Char, I have to get out of here."

"You're feeling faint?"

"Out of *here,* this place, away from being chosen. From that man," she whispered, even as Gabe and Bright Star walked over to join them. "Don't tell Gabe. Force won't work," she added, speaking so fast Char could hardly catch her words. "Fewer know the better."

Char fought to keep calm. No reason to make a fuss now. Gabe would be furious, and they were outnumbered. Besides, the children weren't here and could be held hostage or even spirited away by the time Gabe got help in here. One hand on Grace's arm to steady her, Char stood stock-still, as Gabe gave the young widow Tess's condolences and Kate's, too, explaining Kate was out of state and that Tess was pregnant.

Char saw Grace's hand drop protectively to her belly.

"That's wonderful. Please tell Tess I wish blessings on her."

Char knew she had to get a moment alone with Grace. Just then, Bright Star stepped between the two women and murmured something to Grace, who nodded. He stroked her upper arm, just once, shoulder to elbow, but Char thought in a possessive rather than a comforting way.

The next hour was a blur. Everyone stood during the funeral service, including Grace, who seemed to waver on her feet, but Char was too far back in the lines of the faithful to get to her. Bright Star gave a eulogy, rambling on about how starlight could guide Lee through the dark valley of death and about a shepherd losing one of his sheep. But Char wasn't really listening. She was racking her brain for some way to spring Grace and her two kids out of here, despite the guards, the cold weather, not to mention Grace's condition. It seemed Grace was ready to run, and, whatever it took, Char was going to help her.

Caped and cloaked like pioneers of old, the Hear Ye members stood outside in brisk wind on a barren plot of land—the new Hear Ye cemetery. In Char's sorrow, it seemed just right to see a beautiful winter sunset with the clouds catching the red rays of the sun, smearing crimson across the sky before it all disappeared—just like Lee. The wind howled as his coffin was lowered into the frozen earth that must have been hacked open with the pickaxes Char saw leaning against a nearby tree. She felt numb, not as much from the cold as from the unreality of all this. Thank God, Gabe stood beside her, but she wished it was Matt. Yet neither of them would understand what she had to do.

It annoyed her when Bright Star recited the common words of comfort for a funeral:

> "In My Father's house are many mansions. If it was not so I would have told you…"

He emphasized the *My* and *I* as if he were the Lord himself speaking. She could tell Gabe caught that, too, when he stiffened and gave a little snort beside her, but the flock of the faithful stared transfixed like loyal soldiers.

Bright Star stood over the grave while four men quickly filled it with shovels of soil that thudded like heartbeats on the wooden coffin. Char quickly went to Grace, hugged her again and whispered in her ear, in the wail of wind before anyone could come near. "I'll be waiting in that western line of trees tonight from seven to eight, and every night for a week. If you can get Kelsey and Ethan, come here to the grave, and we'll get away."

Grace blinked back tears half-frozen in the wind. "So soon? I—I— They'll chase us. The master wants this child."

Char was getting panicked as others came closer, including Gabe. "If you get stopped before coming here, say you just had to say goodbye again at his grave—with the children," she told Grace.

"Yes, I want to. I'll try..." was all Char heard before others put their arms around Grace. Their capes and cloaks seemed to open, then swallow her as they led her away.

18

Matt struggled to keep his mind on his work. He had a lot of it, but his thoughts kept skipping to Char making another visit up on the mountain this morning, while she was grieving Lee's loss. Meanwhile, he'd fielded questions on the phone and in person from home owners. He'd done more research about Green Tree and Lacey Fencer, who had just married her right-hand man, Darren Ashley. From their wedding photos on her Facebook page, Matt saw he was the burly tobacco spitter in the picket line.

He kept watching the clock, wondering when he'd hear from Char and when Joe would be back from Columbus so he could find out about the water sample. As the early winter sun set, he fought to focus on the here and now, still worried about Char at that crazy cult funeral, even if Gabe was with her. He was about ready to head home when Ginger knocked on his door for the meeting he'd set up with her and had forgotten. As she came in, quiet for once, he moved out from behind his desk, closed the door and sat across from her in the other chair.

She was looking at him warily so he went right to what he wanted to ask. "I told you earlier about the arrow that was shot into the back of my house on Saturday evening. The sheriff has it now, but, just looking at it as an amateur, I think the arrow could have been one of yours."

"You all should have showed it to me. That sketch you made of the first arrow wasn't enough for me to go on. But you said to think it over and, yes, it could have been mine. And no, I don't have a clue about who would have shot it, 'cause it sure enough wasn't me. I don't go 'round setting those kind of fires, Matt, if you know what I mean. As for me setting my sights on living targets, pheasants, wild turkeys—the occasional wild human male—sorry, don't mean to make light of that. The thing is," she said, uncrossing her legs and leaning closer to him, "lots of folks hereabouts could have my arrows. I ask students to buy their own either at a sports store or from the commercial ones I keep here, but I use mine on the archery range. Students could retrieve or take a couple I'd never miss. But let me tell you," she said, recrossing her legs and leaning back in her chair, "I don't miss much."

Matt could think of a couple of smart follow-ups, but he kept his mouth shut. Besides, he knew from Char that Henry Hanson had taken some of Ginger's arrows out of the trash. He planned to question him, too, but he had to be careful with what Woody had called "mountain pride." Char was so happy Henry was going to drive the new school van that, if the guy took offense at Matt's implications and quit his new job, there would be hell to pay from Char and Royce.

"Oh, I also meant to ask," he said as if it were an afterthought. "Have you ever shot birds from a tree stand?"

"No way. I don't like heights, and tree stands are for big game where you have to let them come to you so you don't spook them. I shoot in the open field. You can get plenty close to game birds if you sneak up on them real quiet. Was there a tree stand behind your house?"

"No. Just curious. But back to people having access to your arrows. What about Orlando?"

"Ha! Sports endeavors, except the kind that's private, are not up his alley. He thinks he's using me, but it's the other way 'round. Okay, I know I speak too frank sometimes, but if someone's using my handmade arrows to make me look bad, I don't know who it would be. You don't think little old me has a motive to do that?"

"No, I don't. I think you'd be shooting at Royce, not me."

"Right, and I don't dare to really cross him any more than you do. He doesn't care about me, but he loves you, Matt. Really, he does, like the son he never had. I can tell that kind of irks Orlando, who worships the ground Royce walks on." She chattered on about Orlando's rough childhood, then his graduating from the "school of hard knocks," and how that made him different from others she'd "known."

For someone who was admittedly using Orlando, Matt thought she cared about him more than she admitted. That spoke well for the man, didn't it? Maybe Matt was looking at the guy in the wrong way. After all, he had to admire his loyalty to Royce, even if he was well paid for it—and Matt realized he had no clue how much Orlando was paid. The man was always at Royce's beck and call.

Though he'd intended to head home, it really was a house and not a home, so he stayed after Ginger left. He knew he'd become a workaholic over the years, but now it didn't seem fulfilling. He stood, looking out his office window into the dark night. He'd meant to ask Ginger about that handmade quiver of hers, but no way was it beaver. He really didn't think she was a liar. On the contrary, she usually blurted out too much, and he preferred that to someone not telling him the truth.

Char hated lying to Matt, but she'd done it, told him on the phone she was exhausted and grieving, so could they please postpone dinner so she could rest up. He'd been concerned but had agreed, said he still had a lot of work to catch up on and he'd be in his office if she changed her mind about later. *Later?* How would she ever put him off a second night if Grace didn't show up tonight? He'd insist on going with her, call Gabe or his deputy in if she leveled with him. They might gang up on her and refuse to let her go at all. And she was convinced that a posse would spook Grace even if she did show up.

But worse, what if she was being set up by Grace? She didn't think so, believed Grace was sincere about getting out of the cult with her kids, just the way she'd believed Lee about *big bucks* and *poison water.* Lee's death must have opened Grace's eyes. Maybe she knew something about it not being accidental. Maybe Lee had been the one making her stay.

But as Char thought back on it now, Grace had made one quick comment that could be both monumental and devastating: "The master wants this child." So then, wouldn't Bright Star be watching Grace like a hawk, her kids, too, in case she tried to flee? But she didn't believe she was being set up by Bright Star because the man had hovered over Grace so. If he'd told Grace to lure Char onto their grounds, he would have given them more time to talk. As it was, each time Char huddled with Grace, Bright Star or the others had quickly swarmed her.

Char also agonized over what it could mean for Grace to be "chosen." *Just because new lives in the cult were precious?* If she was chosen to bear Bright Star's child, was that why Lee turned against him the only way he could—to let her know that he was in cahoots with Royce, who was poisoning the water with his fracking…

She stopped pacing and looked out the front window for the tenth time, grateful Matt had not come to see her, because she would surely have blurted out to him what she planned to do. Her thoughts were dark, just as it seemed outside, even with the streetlights on the snow, the pale moon and the blinking red-and-green early holiday lights on a house nearby.

She closed the curtains and sat at the kitchen table to study her cell phone screen again. She'd used an on-line map to find a place to park her truck near the old asylum property. She'd even chosen a way to walk into the forest that edged the plot of land where they'd buried Lee. Her plan was to stay hidden in the trees until she was sure Grace and her kids had come alone.

She wondered if Tess had called their dad out West to tell him that Lee, his nephew, was dead. Lee, who used to be such a gangly, happy kid. Lee, who, like his father and her own dad, had inherited the gift of dowsing to find pure drinking water on the old Hear Ye grounds. *What if that was polluted by the fracking, too?*

She shook her head to clear it. Again she made sure the note she'd left for Matt in case anything went wrong tonight was propped up on the kitchen table where they'd shared a meal just two evenings ago.

> Dear Matt, I have a chance to help Grace and her kids escape B.S. and I had to take it. She begged me to come alone. No one else knows yet. I plan to take her to Gabe and Tess's until she can find a place to hide, to have her baby safely. I pray you will understand. Char

She pulled on her black jacket, cap and earmuffs, put her phone on vibrate, locked up and hurried out to her truck.

* * *

A little before seven that night, Matt was still at his desk, eating a cheeseburger from the lodge kitchen, and finishing up. He'd just decided to phone Char when someone knocked on his office door, and he looked up.

"Joe! Come in. I was getting worried. You should have called. I'm going to get you a cell phone, necessary for the job around here, anyway. I should have thought of that last night. Sit down. Can I get you something from the kitchen?"

"Sorry it took so long, but your friend Clint had an emergency with bad-smelling city water when I got there, and your testing had to wait. I didn't let the water sample out of my sight, though. Like you said, guard the chain of possession."

"And he did the test?"

"He says he'd like to come here to retest, get control samples of groundwater and more surface water. But it has traces of bromides, which made Pittsburgh and other cities change how they treat their drinking water. I've got a written report here for you," he said, digging it out of his jacket pocket. "Bromides aren't toxic per se but can combine with disinfectants in drinking-water treatment plants—"

"Which is how we get our water here."

"Right. When they combine, it can produce cancer-causing compounds. Man, I'm glad I'm moving my family now—just in case. Also, see there," he said, handing him the paper and pointing. "He wrote a note about naturally occurring radiation that was brought to the surface by drillers. It was found in a Pennsylvania creek that flows into the Allegheny. There's a big risk of wastewater from fracking leaking into ground or surface water. It could even get into the fish."

And maybe beavers, Matt thought. "I see, below all that, he's noted here there were also traces of methane in the sample."

"Yeah. He said there's not much research done on if that harms humans."

"But I also see," Matt said, skimming the paper, "that four years ago natural methane gas leaked into a well in Ohio. The methane had escaped from an inadequately cemented vertical well drilled into sandstone. Local drilling is into shale, but it could react the same. And it says here, if methane gets into basements or sheds, it can cause explosions! Damn, that's all we need."

"Bottom line, your friend Clint says the stuff from runoff water, which can bubble up outside fracked shale wells and those so-called lagoons, can really cause problems."

"Cause problems, for sure," Matt echoed. "But this is all still in the *what-if* stage around here. We'll have to get him here, let him retest. Joe, I'm asking you to keep this quiet until we do. I guess I needed an assistant around here as much as a new head groundskeeper."

"Sure, 'cause I know you're on it and will make it public as soon as you can. He said call him again, and he'll find some time to come down and do controlled samples. And I told him he needed to keep this quiet for now, tell no one but you—well, and me, too."

"I hate keeping secrets, cloak-and-dagger stuff. But sometimes, it has to be done."

Char wished she'd told Matt and Gabe, but too late now. She parked her truck about a half mile from the outer edge of the old asylum grounds and hiked in through what she was certain must be the edge of the woods that went up to the cult buildings and the snowy field with Lee's fresh grave site.

She tried to tell herself it was possible that food poisoning *had* killed Lee—since others were sickened, too—but she still believed Bright Star would sacrifice others to protect himself, and maybe, his business partner, Royce Flemming. After all, it was Royce's money that had allowed the sect to move to their spacious new grounds and build anew there. Maybe Royce kept donations flowing in—especially if Bright Star knew something about the poison water Lee had alluded to in his note. She didn't put it past that phony messiah to bribe or threaten someone as powerful as Royce, let alone Lee.

As she crunched through the snow or accidentally snapped a broken tree limb underfoot, Char told herself no one would be out in the dark woods to hear or see her. Surely hunters didn't hunt at night, perched in their tree stands.

She stuck to the fringe of the field, her steps lit only by fitful moonlight through the clouds. The wind sometimes sighed and sometimes howled, as if it sensed her feelings. *Should she have brought coats or blankets for the kids? Would they have shoes or boots to wear when they should not be outside this time of night?* She had a flashlight in her backpack, but she figured she dare not use it this close to the cult grounds. She passed one of the historic graveyards here. Perhaps insane people years ago had tried to flee this place, only to be caught and brought back and punished.

When she could see the barren field where they had buried Lee, she leaned against a sturdy tree trunk. In the distance, wan lights shone from the main cult building. She both blessed and cursed the moonlight. She could see if someone was coming, but then she might be seen, too. Were the usual guards out at night when it was this cold?

She guessed at the time. Surely, after seven by now. She walked around, hugged herself in the cold. Why had she told Grace she'd come here, wait for them for an entire week? Since she was scared, she'd probably put it off. Matt would catch on when she couldn't spend time with him—if he still wanted to be with her after she went behind his back like this.

She feared Grace wasn't coming.

Her teeth started to chatter. She took off her backpack and poured a bit of the hot chocolate she'd brought for Kelsey and Ethan in a thermos. It helped some.

And then she heard a distant, shrill voice. Had someone spotted her?

She kneeled and screwed the cap on the thermos, stuffing it back in her pack, peering all the while out at the field. Unless the wind was playing tricks, the voice had surely come from over there. She stopped breathing so her puffy white breaths wouldn't obscure her vision.

Someone was coming. A guard? No, thank God, a woman, but she seemed to be alone. If it was Grace, had she come to tell Char she would stay, that she couldn't get her kids away? But no, two small, dark figures appeared from behind her as the three forms paused in the middle of the field, probably at Lee's grave. It must have been a child's voice she'd heard.

Her heart pounding, Char sprinted out of the forest, her eyes not on her cousins but the area behind them. No one. Not yet at least.

"Grace," Char called to her, half whisper, half hissing. "This way—the woods," she added, windmilling her arm.

"Oh, no," she said as Char reached them. "I promised Sister Kelsey and Brother Ethan we were going to the playground with our cousin Sister Char, or they said they would not come along and leave their friends. Bright Star's rules say we don't go out at night, so we're pretending it's daylight."

Char couldn't believe it. Sister Kelsey and Brother Ethan? And brainwashed so that Bright Star's rules held sway even out here? Maybe they could never escape him, but they had to try. Char picked up on Grace having to play along with her kids or else. What if they defied her, refused to flee—or called for help?

"All right," Char said. "Of course. I was just thinking the woods was a quicker way to the swings and slides." In the pale moonlight, she studied the serious faces of the two youngsters. Neither showed fear, excitement or curiosity. *Were the Hear Ye followers drugged? And maybe Grace was not drugged now since "the master" didn't want to hurt the child she carried.* Char felt sick to her stomach. These kids seemed more lost than those on the mountain.

"I also told them we'd play fox and geese on the way," Grace added. "You know, Sister Char, walk in all kinds of patterns and paths so no one quite knows who went where. It would make us geese hard to follow," she added in a whisper the wind tried to rip away.

"Oh, great. Good idea, Sister Grace. Let's do that real fast and then head for the playground."

"We don't get to play much," Ethan said as he started to run in patterns. "Sisters, don't go near Brother Lee's grave now," the boy called back over his shoulder.

"And remember," Grace told Kelsey as she still stood staring at Char and her mother. "We are going to be quiet doing this. Brother Lee is asleep in the ground, and we don't want to wake him."

So Grace had a plan of her own, one of necessity because she no longer held sway over her children. According to the cult she hadn't lost her husband but just one of many "brothers." These kids had been indoctrinated by Bright Star's polluting poison. These kids, maybe Grace, too, would need deprogramming and support, maybe from a dedicated social worker like herself or a child care worker like Tess.

Meanwhile, Char's carefully laid plans to flee through the forest had to be abandoned. How long before Grace and these two kicking paths in the snow would be missed and the search begin? Keeping an eye on the cult building, Char ran clear to the forest, back and forth, making paths in the snow, now that they weren't going that way. Grace moved slowly but, to leave even more confusion in the snow, she headed toward the shoveled-off path that led to an old building that had not been rebuilt.

"Enough," Char told Grace after just a few minutes. "Time to go."

"I know," she said, out of breath. At least she looked hardy enough to make this trek. "Let's head toward the playground."

As the four of them trudged down a shoveled-off path, Char tried to plan a different way to get them to her truck from the playground entrance of this vast property. Once the kids realized they weren't going back to their friends, to Bright Star and his rules, would they agree to get in her truck and be driven to Aunt Tess's house? Well, Grace had planned part of this, so she'd have to take over again then.

They walked single file, Grace ahead, Char at the back, away from the big cult building.

Suddenly, pole lights snapped on behind them. No, Char realized, glancing back, not pole lights. Flashlights or lanterns, at least four of them. Someone from the main building was out, sweeping big beams across the field.

"Okay, sisters and brother," Char told the little party ahead of her, "time to switch to another game. That's the sign Bright Star wants us to play hide-and-seek."

19

"If they find us, should we play dead?" Ethan asked. "Is it like that game where Master Bright Star brings us back to life?"

Ordinarily, Char would have carefully questioned both Ethan and Kelsey about things they'd said, but it was survival time. Those beams of light were bouncing closer across the snowy field. Their game of fox and geese helped as four men—no five—stopped to play their lights across the maze of footprints beyond the area the funeral crowd had beaten down around Lee's grave. Two men went off toward the woods; three continued on their trail.

The women and children picked up their pace around the side of the building. *At least we're all in black,* Char thought.

"If we really want to hide," Kelsey whispered, tugging at her mother's sleeve, "I know a way into this building. I saw Sister Amy sneak in with Brother Paul, so I told on them. I was sad they got chastised."

Chastised? Evidently a Bright Star word. Char was sweating, but a shiver snaked up her spine. These children were innocent and yet dangerous. They'd been warped. Would they give them away if they hid? No choice now. She hoped that their pursuers didn't know that Sister Amy and Brother Paul—and little Kelsey Lockwood—knew a way into the derelict, four-story building that loomed ahead of them—unless the entrance had been sealed.

Kelsey showed them a door that only looked as if it had a padlock closed through its hasp. Char opened the padlock. The door shrieked in protest as they hurried into utter blackness on sagging floorboards. The cold, old building seemed to creak in its very bones. They closed the door carefully behind them.

"Just a minute," Char said. "I'll use my flashlight so we can see where to hide. Sister Grace and I will be with you, and we'll all have to keep very quiet."

Char fumbled for her flashlight in her backpack and shone it down the narrow hall. Cobwebs were laced overhead; the scurrying sound of mice or worse skittered away.

"Everyone, hold hands," Char told them, taking Kelsey's while Grace took Ethan's and came last. Grace was holding up so far, especially since she'd looked so bad earlier today. But Char could tell the poor woman was running on raw fear.

As she led the way down the hall, Char whispered, "Sister Kelsey, did Sister Amy tell you what's in here?"

Ethan piped up a bit too loudly. "In here they used to do tummies."

"Lo-bot-o-mies," Kelsey corrected him. "Sister Amy said that. Then I heard Master Bright Star say he'd like to do that to Brother Lee, but he had to do it another way."

Char gasped. She heard Grace start to cry. *Lobotomies?* Kate had said they used to do those here and in other mental wards in the last century. The operation severed parts of the brain to make a mental patient more passive, rob them of a restless or rebellious personality. But could Kelsey ever testify in a court of law that Bright Star wanted to get rid of her father and had a plan to do so?

"Bright Star didn't really mean that, didn't do that—lobotomies. Oh, poor Lee..." Grace whispered.

"You should say Brother Lee," Kelsey said, crossing her arms over her chest. "He's not yours anymore. You are the master's. You are chosen."

Char blinked back tears. This was a nightmare. How dare Lee and Grace take their precious, impressionable children into that cult? How dare Bright Star ruin lives and send men to hunt them down.

She put a hand lightly over Kelsey's mouth as the child started to say something else. Just around the corner where they huddled at the bottom of the stairs, the door they'd come in groaned again and the floorboards creaked under the weight of more than one man.

Matt tried Char's phone, but it went to voice mail again. He didn't leave a message. Despite the fact it wasn't late, only around eight o'clock, she could have gone to bed. She'd been exhausted, emotionally drained yet angry. He knew the feeling.

He was going to head home for a shower and bed. But just as he got up from his desk, Royce appeared in his doorway. He walked in and took a chair so Matt sat in the one Ginger had occupied earlier.

"Didn't hear you coming," Matt told him. "I thought you'd gone out."

"I did. An early dinner uptown with Orlando, Brad Mason and my local fracking foreman. On our way back, we—Orlando and I—saw the picketers have finally called it a night, but I'm sure they'll be back at the crack of dawn. Hope they freeze their tails off. Clever, though, that sign about 'Frackenstein.'"

"Clever but cruel. I confronted them earlier about it."

"I appreciate that, Matt. You can stand up for me—be on my team—anytime."

"But reasoning with them didn't work. I told them to keep off the property, or I'd have the sheriff after them."

"Reason never works with the likes of them, short-sighted bigots who can't see the forest for the trees. I saw your light on here. I'm surprised you're not with Charlene."

"She's exhausted after her cousin's funeral today."

"Sure, I understand. You don't look too alert yourself, my boy. Listen, I hate to hit you with something else right now, but I wanted to make this clear before the Thanksgiving holiday hits and Orlando and I head back to Columbus so I can see Veronica. Look, I realize you're indirectly linked to Gabe McCord through his sister-in-law. But I'd like you—Char, too, because she owes me—to get him off my back. All I need is incriminating questions from the sheriff while these do-gooder picketers are loose around here."

"Gabe questioned you? Why?"

Royce nodded. "He even asked me to come to his office for it—real official. McCord thinks Woody McKitrick's death might be a homicide, not an accident. Now, whether that could be tied to the attack on you or not, I'm not sure."

Matt sat up straighter. He agreed completely about Woody but didn't want to make accusations. And he'd never bring himself to blame Royce. "Let's face it, Woody was sure-footed, in good health and used to heights."

"McCord wanted to know how upset I was with him since he organized that first attempt at picketing from locals. I admitted I wanted you to fire him and you wouldn't, freedom of speech and all that, not that you agreed with his point of view. The same point of view we've got parading back and forth outside our entrance again. You refused to fire him on principle and because you liked the guy, not because you thought he should try to stop the fracking, right?"

"I wanted to honor Woody's sincere concern for the people and the place where he'd lived all his life. You and I have been over this, and, like I've said before, the drilling fractures more than the bedrock here. It breaks community bonds that Lake Azure damaged earlier. It makes some rich, keeps some poor and feeds the disagreement over whether drilling hurts the environment. Like strip mining and shaft mining, Woody called fracking the newest rape of the area."

"Rape? Well, hell, it sounds like you ought to go join the Fencer girl on the picket line and change your PR speeches around here!" Royce roared, hitting his fist on the arm of the chair. "And now we've got her cousin Joe Fencer in the same position your buddy Woody had here at Lake Azure. Damn it, Matt, I want to know you're on my side."

"Don't you think if I come down on Gabe McCord, he'll think we're in cahoots, as they say around here, covering for each other? You're innocent, so let's just let the investigation roll."

"And have everyone suspect me? Besides, I'd rather have you in cahoots with me than him. I get your point, but just be sure you let me know if anything else is brewing about the local law watching me. I didn't have a thing to do with Woody's death, however much it might look like I have a motive. Even his own son had a motive, because I hear they were at bad odds about things. And I cared about Woody, too, had Orlando drive me up that damned mountain to tell his widow I was sorry about her husband's death. While I was talking to her, Orlando had to deal with that crazy son of hers. Next we'll see Sam McKitrick down here, like the Abominable Snowman off the mountain, getting in that picket line!"

"Sam sticks tight up the mountain, searching for nonexistent terrorists. Where did you hear he and Woody didn't get along? Sam was away for several deployments in the Middle East. I guess when he came back, sick with PTSD, Woody couldn't understand why he didn't pick himself up, get a job and be a better husband and father."

For once, Royce didn't have a quick comeback. He looked flustered. "I heard that about Woody and Sam somewhere. Maybe Brad told me. My local workforce has ears to the ground. I'll see you tomorrow before I leave. And you never answered my question about whose side you're on."

As he got to his feet, Royce reached over and rapped twice on Matt's desk as if he had to knock on wood for something he'd said. As Matt stood, too, Royce threw an arm briefly over his shoulders and Matt hugged him back before he went out.

When Matt heard low voices and more than Royce's footsteps in the hall, he glanced out and saw Orlando had been waiting for him, maybe listening, too.

The staircase didn't creak as much as the hall floorboards, so Char decided to risk going up only one flight to hide from their pursuers. They tiptoed up the stairs. Men's low voices moved around below, then came closer to the second floor.

The women and children ducked into a room at the far end of the hall, slowly, silently closing the door after them.

"Now, we'll have to be very quiet, especially if they

open the door," Grace said. "In hide-and-seek, they could be really close, and we could still keep hidden and win. And we won't call out if they don't find us. We'll just tell Bright Star we won when we see him next time."

Char flicked the flashlight beam back and forth. The skeletons of four rusted cots sat against the walls. There was one big piece of furniture, an old wooden gurney. At first glance, it looked like the table in the shed in the valley, but it wasn't the same. She jolted when her light caught in a broken mirror over a rusty sink and shot itself back at her. The dusty room had cardboard boxes lined up along the other wall.

"In case they look in, let's put the boxes on the old metal bedsprings, then we'll get under the beds," Grace whispered. "Me with Brother Ethan, Sister Char with Sister Kelsey."

"And the two adults will be on the outside, curled up with our backs to the door in case they shine lights at us. Hold this flashlight," Char told Grace as she bent to lift the first box. It wasn't heavy, but it was coated with dust. At least four mice leaped out of it. Her instinct was to scream, but she fought it, then carried the box to the rusty springs of the first cot and placed it there, then put another box next to it. The men's voices came closer. "Grace, get under here with Brother Ethan and Sister Kelsey can hold the light. We're out of time."

More like out of our minds, Char thought. All those jokes people made about the crazy cult on the old asylum grounds, now here she was risking herself and these lives. Who knew what Bright Star would do if he caught them? He wanted Grace's baby for reasons that terrified Char, but he no doubt wanted all of them right now. And he'd blame her as the outsider, the instigator, so that he didn't have to admit Grace wanted to flee.

They heard footsteps in the hall, creaking and banging doors, coming closer. They must be doing a thorough search of every room on both sides of the hall.

She put two big boxes on the cot in the corner, took the flashlight from Kelsey and turned it off as they scooted under, Kelsey against the filthy wall, Char tight to her, closer to the outer edge of the bed. She heard Grace sliding under the other cot, but, thank heavens, no sound—except heavy feet in the hall and then the creak of the door to the room. As it opened and a sliding beam of light intruded, then another, Char lay rigid with her finger jammed under her nose. She prayed they could trust the children not to call out, not to sneeze. Lights snaked around them for what seemed an eternity. She heard—even felt—another mouse skitter away. When the men went out, they didn't close the door.

"Next two floors up, just to be sure, Brother Allen," a voice called so close that Kelsey bucked and grabbed Char's arm. Char gripped the girl's wrist, then hugged her. How much was it going to take to turn these brainwashed children around? Tess might be even better at that than she was. After what Tess had been through as a child, the horror of imprisonment and mental torment, maybe she could really help them—if they got out of here.

"What now?" Grace whispered after a long silence

in the hall. "I think they went upstairs, but they'll come back down pretty soon. What if they close that padlock when they go out?"

"I'll look out in the hall and give you the all clear," Char whispered.

"Let's not wait to tell Master Bright Star we won. We can tell those men," Kelsey said, crawling out behind Char and sticking close.

"We are going to the playground first," Char told her. "Because we get more points that way. There are more parts to this game."

She felt the girl nod as she clung to her. Here she was, Char thought, lying to this child just as Bright Star and his people had ever since she'd been in the cult. But no more time for agonizing now.

"The coast is clear," she told them. Ethan scrambled out from the end of the cot, but Char had to go back to help Grace. Even in the dark, she could sense that the woman's strength and courage were flagging. "Are you all right—the baby?" Char asked, praying that they wouldn't have to deal with premature labor in this mess.

"Yes, I— Let's go. I was thinking there must be a back staircase, but they'd probably look there first, and we might get trapped. I'm sick and tired of being trapped. Do you think Tess will stay with me when I have the baby?"

"Come on!" Kelsey interrupted. "Just don't get on the swings and slide then, Sister Grace, if you're worried about the master's baby."

Char gasped. Grace grabbed her shoulders hard and

whispered. "All born within starlight are the master's babies. Don't judge me, Char. Don't leave me—us. But if I can't make it, get them away—to win the game."

"Don't talk like that. Kelsey—I mean Sister Kelsey—take Brother Ethan's hand. We are going downstairs and out toward the playground. I'll help Sister Grace. Our eyes are pretty good in the dark now, right? I can't use the light or the other team might see us and win. We don't want them to stop us before the playground, so shh!"

Like fleeing felons, they crept down the stairs and out into the brisk night air. It felt so good. Grace was faltering, but Char put her arm around her and hustled her along past the graveyard with just numbers and death dates for the poor souls who had once lived here. When they got near the swings that were in the section on the grounds that was now a public park, Kelsey started to run, but Ethan hung back a minute as if waiting for permission.

"How far to your car?" Grace whispered, out of breath. "I—I'm not sure I can make it now."

"It's farther than when I thought we were going through the forest. I'll have you hide here. I'll hike to it, pick you up."

"I can help pick her up if she falls, but why do we have a car?" Ethan piped up.

Desperate, Char ignored him. "You can't stay out here on the swings and slides while you're waiting," Char told Grace. "I'll call Gabe and have him pick us up. He'll come, be fast."

"Wait till we tell Sister Martha what we did, that we won," Kelsey called out to her brother as she climbed the ladder to the curved slide. Ethan stayed tight to Grace, though the whites of his eyes were big in the darkness as he watched Char fish out her phone. She'd seen young, rural Navajo and mountain kids stand in awe of smartphones or tablets. She should have realized that Ethan had been sheltered that way, too.

The boy came closer. The light from her phone screen seemed terribly bright and could make her a target. She hunched over it and noted she had two voice mails and several other calls, but she ignored that and dialed Gabe's home number.

"Char, what's up?"

She turned away from Ethan and covered her mouth and the phone. "I'm on the playground at the edge of the asylum with Grace and her kids. She's running from the compound so I met her, but we came out a different way from where I had my truck. Can you or your deputy come get us—*fast?* Bright Star has men after us…."

"I can't believe that you— Oh, yes, I do. Hide. I'll be there as fast as I can."

She was pretty sure she heard some muffled cursing, but he was right. They had to hide again. The lights—three of them—were coming down the path they'd just walked, coming fast.

20

"We've got to hide in the trees now," Char said to Kelsey as she whizzed down the slide where Ethan stood at the bottom, looking up as if suddenly shy—or finally aware something was very wrong in his controlled, little world. "It's still hide-and-seek."

"But we've won now," Kelsey said, her voice defiant. "Sister Grace promised us this playground. They can't stop us now, and wait till everyone hears we got this far. But I'm going to tell those men we won't go back till we've had time to play!"

At the bottom of the slide, the girl turned toward the men, cupping her hands around her mouth. Char raced over and pulled Kelsey to her, clapped her hand over her mouth and half dragged, half lifted her away toward the elaborate jungle gym. At least, Char thought, they hadn't beaten her Lockwood backbone out of her.

Shushing Ethan, Grace followed until zigzagging, jagged lights swept ahead of their path. They jumped back, not going out the other side of the jungle gym, but huddling under the monkey bars. "If they find us here, we lose all our points. You have to keep quiet," Grace whispered to Kelsey.

Char sensed that this child not only had backbone but a good brain. It was time for a dose of the truth. "Listen to me, Sister Kelsey," she said, kneeling in front of the girl, nose to nose. "Those men want to hurt us just like they hurt Sister Amy and Brother Paul. Maybe like they hurt Brother Lee, and you know he loved you and Eth—Brother Ethan, Sister Grace, too. Please believe me—right, Sister Grace?"

"Yes. Yes, Sister Kelsey—please! Look, they've gone into the woods where we were going to hide."

Ethan spoke, his voice soft and trembling. "Do we have to go look for them in the dark? I think Master Bright Star and his guards can be mean."

Thank God, Char thought, *little breaks in the hard exterior of these abused kids.* "Listen, now. All four of us have to run into those bushes way over there, get behind them. It's not as good as the trees, but we have to go away from the men. Okay," she said, not giving them a chance to answer, but planting a fast kiss on Kelsey's sweaty, dirty cheek. "Let's go."

The two kids ran together, while Char helped Grace. They hunkered down behind two small shrubs. Tears blurred Char's view of the three lights when Kelsey still stuck close to her and Ethan managed to plop himself in his mother's almost nonexistent lap. Char wasn't sure they could run farther, even when the lights started toward them again. The men's voices carried in the wind.

Open lawn lay behind them. They were trapped. How long would it take for Gabe to arrive? Could he get them away from these men if they were caught?

"They're coming," Grace gasped, sounding even more out of breath. "Take these two and run, Char. Hide them. You and Tess take care of them. Please!"

"We need to stay together. We can stall for time even if they trap us here, make something up."

"The games were made-up, weren't they, Sister Grace?" Kelsey asked her mother. In their panic as the men came closer, they didn't answer her, but Char put her hand on the girl's shoulder. She was shaking, but weren't they all?

"They won't harm us," Char told Grace. "Not at first—if you pretend you've gone into labor. I'll be helping you. It will stall and protect us until Gabe can get here. I'll bet it's only been a little over five minutes, and he'll need more time."

"What kind of labor?" Ethan asked in a whisper as he huddled next to his mother.

"This kind means hard work to bring a baby into the world," Char told him. "But then everything turns out okay. Grace—what do you say?"

A man cried out. "Here! Over here, behind these bushes, Brother Stephen!" A light beam flicked past, then fixed on them. "All three of them—no four! 'You do well to heed a light that shines in a dark place, until the daystar arises!' I feared for us if we didn't find her!"

A third man ran to join the others. The first two who tried to drag them out fell back when Char shouted at them. "Sister Grace is in labor to have her baby! She's a chosen one! Get back! I'm helping her. She wanted to have her baby outside the community to be sure it was safe!"

"Is that true, Sister Kelsey?" the third man asked the child instead of Grace.

Char held her breath at what the answer might be. She could hear the high-pitched but distant whine of a siren. But these men still had time to pull them back onto Hear Ye land.

"Of course, it's true," Kelsey's thin voice rang out. "She's in labor to bring a baby into the world. See?"

Their lights illumined Grace, bent over, clutching her stomach, groaning. "You go fetch the master—fast," one man said. "Bring help!" They heard feet crunching the snow as he sped away.

Down to two men, but two too many, Char thought, as she put her arms around Grace's shoulders to help support her. Kelsey, God bless her, hugged her, too.

"Hey," one man said. "What if that siren's coming here? What if this outsider called an ambulance?"

"No, it's Brother Gabe," Ethan said. "Please don't hurt us."

"I'll just leave her to you, then," Char said to the men. She needed to get to Gabe. "I've got to get help, or she'll lose the baby! Let me pass!" she cried. "Watch over her until your master sends help."

"No!" Kelsey cried and clung to the hem of Char's jacket. "Don't leave us!"

Despite Kelsey's weight, Char barreled at the closest man, rolling at his knees, knocking him off his feet. Grace's scream shredded the air. "My baby! Help me!"

The second man got a hand on Char, swung her around, and she saw he was holding a knife. She tried to pull away, put a hand up to stop him. The siren was piercing now, close. She saw the sheriff's car, its light bar pulsating with colors. "Wow!" she heard Ethan shout in the chaos. The car's headlights slashed across her, blinding her—the man who held her, too. She kneed him as Grace screamed again, so loud she almost drowned out the siren.

Gabe jumped from the car "Police! Hands in the air! Now! Do it! No one moves!" he shouted.

But everyone moved. The Hear Ye men fled into the darkness. Grace sat up and, with Char's help, got to her feet. "We're over here, Gabe!" Char called. "We're okay!" It was only when she picked up Ethan to carry him to the sheriff's car that she saw the man had cut her. Her jacket was ripped, and her hand was bleeding. But it was such a small price to pay.

At Tess and Gabe's house, Char and Tess got everyone settled while Gabe phoned his deputy, Jace Miller, to come over, then called Grant and Matt.

"You called Matt?" Char demanded when she heard. Tess had washed her up as if she were one of the kids, then wrapped her hand, cut across the palm, but it was bleeding through the bandage.

"We need support here for the night. I've called Dr.

Phillips, too, to take care of your cut and look the kids and Grace over."

"Gabe, I'm sorry I didn't tell you, but you wouldn't have let me go."

"You got that right. By the way, Matt's more furious than me. He says you lied to him, said you were home."

"I had to go alone or Grace wouldn't have come with me."

"It's called backup, Char. You should have had backup, even if we had to hide in the woods. I don't want Bright Star and his loonies here tonight, trying something. It won't take him long to find out where 'his people' are, and if they know enough to squeal on him, he could be desperate. And, like you said, if he wants Grace's baby..." He lowered his voice even more. "It is Lee's baby isn't it? What's that you told Tess about the master's baby?"

"I'm not sure it's Lee's. Tess and I will talk to her, but not tonight."

"If Bright Star's the father..."

"Could he be prosecuted for rape?"

"Depends on if it was consensual on her part."

"No way!"

"Look at these people. Look at those kids. Brainwashed."

Raising her arm, hoping that would stop the bleeding, she told him what she'd heard. "There could be more than rape." She was whispering, too, though they were in the hall and everyone else was in the living room. "Kelsey overheard Bright Star say he'd find a way to get rid of Lee."

Gabe's eyes widened. "Everyone there talks in riddles and generalities," he said. "Are you sure? A sharp lawyer would take that child apart on the stand, let alone Grace. But I'll look into it. I'll make sure Kelsey gets a child psychologist to interview her—and a lawyer for Grace. Don't you question or prompt either of them, or we could be charged with bias at the least, tampering with a witness, too. We'll have to find them a safe house, and I've got an idea for that. I have to admit, though, as risky as you acted, Tess was thrilled, and she's looking better than she has in quite a while. Now, would you sit down and rest until the doctor gets here?"

She was not sure she could really rest until Matt arrived. "I'll be all right," she insisted and went into the living room. Grace had fallen into exhausted sleep on the sofa, covered with a quilt, one arm flung protectively over her big stomach. Char heard the kids somewhere nearby. Tess had bathed them and dressed them in her socks and Gabe's T-shirts under his flannel shirts. Ethan especially looked like a dwarf in a huge nightshirt and loose plaid robe.

Char went down the hall and saw the light on in the day care center. Ethan played with LEGO blocks, and Kelsey was painting with watercolors at the easel—painting a star under a strip of sky that ran across the top of the paper, and then a frowning face on the star in black, so all the colors ran. Tess had done some art rehab years ago, so maybe that's why she had Kelsey painting already. Too bad Gabe had ordered them not to probe Kelsey's or Grace's thoughts—or accusations.

"Char, sit down before you fall down," Tess said. "We told the doctor you'd need stitches, and he said he could do it here as a favor to Gabe."

"That bad man, Brother Allen, cut her," Ethan said.

"They were very bad losers," Kelsey added. "Sister Grace says we won the game."

"We did indeed," Char told her and went over to put her good arm around the girl's shoulder. "So far we did, at least," she said, glaring at Kelsey's painting. She was starting to feel light-headed so she sat down in one of the beanbag chairs to wait for the doctor.

Matt could have chewed nails. What was Char thinking, taking on those crazy cult fanatics alone. Gabe said she was injured but she could have been killed. She hadn't trusted him enough to level with him. She'd lied. There was no way to build a relationship on that sort of behavior. He wouldn't even have come except Gabe said he needed some help tonight to protect Grace and her two kids.

He jerked his car to a stop on the street in front of the Lockwood house and day care center. The sheriff's car was parked in the driveway and the deputy's car—with Jace Miller in it—was blocking that. Grant Mason pulled up right behind Matt.

"I'm glad Char got Grace and her kids out," Grant called to him when they got out of their vehicles. "But she could have been hurt."

"I heard she is hurt. I'm sure Kate will be upset."

"Oh, she was when I called her," Grant said as they hurried up the front walk together. "Upset she wasn't here to be a part of it. Of course, she would also explain to us the psychological fallout for prisoners, the Stockholm Syndrome and who knows what else. If you want one of the Lockwood women, Matt, you pay a price, but—damn—they're worth it. At least Kate is."

He didn't want a Lockwood woman anymore, Matt told himself, as Gabe opened the front door, shook hands with both of them and brought them in.

"I trust Bright Star about as far as I can throw his entire cult," Gabe told them. "Thanks for coming. We've got a fortress mentality going on for the night. I'll make us some sandwiches later, and the doctor should be here soon. Matt, Char's in the day care area with Tess and Grace's kids. She's been cut on the hand, and I was afraid Grace would go into labor, but she's resting."

Matt was surprised to see Gabe in his uniform, with loaded utility belt on his hip and his small radio strapped on his shoulder. As he walked away, Matt heard him talking to his deputy outside. This was serious stuff. Matt went down the hall toward the front, lighted room, thinking he should walk away from Char right now. But he kept going.

The Lockwood women. Tess was married to a man she had loved for years. Kate was engaged to be married soon. Char, the middle girl…didn't they always say the middle kid could be trouble?

He stood in the doorway, quiet at first, taking it all

in. Tess sat across the room in a beanbag chair, leaning her head against the wall, asleep, with a young boy in her lap, sound asleep, too. A young girl curled up next to Char, who looked barely awake and seemed to be guarding them all. As angry as he was, he was so glad to see her in one piece.

She stood carefully, to not disturb the child. They went out into the hall and, not touching, sat on the stairs leading up to the second floor. He could see blood had seeped through the bandage on the palm of her left hand.

"I'm sorry, but it had to be done," she said. "I didn't want to mislead you. I left you a note at the Mannings' in case anything went wrong."

"Oh, great. Very helpful after the fact in case you ended up hurt, missing or dead. Mislead me? Is that a nice way of saying you didn't want to lie to me? Because you did."

"I thought it would be easier to get them out of there than it was. I had a plan that didn't work out and had to go with theirs—Grace's—to make the kids cooperate, to con them into going along."

"Yeah, well, I know how they feel. Everyone I trusted lately is suspect—even Royce—for a con job, but I thought I could trust you."

She sniffed. Tears shimmered in her eyes but she didn't cry. A strong woman. He'd said before he wanted a strong woman, didn't he? One who didn't wring her hands when a car was ready to crash off a cliff?

"How's your hand?"

"Throbbing now—like my heart."

"Char, it's just I—I couldn't stand it if something happened to you."

"I feel the same about you," she clipped out. He saw a single tear slide down her cheek. "I understand why you're upset," she said with a sniff. "I agonized over misleading—lying to you, but I had to go alone. Why should you be involved with my family mess—with me?"

"Because, damn it," he blurted before he even knew what he would say, "you have come to mean so much to me in such a short time. I need you, need to trust you, want you—"

He didn't finish because they came together hard.

"Watch your hand," he muttered as he lifted her into his lap.

"Watch your heart, Matthew Rowan, because I've lost mine to y—"

She held the injured hand up as he silenced her with a searing kiss. He had never wanted a woman so badly. It still galled him that she'd lied to him, yet he understood why. But all that meant nothing compared to the pounding in his head and heart for her.

He held her in his arms, telling himself to be gentle, but feeling beyond that. She gave as good as she got, moving her hips in his lap, opening her mouth to him, kissing him back. They were breathing so hard they didn't hear anything at first. Someone knocking, a distant voice?

Matt lifted his head. Glassy-eyed, he blinked to clear his sight. Gabe was close. Just down the hall.

"The doc's here and ready to stitch Char up," he said, and beat a quick retreat.

"Mmm," she said, her voice shaky, her face flushed. "As far as I'm concerned, the doctor's here already, another one that makes house calls."

Matt steadied her while she stood. "You know," he said, "speaking of that, sometimes I think I could get used to a house full of kids, even sisters- and brothers-in-law. Thanksgiving's coming. With all that's going on with your family and Kate still out of town and now this, how about all of you coming to the lodge for turkey dinner on Thursday, my guests?"

He walked her down the hall toward the kitchen, where they could hear the doctor's voice. He held her elbow. He was shaking, too. "I was thinking of trying to make reservations," she said. "But I figured it was too late." She stopped, lifting her good hand to try to smooth her wild hair. "If we get through this night, we'll have a lot to be thankful for. Yes, I'll ask the others. How lovely in the midst of everything."

With a gentle hand, he helped her brush her hair back from her face. "I thought it was too late, too—for us—but when I saw you hurt—I knew it wasn't."

Gabe's voice cut in behind them. "Char, get in here and get stitched up. Jace reports that a van with Bright Star's band of brothers just pulled up in front. Matt, let's get the kids and Grace upstairs."

"I'll help," Char said. "This cut can wait. They might

be scared by men they don't really know. Tess and I can help."

Gabe just shook his head. Matt rolled his eyes and shrugged. "Okay, fine," the two of them said almost in unison as she darted away from them.

Matt thought about poor Sam McKitrick always fearing the Taliban were outside in the dark. These cult members were terrorists of another kind.

21

This time when Char huddled with Grace and her children, she wasn't afraid. They sat cross-legged, close together on the bed in Tess and Gabe's guest room. Tess was with them, and Matt and Grant were downstairs with Gabe and his deputy. Still, she jumped when Bright Star's voice, metallic, piercing, sounded outside. He must be using a megaphone since he always talked so softly.

"Sister Grace, Sister Kelsey and Brother Ethan, come home! Come home right now."

"I'm surprised," Tess said, speaking loudly as if she could block him out, "that he isn't giving us some warped Bright Star quote. Gracie, he thinks he's the messiah, and he's not."

The unmistakable voice boomed out again, repeating word for word what he'd just said. Grace was visibly shaken, yet she looked defiant.

"Gabe can arrest him for disturbing the peace—for starters," Tess muttered.

"Now that we're safe here, I know what to say to him to make him go away. I used it on him after—once after he was mean to me," Grace whispered as if Bright Star could hear her.

Char wondered if that was about nine months ago, but she remembered all too well that Gabe had said not to question Grace about whether the baby she carried was Lee's or if she knew more about Lee's death. "Do you want me to take Kelsey and Ethan into another room?" she asked. She gave Tess a look that meant, *some big reveal is coming.*

"No, Kelsey and Ethan can stay," Grace said. "All I need is pen and paper. I found the words myself, memorized them. It will send him away. Only, if I do this, Gabe has to get us a different place to stay, like he said, where that man can't find us. And, Char, I'm worried for you now, too—all of you."

"We're not afraid," Tess assured her. "And Gabe's been working on a safe place for you to stay away from here. We have a friend, Vic Reingold, who works for the Ohio Bureau of Investigation. He promised he has a good home for all of you, until Bright Star can be stopped. I'll get you something to write on. Is it some kind of threat?" she asked as she scrambled off the bed and rummaged in the drawer of the bedside table.

Grace put her arms around her children. When Tess came back with pen and paper, Grace spoke. "Please write this down, will you, Tess?"

Tess wrote down the words Grace dictated.

> And a great star fell from heaven, burning like a torch, and it fell on a third of the rivers and on the springs of water. The name of the star is Wormwood. A third of the waters became wormwood, and many men died from the water, because it was made bitter.

"See," Grace said, breaking into the first smile Char had seen from her in years. "That is from the book of Revelation, because I've had a revelation. I have to stop that man. And, thanks to Char, I have learned to fight fire with fire."

Even as Bright Star's magnified voice rang out a third time, Char took the note and headed downstairs. To her surprise, Grace followed her into the hall.

"Char, I can't thank you enough for helping us—to shed blood for us, a sacrifice. You risked your life." She glanced back over her shoulder and whispered, "I want you and Tess to know that this child I carry—well, I don't know if it is Lee's or Bright Star's, but who fathered him or her is not the child's fault. It wasn't allowed, but Lee and I sneaked some time alone. Maybe that's why Bright Star turned against him, since he knew I still loved Lee. But I will bear and keep this child, claim that it's Lee's legacy to me. But to the master's—I mean Bright Star's—mind, my baby may be the awaited one. If it's a boy, that is. And," she said, frowning and looking down at her belly, "I'm carrying the child high, like I did with Ethan."

Char forced herself to close her mouth.

"You don't ask if I was willing," Grace whispered. "I wasn't. Maybe I was drugged, I don't know. But I do know, with my three children, I must hide until that man is imprisoned or dead."

"Does he—did Bright Star have people's food drugged?"

"You mean, could he have intentionally put something in Lee's food and the others who took sick? It could be. Anything is possible with him."

"And the water below the fracking site? Is it poisoned? You allude to bitter water in this note."

"Lee said there were dead fish, dead beavers. He thought Bright Star knew but ignored it, or maybe wanted to use that knowledge somehow to profit himself. He sent Lee there to tear down an old chastisement room, but Lee said he left it as proof of Bright Star's evil ways. I think Lee hoped someone would discover the horrors of that valley. It was all Lee had to fight back with, since Bright Star held us all. When Lee died, Bright Star dropped his guard—and now I've betrayed him, too. So," she said, clasping Char's hand that held the note, "I found a way to fight back just like Lee. And you helped me."

She gave Char a quick hug and went back into the bedroom. Char stood staring after her a moment. Of course, she'd tell Gabe and Tess this later, tell Matt that Lee thought the fracking water might be polluting the river and that Lee was the one who intentionally left the waterboarding shed as it was.

At least she hadn't exactly gone against Gabe's warning not to question Grace, because she'd volunteered her information. Char was now the keeper of what not only threatened Grace but her, too. A little knowledge was a dangerous thing, as they said.

She hurried down to Gabe and Matt, who were outside on the front porch in the dark, keeping an eye on Bright Star and the four men with him. Char heard someone out there speak. "That's her, Master. The one who was with them." Did they have night goggles like Sam McKitrick, or had she just been silhouetted in the door?

Before Matt hustled her back into the house, she glared toward the men on the curb, handed Gabe the note and explained that Grace said it would make them back off. They were barely inside, when Matt put his arms around her and pulled her away from the door.

"Where's Grant?" she asked.

"Watching the back door. Deputy Miller's outside by their van. Did you hear one of those men point you out?"

They were both startled as Gabe's voice boomed out, without a megaphone. Peeking out, they saw he was reading from the paper with a flashlight.

"Bright Star. A message for you from Grace Lockwood, Mrs. Lee Lockwood."

"Send her out. I wish to talk to her."

"She doesn't want to see you, but here's her message." He read out the note.

Char tensed, waiting for Bright Star's voice, but all they heard was the van pulling away.

"You realize what those words could mean, don't

you?" Char asked Matt. "Lee's note for me about poison water was short, and that one is cryptic, too, but it implies the same thing. Bright Star, at the very least, knows about polluted water, but is keeping quiet. Grace told me Lee wasn't really sure about it, only that he saw dead fish and dead beavers—and he's the one who left the waterboarding shed there when he was sent to take it apart. I'll bet his mistake was telling Bright Star he'd be a whistle-blower, or use all that against him somehow—for his making Grace the 'chosen one.'"

"Damn," he whispered, his lips against her forehead. "I'm going to get that Cold Creek water retested fast, then report to Royce. Since the Hear Ye people lived there for years, fished and hunted—punished people in that shack—maybe they still went back after they sold out. Maybe they saw the signs of pollution but kept it quiet. Or what if he's been blackmailing Royce about it?"

"Then Royce knows and should do something, not about shutting up Bright Star but taking care of the water. Matt, I know he's dear to you, but doesn't he *have* to know if the fracking's poisoning the water?"

"I swear, if he knew, he'd do something, and I'm not going to make accusations or confront him until I have all the facts. At least Grace is getting protection, getting out of here. I don't want to lose you, but, for now at least, I wish you could hide somewhere, too."

Just after 2:00 a.m., Gabe roused everyone from where they were sleeping all over the house. Char and

Matt had been on beanbag chairs in the day care, utterly exhausted. "The BCI men are here," Gabe told them. "Time to say goodbye for now."

They went out into the kitchen, where a man Char remembered from years ago as well as from his later visits, including Tess and Gabe's wedding, sat drinking coffee. Two other, younger men came in and leaned against the wall. Behind them, she glimpsed their van, which they'd driven into the now-closed but lighted garage. The side of it read Bureau of Criminal Investigation. The vehicle also boasted the rising sun symbol of Ohio and the attorney general's name. But would any of that scare off Bright Star's lackeys if they were spying on the house?

"Can't stay long if I'm going to get our refugee family to their new address," Vic was saying. He greeted Char by name and was introduced to Matt. Vic was in his sixties. He had an unruly shock of white hair and sharp brown eyes. Char was relieved he'd brought two strapping young agents with him for reinforcement.

They all crowded around the table or leaned against the kitchen counters, drinking coffee or orange juice and eating doughnuts. Tess had mentioned that Vic was long-distance-dating Gabe's widowed mother, who still lived in Florida. Char recalled how smitten the couple had been at the wedding, and it cheered her—gave her hope—to know they were building a relationship that had started so suddenly.

Char's memory of Vic Reingold from the nightmare days when Tess was missing was vague, but he was still close to Tess and Gabe after helping them out again last year. He seemed to exude confidence and control, somewhat, she thought, like Royce, but without the sharp edges. Surely, Grace and the kids, still upstairs getting dressed in modern clothing the men had brought, would like him. At least the coast was clear, as far as Deputy Miller could tell. There was no sign of Bright Star, the cult van or his men.

"No one else we'd rather trust with this than you," Gabe told Vic.

"So you said she's almost ready to deliver?" Vic asked. "It sounds like she's as strong as the Lockwood girls, and I'd love to see that bast—that phony guru Brice Monson, aka Bright Star—get what's coming to him. So," he said, turning to Char, "you have now managed to put yourself on that sicko's hit list. You be careful, understand? Gabe's shorthanded here, something I'm trying to weigh in on. But it sounds like Bright Star's finally trapped, and trapped animals are dangerous."

"I'll be careful," Char promised, lifting her newly stitched up and bandaged hand, as if making a vow. "But I'm not going to hide out or let him run my life. I'll try to have someone with me all the time—I mean, during the day."

Vic's hooded eyes flicked from Matt to her, then back. "Good," he said. "But even at night, maybe stay here with Gabe and Tess till this all gets sorted out. I'll have Mrs. Lockwood—Grace—make a statement, and we'll go from there. And I'll call you, Tess, the minute she goes into labor, then Gabe will bring you—make sure you're not gonna lead anyone to her."

When she came downstairs with the bleary-eyed kids, Grace embraced Tess and Char. Char was deeply touched when Ethan hugged her goodbye and Kelsey said, "Even if you're not really a sister, can you be my aunt?"

Grace and Char exchanged teary glances. "I'm really your second cousin, but yes, I'd be happy to have you call me Aunt Char—and we'll be good friends after your mother has her baby, and you can all come back here."

"When?" Ethan asked. "I won't have any friends here since we ran away."

Matt was closest to him and crouched to get down to his level. Both children were in jeans, boots and sweatshirts and unzipped, warm coats. "Gabe's your friend, Grant is and I am, too," Matt told him, brushing the boy's mop of hair back from his forehead. "When you get back—after you and Kelsey have helped your mother for a while with the new baby—we'll go to the swimming pool where I live, learn to ride horses because we're going to build a stable there, and other fun things. And that's a real promise."

The little boy and the big man shook hands on that. Tears prickled behind Char's eyelids. For one moment, she glimpsed some sort of summer day camp at Lake Azure, where the mountain kids could come. Ethan's sad face lit up, and Kelsey clung to her for a moment. She broke down when the BCI van drove away. She was angry, grateful and scared, but most of all, she was falling in love.

Tuesday morning, Char awoke in the guest bedroom at Gabe and Tess's house. Matt had ganged up on her with them, and insisted she couldn't be alone. Emotionally and physically exhausted, she longed to stay in bed, but Matt would be here soon to take her to retrieve her truck, and she'd arranged to meet Henry Hanson for his first day of delivering the mountain kids to school. She had planned to drive on her own, following him up Pinecrest, but, once again, Gabe and Matt had laid down the law that she had to go in the passenger seat of the new van Royce had provided for her project, not by herself.

"What a night," Tess said as she sat down across the breakfast table from Char and glanced at the newspaper on the table. "Gabe's already gone, but Jace Miller's going to drive by every half hour or so, since we'll have the day care kids here soon. You and I are dedicated to children, Char, and I can't wait to bring this one into the world."

Little Kelsey's bold words about bringing a new baby into the world to the men who almost captured them last night echoed in Char's head. Kelsey and Ethan had both parroted things they'd overheard, and they had so much to learn out in the real world. But would Kelsey's claim that Bright Star had plans to get rid of "Brother Lee" stand up to scrutiny? And would that maniac's hit list stop at that?

"You're eating cereal and bagels?" Char questioned Tess as she dug into breakfast. "Won't it set your stomach off?"

"No nausea today, only hunger. Maybe I'm in a new phase. Speaking of which, I guess you and Matt have taken it to another level. Gabe said you two were pretty hot and heavy on the stairs last night. It happened fast, didn't it? I mean, it did with Gabe and me, too, but we'd known each other years before, had emotional ties back then, because of my tragedy."

Char reached across the corner of the table and took Tess's hand with her uninjured one. "I can't believe I found someone here in good old Cold Creek. But there are complications, things happening right and left, things that could be trouble, despite wonderful things like all of us being together at Thanksgiving at the lodge. I'm glad everyone agreed to that. I'm sure Kate will, too, when she gets back. It's something to look forward to in all this."

"But as Vic said last night, you have to be careful. I think that master manipulator Bright Star's a coward, but his yes-men robots could be dangerous. Just remember Gabe told you that 'I'll be careful' are famous last words—I almost learned that the hard way and Kate did, too."

"Then how about I'll be very, extraordinarily, extremely, overly, really careful?" Char asked. "Good things are happening up on Pinecrest Mountain today, and I'm going to be there to see them!"

22

When it was barely light, Matt picked up Char at Gabe and Tess's and drove her to retrieve her truck, which she'd forgotten about during the chaos last night. As they walked toward it, hidden among pines not far off the road, they saw the back tires had been slashed.

Char gasped. "Those Hear Ye vandals had to look hard to find it!" she cried, stomping around all four sides of the truck. The front tires were cut, too. She saw footprints she hadn't made, apparently only one other pair, going off into the trees. "I'm going to check if there's a note on it, or if they even scratched something in the paint."

"No, you're not. Get back in my car." He grabbed her arm and hustled her away. "Think! They found your hidden truck, so they could be hiding here, waiting for you to come get it." He unlocked the door and pushed her back in the passenger seat. He strode around to the driver's side, got in, slammed his door and locked them in. He backed out onto the road, then sped off until they were a good mile away before he pulled over.

"I wasn't thinking, either," he told her. "I keep wanting to deny how bad this could be. We could have walked right into a trap. All we need is another arrow coming at us. Grace told Gabe that Bright Star has forbidden guns, but some of the cult members hunt with arrows and recurve bows."

"But the two incidents with arrows came before I caused them any trouble, so how could it be them behind it? I'll bet they hunt beavers, though. Remember I told you about all those hunt quotes Bright Star had all over the walls? And I know from close up and personal that they have knives to slash tires." She frowned at her bandaged hand.

"The bastards knew you had a vehicle out here somewhere since you and your family fled with Gabe." He took his cell phone out of his jacket pocket while he let the car idle. "After helping Grace last night, you've got to be more careful than we even imagined."

"But if that maniac strikes out at me, it would be so obvious who did it."

"I think we've seen he's willing to sacrifice useful members like Lee, even risk poisoning others to make a death look like an accident. What scares me is that he'd think nothing of getting rid of a nonbeliever like you—the infidel enemy."

"But he's a coward."

"So he uses robot slaves," he argued, punching in a phone number he had on speed dial. "We're both exhausted, not thinking straight. Worse, if someone was after me before, you've got a target on your back now, maybe just not from the same source."

"Are you calling Gabe?"

"You bet I am."

Char pictured the viciously slashed tires. She struggled to calm her shock and anger, control her fear. Matt was right. She had to be more wary, but she hated to run scared. At least he'd handled everything back there, so she could rely on him. Actually, someone had done him a favor because he didn't want her driving anywhere alone, and now the only wheels she had were slashed, just like her hand.

After arranging for Gabe to send someone to inspect and tow Char's truck, Matt drove them to the lodge. He found he had an upset home owner waiting to see him so Char sat down in a rocking chair by a planter in the lobby to wait for Henry Hanson. The new van he would drive was still parked out front. She'd seen a truck that looked like his, too, so he was probably in the restroom or just waiting for the time he'd said he'd begin their run up the mountain.

Three students would be picked up today, Penny Hanson, Jemmie McKitrick and Bethany Antrim, but Char hoped there would be five or six next week. She had more to visit if she could get four new truck tires and, if Matt had his way, a full-time bodyguard. Maybe she could talk Henry into driving her in the van to talk to other mountain families. At least she could afford to pay for his gas if not his time. She didn't want to ask Royce for more, not now, anyway.

She was exhausted, and the winter sun coming in through the lobby window felt so good that she almost nodded off, but she snapped alert when her head bobbed. From down the hall the other way, toward the back, she heard Royce's voice. He was up early, but then Matt had said Royce was leaving with Orlando tomorrow for Thanksgiving in Columbus, so maybe he had a lot to get done here first. She'd like to thank him for the school van again before he went, remind him today was the first day his generosity would benefit the mountain kids. She wondered if he'd heard what had happened last night. If he and Bright Star still communicated, maybe he'd heard about it from him.

She felt a stab of remorse as she hefted her big bag over her shoulder and headed toward Royce's office. Here she was, helping Matt to possibly prove pollution caused by the fracking. If that came out, would Royce blame her, take the van back, leave poor Henry unemployed again?

Then she realized the other voice was Henry's, so maybe Royce was wishing him the best or telling him to be careful. Matt could have put Royce up to that, because she knew he didn't want her going up on Pinecrest, even before she defied Bright Star.

She leaned against the wall, not wanting to interrupt the two men. But she stood alert as Royce's words floated to her. "Just remember, the extra cash means you'll take care of Charlene, too."

"Oh, yes, sir. Got that loud and clear. Well, better get out to meet her. I'll report in later."

Char hustled down the hall, so she wouldn't be seen hovering. She didn't know whether to be comforted or incensed. *Take care of her* could mean two opposite things. Royce was paying Henry a decent salary for only two drives a day, so what was with the extra cash?

Pulling on her coat, she hurried outside into the sun and cold wind. She couldn't barge in on Matt right now to tell him what she'd overheard. He'd stop her from going at all. Should she refuse to go? No, she was paranoid. She'd already decided she could trust Henry, and this didn't change that. He had clearly and openly explained that he did have some of Ginger's arrows, and why. She felt they had come to a good agreement and for good reasons. It was all set up for her to go with him today. Everyone from Gabe to Matt, now to Royce, knew about that. She was just exhausted, seeing danger behind every tree.

But then, there were a lot of trees up on Pinecrest.

Although Char hadn't noticed it, Henry's daughter, Penny, was sitting in his truck, waiting for him to unlock the new van. As he joined Char outside the lodge, he waved to the girl.

"Said I'd pick her up later each morning," he explained. "But she was so excited she come clear down with me just for today." He unlocked the van doors, and Penny came barreling out of their old truck with what looked to be a fairly empty backpack. Then Char saw

Henry had also brought one of his sons—let's see, his name was Crayton—though Char hadn't registered him since the boy made it to school now and then. But this was perfect. Next year Henry's son Simon could ride this van, too, if there were any seats left. She'd had to promise the elementary school principal that all the kids would wear seat belts when she'd submitted the legal permission papers for Henry to drive.

"I'm glad to meet you, Crayton, and see Penny again!" Char said with a pat on Penny's shoulder. "Climb on in the second seat and put your seat belts on." She turned to Henry. "But in weather like this, if they ride down with you in the morning, bring them into the lobby to wait where it's warm."

"Sure. Didn't know if that was okay. Don't you fret none. Didn't plan on taking time talking to Mr. Flemming today. Real kind of him to wish me good luck and all. Beholden to both of you."

Henry's admission that he'd talked to Royce, and Penny's crooked-toothed grin soothed Char's nerves. Henry wasn't trying to hide something dire from her. It wasn't his way. After the terrible happenings yesterday—with the good result of Grace and her kids being free—everything would surely go great today.

By the time Matt solved the home owner's problem, Char was gone with Henry in the new van. He went back to his office and called Clint Parsons in Columbus. They didn't spend much time talking about the old days.

"Clint, any chance you could come down real soon

to retest the water? I know with the holiday this week it's a bad time, but a lot of folks' well-being could be at stake. I'll feed you well at the lodge, be glad to pay for gas and your time. I feel like I'm sitting on a tinderbox with this situation."

"I can see why. Each well the frackers dig uses between three million to seven million gallons of water, and then wastewater has to be put into disposal wells and holding tanks until it can be shipped away. The risk of contaminating the aquifer, let alone surface water, is huge. But unless you want to get someone else involved—and then keeping this quiet for a while longer could be a problem—I can't come until Saturday. Susan and I are taking the kids to her parents' house in Cleveland for Thanksgiving, and won't be back until Saturday morning. I could drive down then, see you for lunch, and we'll take those samples."

"Great. I can't thank you enough. Meet me at the lodge."

"Listen, Matt, I know that's old coal country nearby, right?"

"For sure. Some strip mining around, but up in the hills—the nearest would be Pinecrest Mountain—there used to be a lot of shaft mining."

"Okay, here's the deal with that. Fracking's getting the media spotlight lately, but runoff pollution from coal mining has caused water problems for years—dead fish and on up the food chain."

Despite that terrible news, Matt breathed a sigh of relief. That could be it. Coal mining runoff. Then Royce and his fracking would not be to blame. But it was probably wishful—desperate—thinking since that fracking site was right above the polluted water.

"The thing is," Clint went on, "it's highly unlikely that the contaminants from coal mining and fracking would be the same. We'll see."

Yeah, Matt thought, *we'll see about a lot of things.* Was he crazy to try to protect and excuse Royce? But even more than that, he'd give anything now to protect his stubborn sweetheart Char.

After they picked up Jemmie and Bethany, Char noticed the kids handled their excitement in different ways. Penny acted really shy, even when Bethany tried to befriend her. The two girls pretty much ignored Crayton, who was humming, and Jemmie McKitrick seemed almost giddy.

"Want to hear something funny, Miss Charlene?" he asked from the seat behind her.

"Sure. Let's hear it."

"My Pa still works for Uncle Sam and his name's Sam, like he was named for him, he says."

"But he's out of the army now, ain't he, boy?" Henry asked.

"Still getting a big paycheck," Jemmie boasted. "'Cause he's sick, needs vitamins and all that."

Char heard Henry give a snort. He shook his head, but Jemmie wasn't to be deterred. "Someday soon just him and me's going on a trip out West to see Indians and a rodeo, but I'll miss my mom. Miss Charlene, if you see her down in town, would you tell her I'm in school and I'm gonna work hard, 'least till Pa and I head out?"

"I'll try to see her real soon, Jemmie. My truck is broken right now with bad tires. But if you're going out West to see Indians—only during your summer vacation so you don't miss school—I'll tell you all sometime about the Navajo tribe and where to find them out West."

"Aw, great. I'll tell Pa. I hope there's trees out there. He has a really neat suit with leaves stuck to it, tree colors but he says it don't work good in the winter when he's on patrol, 'cept at night."

"An army camo Ghillie suit," Henry put in. "I seen him in it with his gear."

"All right, here we are," Char told them as Henry turned into the driveway of the consolidated district elementary school. "Mr. Hanson's going to pick you up at this same spot after school, so take a good look at the van again when you get out. Since this is your first day, I'm going to take you in and have you meet the principal."

"Even when we didn't do nothing wrong?" Jemmie asked.

"Even when you didn't do *anything* wrong," she repeated, hoping the kids would pick up on the correct grammar. "The principal's office is for all kinds of good things, too," she added as she got out and slid the van door open for Jemmie and Crayton as Henry let the girls out the other side.

Penny hugged her father goodbye, though her

younger brother hurried ahead. Henry gave Char a big, proud smile. Oh, yes, she just knew she could trust Henry Hanson. Things were working out so well, at least here.

Penny slipped her hand into Char's. "I brought the crayons you gave me," she whispered, taking little skipping steps. "Can't wait to color something real pretty, and it will be for you."

Char blinked back tears. All she'd been through with needy kids lately made her want to cry. Oh, yeah, she was as needy as they were, to help them, to keep herself safe. And above all, for the first time in her life, she needed a man, and that tore down the walls she'd built up around herself for years, maybe ever since her father deserted the family years ago.

The ringing school bell jolted her as the five of them went into the busy building together.

"You know," Henry said as he drove Char back to the lodge, "truth is, Jemmie's pa Sam's sane as they come, only crazy like a fox. Sly like one, too."

"I've met him—twice," she said. "He seemed really strange. His family says he still has PTSD and acts really weird, looking for terrorists at all hours."

"Naw. 'Acts' is right. Seen him in his right mind. Got him a good con going, bilking the gov'ment, not that lots of others don't. His pa, Woody, was onto it, said Sam was just getting out of a job once he got home, drawing pay he wasn't working for. They got into it pretty bad. His wife, Mandy Lee, she done smelled a rat, too,

I bet, gone down to her Fencer kin, and that rat is Sam McKitrick. Why, bet he's even conning his boy. Going out West to see Indians and go to a rodeo—baloney."

Was Sam crazy like a fox or one of hundreds of traumatized former soldiers? Char wondered. If his strange behavior was an act, that was shameful, considering what some vets were still going through. He was cheating those mentally wounded soldiers as much as the government.

Maybe she should go talk to Mandy Lee McKitrick at the Fencer place. Char had heard something about the doctors at the vet hospital concluding Sam wasn't disturbed. But in that case, he wouldn't be getting disability pay. Maybe his game was to fool people so he could avoid getting a job, get his boy and take off. How many times had that happened when the parents were estranged? But why would Sam be planning to run if he had a good scam going here—unless he had something much bigger to hide?

23

Back at the lodge, Char figured she'd try to hitch a ride from Joe Fencer to visit his sister-in-law, Mandy Lee, if he was going home for lunch. She'd glimpsed him on the Lake Azure grounds this morning.

But it irked her to be a moocher like when she was putting herself through college at Michigan State in East Lansing. She'd try to snag rides from anyone who had a car. How had it come to this helpless feeling again, and not only because her truck had been sabotaged? Back then she'd been in love with the wrong man, but now, surely she was falling in love with the right one. But if they were both in danger, how would it ever work out?

She said hi to Matt's secretary and peeked into his office. He was doing desk work, frowning at his computer screen and taking notes. He looked up and visibly relaxed. A smile lit his face. He closed the lid of his laptop.

"It went okay?" he asked, getting up.

"Yes. Mission accomplished. Henry drove well, the

kids were happy. Matt, Henry says Sam McKitrick is just putting on a show about his protecting his place from terrorists, that he's conning everyone. What if Woody knew that, called him on it?"

"It's possible," he said as he came over to close the door behind her. "I thought it might be just that Sam didn't want to look for a job since he had saved some money, was getting disability pay too at first. That could be what came between them, and they argued—up on the cliff. Okay if I call Gabe to fill him in on that, or will you? And I'd like you to stay with Gabe and Tess awhile longer. Actually, I'd like you to stay with me, but I don't want you to get the wrong idea."

He moved closer to her, slowly pinning her against his office wall with his hands beside her head.

Her breath caught in her throat, and her pulse picked up. She'd been tempted to just run in here and throw herself in his arms. "What about that would be the wrong idea?"

"That I can't keep my hands or thoughts off you."

"I repeat, what's wrong with that idea?"

"Nothing in my book, but so much has happened. We've had ups and downs since we found each other—ah, just one week ago today. I didn't want to push my luck. But talking about someone being crazy, I'm that—for you."

He bent his head to kiss her. She looped her arms around his neck and kissed him back hard, open-mouthed. She wanted his attention, his love—she wanted him. He pushed her closer against the wall, gently, but the kiss was wild, and she returned it mindlessly as his hands moved inside her unzipped coat and grasped her waist, then lowered to cup her bottom.

After what seemed a mere moment, he came up for air first. "I don't…mean to do this here," he told her, drawing in deep breaths. "Let's go to my place for lunch."

"Can't," she told him breathlessly. "I've got to ask Joe Fencer if he'll take me to talk to Mandy Lee. I promised Jemmie I would talk to his mom and I might get a better reading on Sam if I do. Then we can let Gabe know that, too. And about two o'clock, Henry's driving me up Pinecrest to talk to two other families with truant kids."

They stayed in their embrace for a moment, nose to nose. He looked dazed. "I can take you to see Mandy Lee. I don't want my woman being driven all over the county by other men."

He winked and squeezed her bottom, then guided her to sit in a chair. He pulled the other one up so close their knees touched. He leaned forward and took her hands in his big, warm ones. "Next week, if this isn't all settled somehow, think about staying with me instead of Gabe and Tess. No pressure, but—"

His intercom buzzed. They both jumped when his secretary's voice made her sound as if she were in the room. "Matt, Sheriff McCord's on the line, says it's important."

His eyes locked with Char's before he looked away, leaned over his desk and grabbed the receiver. "Matt here, Gabe."

Char strained to hear but couldn't tell what Gabe was saying. "Are Grace and the kids still all right?" she asked Matt in a whisper. He nodded but held up his hand as he concentrated.

"Man, Vic Reingold has clout!" Matt told Gabe. "Sign him up for future help. So what did the test show? Really? Yeah, I'm surprised, but we can't put anything past anyone now. Okay, I understand. If she argues, tell her I gave my permission for her to be away," he said, and hung up.

"What now?"

"Vic Reingold got Gabe a rush on the DNA test on the arrows. What was there matched the swab test Ginger agreed to give so her DNA could be eliminated, just like ours was. But her DNA and ours were the only trace on the two arrows. If someone else handled them, other DNA would be there, too. Gabe's coming over right now to take her to the station to question her, and he just wanted me to know."

"Ginger! What's the motive? You said she wasn't after you, but maybe she's angry with you—or just wants you to need her help. Maybe she's not really at odds with Royce but helping him. He wants to keep you in line, so she's shaking you up so you depend more on him."

"Sweetheart, all roads do not lead to Royce!" he told her much too loudly, as if he was trying to convince himself.

Well, she thought, glaring at him, however bad this continued to get, at least he'd called her *sweetheart.*

* * *

Matt dropped Char off at the Fencer house across from the huge fracking site. He'd agreed that it might inhibit Mandy Lee if he went in, and he didn't want to visit Joe's house without talking to Joe first. He valued his new friendship with him.

As he backed out of the driveway, he saw Brad Mason in his bright red truck driving into the fracking site. On a hunch, he followed him in, parking just behind him near what must be the main office, a corrugated metal building with a flat roof. They had set up this site in a huge hurry, really, in several months. When he got out, the noise and motion of the place hit him hard. He wondered why they had no security here, or did the fact he drove in right behind Brad give him a pass?

"Hey, Matt, what's up?" Brad shouted as he noticed him and walked toward his car.

Even close up, they both talked loud to be heard. The diesel engines on the waiting tanker trucks and some loud pounding nearly drowned out their words. "Just saw you pull in when I was dropping something off across the road," Matt said.

"Yeah, having that site's sure going to help with expansion. This is the biggest site EEC has in this county, but we are always on the lookout for new ones."

"I realized I haven't looked at the action here close up, not since the grid was first laid out and I came here and walked around the site with Royce."

"He'd still let you buy into the company—or hand

you part of it," Brad said, squinting at him. "You want a quick tour? There's a meeting here soon about the schedule for tearing down the Fencer place, but I've got a few minutes."

"Yeah, a tour would be great."

"I'll get us both hard hats—site rules. Anything for the boss's son." He grinned at Matt. "Just kidding, but you're the closest thing to that. He takes care of all of us nicely, at least *I* think he does. Orlando might argue with that."

Matt scanned the busy site while Brad went inside. *True-blue Orlando was upset with how Royce treated him?* Brad must have read that one wrong.

Matt studied a square structure built of pipes that reminded him of massive, entwined spaghetti. More pipes were piled on the ground. Tall, thin towers—actual drilling sites—scattered here and there seemed to stab the sky. The big lagoon of water glinted in the winter sun. Was the water really tinted the color of tea, or was that just a reflection from the thick plastic shell that encased it? It had to hold toxins in wastewater. *Could that be leaking rather than runoff from the wells themselves?*

"Is that wastewater or usable water?" Matt asked, when Brad returned and handed him a hard hat.

"It's a holding tank for used water. Tanker trucks come to haul it away to be cleaned of pollutants so it can be recycled for reuse. I'm not the tech guy to talk to, but it's all handled by the book. Why? Is there a problem?"

"I sure hope not. Will there be more wells or storage lagoons over on Joe Fencer's land?"

"Oh, I get it. Look, Matt, level with me. Is Fencer getting cold feet again about selling his land and he's sent you over here? It's a done deal. I know he's working for you now, and that's great. But why don't you ask Royce or Orlando about the expansion plans? They'd love to know you're interested. I'm only the head of site acquisition."

"I realize that. Yeah, I'd like to support Royce in any way I can. I've only been leery of the fracking because it split the locals into the haves and have-nots after I'd tried so hard to patch all that up when we opened Lake Azure." He regretted he was partly lying now, but he'd almost talked himself into a corner. "Big changes in an area like this break more human bonds than the fracking breaks the shale."

"Yeah, I have to deal with that, too," he said, sounding almost relieved. Matt thought Brad was jumpy, almost defensive. Did he know or suspect something was not right here but didn't want to rock the boat of a lucrative job?

The most interesting thing about this impromptu little interview, Matt thought, was the fact that Brad had suggested he should talk to Orlando—a disgruntled Orlando?—about it. Was Orlando more than just Royce's driver and bodyguard? Maybe it was time for Matt to mend fences with Gordon Orlando—or pretend to.

"I'm sorry to take your time when you're so busy helping your sister move," Char told Mandy Lee as they each balanced a mug of tea on their knees. Most of the furniture had been cleared out, so they perched on packing boxes in the nearly empty kitchen.

Sam's wife's hair was somewhere between blond and red. She had it scraped back in a ponytail, and that accented her big hazel eyes. She was very thin. Her hands shook when she'd poured their tea and still did now as she cupped them around her mug. She wore tight black jeans and an oversize, gray Go Army sweatshirt. Char thought she looked younger than she must be, but then most mountain girls married early.

"I realize you haven't seen Jemmie for a while." Char steered the conversation toward where she hoped to go. "So I wanted to tell you he's officially enrolled in school, has a ride there and back every day, and he wants you to know he's going to work really hard at his lessons. I promised I'd tell you when I rode in the school van with Henry Hanson, the driver, today."

The woman blinked back tears. "I'm right grateful. You must think I'm a terrible mother, leavin' him like this, but his Granny Adela's always been his second ma. I just had to get away, least for a spell."

Char bit back her urge to say, *Married to Sam, no wonder.* She tried to choose her words carefully. The poor woman was so nervous she was bouncing her right foot hard but didn't even seem to notice.

"Also," Char went on, "Jemmie said that his dad is planning to take him out West sometime on a big trip. I wouldn't want him to miss school now that he's back."

"Oh. Oh, no! Sam shouldn't be goin' off with my

boy. That's pro'bly just big talk. Sam's like that, though he got him some money to back it up from his army checks—for his disability, the PTSD."

"How is he doing with that?" Char asked, not wanting to chance quizzing her on how he could get disability checks if the VA hospital doctors said he didn't have stress disorder.

"Well," she drawled, then took several sips of her tea as if to stall. "If you seen him, you know. Fearful of someone sneakin' up on the house. Puts out a ring of protection, he calls it. He's out all hours, comes and goes. Those doctors tested him was dead wrong 'bout him being just fine. I couldn't abide it no more, livin' with him, needed a break. At least he fusses with his old pickup hid out somewheres in the woods in one or t'other of his haunts. I think he just putters with it."

"I guess he and Jemmie get along well. That's good, since I heard somewhere that Sam didn't get along with his own father."

"Oh! Who said that?" she cried, slopping some tea on her jeans.

Char could have kicked herself for taking the wrong turn when they'd seemed to be getting along.

"But…that's true," Mandy Lee said, frowning at her own thoughts and lowering her voice. "Woody and Sam were oil and water after Sam come back from the war this last time, but that's fam'ly business. Matt Rowan tell you that? I seen he let you off in front. Look, I miss my boy and I'll find a way to see him soon, maybe take Joe and Sara Ann up with me."

"I'm sorry. I didn't mean to upset you or pry. I know Matt thought the world of Woody."

That seemed to calm her some, as her bouncing foot slowed. "Woody cared for Matt, too. But see, the sheriff come 'round, asked me the same about is Sam really sick. And I don't want Sam thinkin' I sicced no one on him, asked him not to bother Sam, but said he'd have to talk to him."

"I guess you know Sheriff McCord's my brother-in-law, but I didn't know he'd talked to you."

"Well, as for family bonds, 'bless be the ties that bind,' like that old hymn says. It don't mean we know what our mate is really up to," she said, her voice bitter as she got up to slosh the rest of her tea in the sink.

Char could tell she wouldn't be getting more out of poor Mandy Lee, at least right now. However much she might love her son, she was running scared of Sam.

And, Char realized, she had learned one new thing of interest. Sam might have a pickup truck hidden in one of his "haunts."

When Matt picked up Char, she told him what Mandy Lee had said about Sam having a truck hidden somewhere that he puttered with.

"She say what color it was?"

"No, but aren't about 90 percent of the ones on the mountains black?"

"You're right. But if he's always just working on it, it sounds derelict. Are you thinking he'd have some motive to try to shove me off the cliff with it?"

"Don't kill the messenger, all right?" she said, putting up both hands as if to ward him off, then yanking her bandaged hand back into her lap. "Maybe he was jealous of how much you and Woody got on when he and his dad didn't. Sorry, Matt. I can tell you're upset, too."

"Yeah. I saw Brad Mason drive into the fracking site across the road and went there to look around a bit. He's hardly one for an in-depth tour but he insists they're really careful about storage of their toxic waste. Their big, plastic-lined lagoon is full of it."

"Bad news if Kate's about-to-be brother-in-law is in on anything shady."

"Worse news if Royce is in on something bad, but I still don't think so. I wish I could have gotten more out of Brad, but I had to lighten up. Anyway, he jumped to the conclusion I was there on Joe's behalf. Listen, you know when you came into my office this morning?"

"Ah, yes. I recall parts of it quite clearly," she said, twisting toward him in her seat and reaching over to punch his shoulder with her good hand. "Especially, the part where I was tight to the wall but didn't feel a bit like a wallflower."

He nodded and seemed to bite back a grin. "Well, when you came in, I was researching more about Green Tree and Lacey Fencer or Ashley or whatever last name she uses now that she's remarried."

"Go on."

"I read where her Green Tree team was picketing a fracking site in Pennsylvania, some of their members were accused of dumping pollutants in the water before testing it. The case wasn't proven, but what if they did something like that here? Dumped typical toxins you'd find with a fracking leak, then come in here with their picket lines and accusations, just hoping someone tests the water. I know, I know, you're going to say I'm probably just trying to keep Royce in the clear again, but there are all sorts of possibilities here."

"You and Woody were friends, but Royce is like a father to you, isn't he?"

He sighed. "Yeah. Brad more or less said the same thing. I lost my dad early, but Royce was always there. Helped my mother out with money before she died. Never missed my birthday, helped pay for me and my sisters' college educations, took me to Europe when I was still in my teens. Not the usual backpacking, either, ritzy hotels. Of course, then he offered me the partnership at Lake Azure. I've learned a lot from him. And I'd bet a lot I'm never going to learn he's doing something bad with the fracking, not intentionally, not risking harm to this area or hurting people."

"I understand. But you're going to keep looking into it, right? I mean now that Gabe knows—"

"And you. And Clint Parsons, who's coming out Saturday to do official sampling. Sure, I'm going to pursue it, and I'm going to prove if the water's bad, that Royce had no idea about it. I'll warn him right away then so he can be proactive and have things on the road to recovery by the time word gets out. I could help him with that, like I've helped patch up things before. Char, I repeat, it doesn't make one bit of sense that he'd intentionally let local water go bad, not with the stake he has in the Lake Azure community. I'm holding to that—and I'm holding to you, if you'll let me."

"I'm not trying to get away, believe me. But how about this? Kate's back. She called and asked me over for dinner tonight, and Brad's going to be there. She's in protective-older-sister mode, wants me to spend the night there. She thinks since she was out of town and had nothing to do with my getting Grace away from Bright Star that it's a safe place for me to be instead of at Tess's, even with the sheriff there. And she apologized ahead for Brad's tendency to drink too much. He'll probably talk about his work and maybe I can steer the conversation around to finding out more about the fracking site and the water disposal. Matt, she invited you, too, but if you weren't there..."

"Brad wouldn't be staying all night, too, would he? You know he's got a place now at Lake Azure."

"She said I could have the guest wing all to myself."

"I want to have you with me, protect you myself, but changing venues does make sense. Look, the protestors are back," he muttered as he pulled off the road onto the Lake Azure grounds. "And damn it, look at that sign on the end."

She gasped. It was as if Matt had been psychic. TEST THE WATER, it read, and the poster on a stick bouncing up and down right next to it said, TOXINS KILL.

"Maybe you're right about them tampering with our water," she said.

"I'm hoping they go h
ing weekend to give us
tempted to tell them to gc
Bright Star's the one whc
site. Let B.S., as you cal
about biblical bitter wate

"Matt, I'm sorry you
wood tragedies."

"No, I'm sorry," he sa
protestors behind. "I'm t
ever since I almost went
panic's been building ins
it, I guess by controlling
I—we—should just leav
swear, someone pushed
me, too, not that it was th
last thing I do, I'll find o

24

During dinner at Kate and Grant's that evening, Brad managed to be the life of the party. They'd only had a glass of wine with the meal but the way Grant was frowning and Kate was rolling her eyes, it was pretty obvious Brad had arrived with something already in his system. Char wondered if Royce knew Brad drank as much as he did. Still, he was a clever, funny drinker, not a sloppy or goofy one.

"We're hoping," Kate said as she cut carrot cake and kept plying Brad with coffee, "Brad settles down soon."

"Double entendre," Brad said, and winked at Char. "Grant and Kate would like me to lose my evening cocktails and find a good woman. So, are you taken, Char?"

"Taken with Matt Rowan, if not by him. We've only known each other a little over a week."

"Well, that's about how long our grandparents knew each other before he proposed, right, Grant? But then, he was going off to war, so that sped everything up. She waited for him while he almost got killed more than once. But times are different now. Got to admit there are pros and cons about playing the field."

"Speaking of which," Grant said, "are you still dating Ginger Green at Lake Azure?"

Char almost dropped her fork. Ginger had had a fling with Brad, too, as well as Orlando and Royce and who knew who else? But not Matt? Could she trust that? She still had the feeling, now backed up by DNA, that Ginger had shot those arrows because she was jealous. Or maybe she was angry because Matt refused her obviously skillful seduction powers. But would Ginger hire someone to try to push him off a cliff over that? Some piece of the puzzle was missing, but she saw her chance to learn something more from Brad, even if it wasn't about fracking pollution.

"Did Ginger teach you archery?" she asked, stirring cream into her coffee.

"Ha! Sure. It gave her an excuse to get her arms around me. And she said my aim at her target was good, just what she liked, and—"

"Brad—" Grant cut him off. "Listen, bro, you're right on the edge so—"

"We're all right on the edge, aren't we? Much closer than we think."

He stared down Grant, then Kate, then Char. Did he intend a hint about Woody going over the edge? Matt almost had. No, she was reading too much into things again to think Brad had anything to do with all that. She was exhausted and needed a good night's sleep.

Kate shook her head at Brad's philosophizing. Char couldn't wait until he left so she could excuse herself and go call Matt about Ginger's links to another possible partner in her crimes.

Shortly after Brad left—Kate had made him drink two more cups of coffee and walk a straight line, especially since it was starting to snow again—Matt arrived.

"A business call, but pleasure, too," Matt said as Kate brought him in. He smiled at Char, then sobered. "Okay, everyone, announcement time. Gabe just called to say that Grace Lockwood gave a deposition claiming that she believes Brice 'Bright Star' Monson had motive and means in her husband's death. Meanwhile, though, I think we'd better sit down for this next piece of news, especially since you ladies look so happy," he said. Char took his coat as Kate handed him coffee and cake and they moved into the living room before the fire.

"What?" Char asked. "What's B.S. done now?"

"According to Gabe, he's threatening to press charges against you for coercion and abduction."

Char bounced up from the couch. "Oh, for heaven's sake! He's the one who does that again and again with poor gullible people!"

"Which is more or less what Gabe told him. Gabe thinks that's a smoke screen. Bright Star's looking for something to bargain with since he'd do anything to avoid having to take a lie detector test, make a sworn statement or ever get into court, so calm down, sweetheart."

She sank back beside him on the couch. "Easy for you to say, since you're not on his possible hit list. But, at least, now that he's shown how he thinks threats like that will hold us off, I feel better. After telling Gabe that, he doesn't dare send his robots to harm me."

"You know," Kate said, "if he and some of his acolytes were dead and buried and someone dug them up ages hence, they'd never know how screwed up and evil he really was." She looked out the large, back window toward the mound tomb.

"Char, you okay?" Matt asked, putting a hand on her arm.

"All three of us Lockwood girls had run-ins with that horrible phony messiah," Kate said. "I hope this at least shuts him up—and at best, closes him and the Hear Ye cult down. Matt, did Gabe tell Bright Star that Grace is standing up to him and might bring down his house of cards?"

"He informed him of the accusations and Bright Star claimed she had to be coerced. He said he'd get a lawyer and heads would roll."

"Sounds like the old days where Marie Antoinette supposedly said, 'Let them eat cake,' and they cut off her head," Kate said.

Grant threw his arm around her. "Let's not go there. Besides, Matt's eating cake."

Matt just grinned and went on. "And, oh, yeah, Ginger still claims she didn't shoot an arrow at me or Char. I'm not looking forward to seeing her at work tomorrow. What? Why are you all looking like that?"

"Brad let slip tonight that he and Ginger were recently more than friends," Char said.

"Well, join the club, and I don't mean me. But we don't accuse people of shooting arrows because they go from man to man. I just can't believe Ginger's to blame for that."

"They were skillfully shot, and she's good at it," Char said.

"Hey, almost forgot one piece of really good news, partly why I came over. I know I could have called, but I wanted to see Char. It's all set for the six of us to have a private room for Thanksgiving dinner at the lodge. I hope Brad has other plans, so we're not leaving him out."

"He does," Grant said. "He's going with Royce and Orlando to Columbus. Change of scenery, I guess."

"Speaking of which," Kate said, "let's turn out the lights in here, cherish the moment and watch the snow fall outside. It's beautiful."

They did that, the four of them, seeing the snow swirl past the window until Matt said he had to go. Char walked him out, even donned a coat so they could stand out in the magical darkness together.

"I don't want you to go," she said, though the wind tried to whisk her words away.

"I'd like to take you with me. You've been a vagabond, sleeping here and there when I only want you to sleep with me."

"Yes—I… Me, too. But everything is happening so fast."

"Darn bulky coats," he whispered in her ear, but held her tight, anyway. "And let's stay away from the front doors and windows," he said, moving them a few steps away into deeper darkness. "At least there's nowhere someone can hide close by to send an arrow our way into the door or wall."

He warmed her lips. He warmed *her.* The soft, thick snow was a blanket protecting them, wrapping them in white, hiding them from other eyes. For once, she didn't feel they were being watched. She clung to him, kissed him back hard. The blowing, twisting snow—no, it was Matt's hands and kisses—made her dizzy. She was giddy with glee that they had found each other. She wanted to run, make snow angels, a snowman, throw snowballs, play Grace's game of fox and geese....

"Gotta go," he told her. "What snow? What cold? I think we're in the tropics, and that's just where we should go when this is all over."

"That's where Kate and Grant are going on their honeymoon—St. Croix," she blurted, then remembered that was supposed to be a secret. "Oh, don't tell them I told you."

"I won't. I need to catch Royce tonight before he heads back to Columbus tomorrow, maybe have a quick word with Orlando, too, start to mend fences, since he may know more about the fracking than I realized. He's always thought I was an idiot not to get into it." He kissed her again, hard. "See you tomorrow," he said, but still kept his arms around her. "I can pick you up here, but you're not going up Pinecrest with Henry again, are you?"

"Not with all this new snow. I'll have to make my other calls on 'should-be' students on Friday, if I can still walk after that turkey dinner you promised. Yes, see you tomorrow. And you did call the gas station like you said to get them to hurry those new tires, right?"

"I'll call in the morning. I still don't want you going anywhere alone."

"Have you found out if the picketers really left for the holiday?" she called after him as he walked to his car, and its lights flickered as he unlocked it. The interior dome light popped on. Out here, his car lights seemed so awfully bright.

"Evidently they're real people with families, too. Any more questions? If we're out here much longer, Kate and Grant will send the sled dogs for us. But I wouldn't even mind an igloo with you."

"Why, Matthew Rowan, I believe that's the most romantic thing you ever told me—and it rhymes, too."

"Then how about 'I have things to do but I've come to love you.'"

"And the next line—Me, too!"

He trudged back through the thickening snow and kissed her again. "Damn sister chaperones," he muttered, glancing toward the house before he headed back to his car. "I'm going for a ride, get the hell back inside," he called to her with a shouted laugh.

Despite her worries and fears, she hugged herself for pure joy as he drove away and she went back inside.

* * *

When Matt called Royce on his cell to see if he could drop by his suite at the lodge, Royce told him he was playing pool in the lodge rec room, so Matt went there. He saw that Royce had failed to mention he was playing with Orlando, but he steeled himself to be upbeat with both of them. No one else was using the other table in the room this late and in this weather, so Matt figured it was a good time for some serious talk.

He gave a quick squeeze to Royce's shoulders and offered his hand to Orlando, who barely managed to cover his surprise, before they shook hands. "So who's winning?" Matt asked.

"Orlando knows to let me win—a lesson that's been lost on you," Royce said with a grin, and leaned over the green felt table with his cue stick to neatly hit a ball into the side pocket.

At least Royce was smiling, Matt thought, though his words hit home. Did it mean more? Matt was having the same problems lately that Char had—overanalyzing every little thing.

"So what's new?" Royce asked. "We'll be done with this game pretty fast, then you can get in with us."

"No, I'm fine. I'm happy to report the Green Tree army must have decamped for the holiday."

"As we all must," Royce said, nodding. "Veronica is missing me. I want you to meet her, Matt. Not sure if I'll bring her here or take you there. When I'm here, I work and worry too much."

"About the fracking?"

"This trip started out because you almost got shoved off a cliff, remember?"

Orlando's shot bounced off two edges of the table and went in, too. He looked up. "Any leads on that from your end, Matt?" he asked.

"I'm working on it. I thought I should tell you both that Ginger has been questioned about the arrows, one that just missed Char and me and the other that just happened to get stuck in the back of my house. Ginger's DNA is on the arrows, but I don't think it was her, just that someone took her arrows. There's no motive and it doesn't sound like her to draw a skull and crossbones and write crudely printed, misspelled threatening notes—or note," he corrected himself, because surely she had nothing to do with putting one in his burned truck. "I think it's someone who wants to shut me up or keep me in line, but for what?"

Royce sighed and rechalked the tip of his cue stick. "I'm just hoping someone's not trying to get to me by hurting you. That's why I put Orlando on your tail, and, yeah, I should have told you—asked you. So how's Charlene? Bright Star's furious to lose a couple of cult members, but I told him not to blame her."

"He called you?"

Royce frowned and nodded. "He has this weird idea—like most of his thoughts—that we're still partners when we're not. He sold me the land for an excellent price, it helped him out—that's all."

"He's threatening to hit Char with charges of trespassing and abduction for helping her relatives leave."

"No way," Orlando said, almost with a sneer. "He'd never want to step into a court of earthly law. That guru has his own laws."

Matt turned to face Orlando. "You've tangled with him?"

"Mere observation," he said, turning away.

Matt was tempted to call it spying, but then, didn't that mean Royce ordered him to watch or confront Bright Star?

The three of them played one game of eight ball, then Royce called it quits and said he was going upstairs to his suite. "Can't be out of gas with Veronica when I get back tomorrow," he told them with a little laugh. "Orlando, we'll head for the big city about 9:00 a.m. See you for breakfast at the lodge before then, Matt. And speaking of lady loves, how's Charlene? You didn't answer me before."

"She's fine. I know it's fast, Royce, but she's the one. I can't help worrying about her all the time. It puts everything else in a new perspective."

"Glad to hear it," Royce said, coming back to put a heavy hand on his shoulder. "Let's the three of us—you, me, her—have dinner when I get back next week. I wouldn't mind a wedding here at the lodge, then some little kids to play with when I come visit over the years. Well, don't mean to be pushy or jump the gun on all that."

"Sounds like you've been reading my mind," Matt said. Ordinarily, he would have left when Royce did, but he wanted to patch things up with Orlando—and find out how much he was really involved in overseeing the fracking here.

"Just remember," Royce said as he headed for the door, "I've known you since you were born, my boy."

When Royce was gone, Orlando said, "Brad mentioned you stopped by the big fracking site today. Any questions I can answer for you? Brad's more or less in charge of local site purchase, and that's all."

"He mentioned I could talk to you. You know everything Royce does about it?"

"Not really, but enough. Royce is my business, so fracking is, too. Is there a problem—other than the fact you don't give Royce his proper due or respect? At least tonight you leveled with him about how much Charlene Lockwood means to you."

"I'm trying to build bridges, Orlando, not burn them—and not get another lecture from you. I know how valuable you are to him, so I regret telling you off after you followed Char and me up on Pinecrest."

Orlando's cue ball broke the new triangle of balls with a click and a series of muted thuds. "Believe me, I had better things to do. But how valuable am I to him? Let's just say I'm working on that. It's you who is sitting on a fortune and don't seem to know it. You could actually use someone like me to help you out."

"You mean, running Lake Azure?"

"I mean," he said, slamming the big end of his cue stick on the floor, "that you're the chosen one, the golden boy. You're his heir to everything, and I think you should start acting like it, go along with what he does, who he likes. And yeah, that means you and me have to get along good, so thanks for the handshake and the apology."

"I do value all he's done for me, our relationship."

"If so, you'd back everything he does and that means the fracking. It's not enough to chat with the Green Tree bunch to get them out of here. He has enemies, so maybe they went after you."

"Listen, Orlando, I don't have to—"

"I'm out of here," he insisted, punching his cue stick back into the rack on the wall. "See you when we get back. I'm having turkey dinner with my widowed sister, but maybe you and I can talk turkey when we get back."

Without another look or word, the man strode out.

Matt leaned stiff-armed on the edge of the pool table, staring at the scattered balls. *You're his heir to everything?* Did Orlando mean in Royce's will, or that he was executor of his estate or what? Why did Orlando know stuff like that if he didn't? Because Royce wanted Matt to care for him for other reasons?

He jumped when his cell rang. He dug it out of his shirt pocket. He saw it was Gabe calling.

"Gabe, it's late. Everything okay?"

"If you call eighty-seven members of a religious cult going nuts okay. Bright Star's missing. Several of the Hear Ye brethren who called me insist he's ascended into heaven and won't be back."

25

"Bright Star's missing?" Matt asked Gabe. "No clues where he's gone?"

"I'm going out there now. I called Char. This may be a ploy to flush her out, so I told her to stay put until I get a handle on this. But I think his flock is genuinely upset. Some of them aren't even making sense, but what's new about that? One guy, Brother Stephen, said like he must have gone out to meet with Moses and Elijah and flew away, ascended from the mountain."

"I wouldn't put it past him to stage something like that."

"I'll get back to you."

"Gabe, if he's hiding out for some reason, maybe he's down by the river under the fracking site. You know, in that hut with the quote about Jonah gone missing in the belly of the whale."

"I can't stage a manhunt for him right now. Technically, I haven't even served him with a warrant. I'll see what I can get out of his people about where he might go."

When Matt strode out into the hall and headed for his car, he saw Orlando in the dim lobby on his cell phone. It was so dark out here that the phone's light threw shadows on his face. Orlando glanced up, ended the call and came over.

"You said you were sorry for coming down on me before," Orlando told him. "I'd like to apologize for lecturing you. For jumping on you about Royce. I'd appreciate it if you wouldn't tell him."

"Sure," Matt said, "as long as what he's doing is right and good."

"Of course, it is. You know that."

Matt was tempted to tell Orlando that Bright Star was missing, but he'd tell Royce in the morning and let Orlando find out from him. As he went out to his car, he felt some weight had been lifted from his shoulders. If Bright Star had taken off because of possible charges against him, maybe poor Grace Lockwood and her kids could come back soon. And his disappearance—if it held up—made Char a whole lot safer.

Word about Bright Star spread like wildfire through the Cold Creek community, mostly because the cult members went door-to-door at first light, asking if anyone had seen their leader. Grant answered the door when the bell rang, but Kate and Char stayed out of the line of vision of a man Char recognized from the night Grace had fled the commune.

"Well," Kate said with a sniff after Grant closed the door, "if they're asking all over for him, they certainly don't think he ascended to heaven."

"More like he went in the other direction," Char said as they walked back to the breakfast table. "Maybe we will have something extra to be grateful for tomorrow."

"Gabe thinks the guy's on the lam because Grace was going to bring charges," Grant said. "I just hope he either gets caught and arrested or gets far away from here and doesn't hang out, lurking. And that the cult doesn't keep blaming you, Char, since you're here as a target and Grace is not."

"I don't think any of that body of worshippers would dare make a move without their master," Char told him. "He does all the thinking for them. I'll feel a lot better going around the area if Gabe locks him up or finds out he's run. Good riddance. I'll bet he had a fortune squirreled away from his Hear Ye members who gave up all their earthly goods to him. Lee and Grace did. Then he got a fortune for selling that land to EEC for fracking. Without him, maybe the cult will disband and the land and buildings can go for something to help the mountain kids, like a park or a summer camp."

After they got up to clear the breakfast table, Kate put her arm around Char. "I thought you were going to ask Matt for something like that at Lake Azure with the swimming area, canoes and the stables he says they'll build. If he promised that to poor little Ethan, maybe he'd go along with it for more—and with you to run everything there."

Char sighed. "I'd love that. And I guess you know I love him. Maybe, at last, things are looking up."

Char dared to believe that Thanksgiving Day would bring blessings. Her sisters and their loved ones were together in the lovely setting of a wood-paneled private room at the Lake Azure lodge and didn't have to do all the preparation for the meal. Even Gabe seemed temporarily relaxed. He'd found no trace of Bright Star. No Hear Ye vehicle was missing, so he hadn't been able to let the Highway Patrol know what to look for. They'd phoned Grace to tell her, and, since there was no way Bright Star could know where she was, she was ecstatic.

"It's too late for Lee," Grace had told them on Matt's speakerphone. "But maybe someone else at Hear Ye got fed up with Bright Star and did him in. Can't imagine who, though. They were all either buffaloed by or scared of him, just like me. Tess, I think I'll be sending for you soon. This baby's getting ready, I can tell. Whether it's a boy or a girl, the name will be Lee, after his—or her—father."

Char had noticed she'd said that emphatically. Yet she'd admitted privately that the baby could be Bright Star's. But as she'd said, too, it wasn't the baby's fault, and she was the mother. Char scolded herself for thinking of that old horror film *Rosemary's Baby,* where Mia Farrow bore the Devil's child and then loved it, anyway.

"Char, you okay, sweetheart?" Matt asked and put his arm around her waist as they gathered at the table for the meal to be brought in. "Tess will be with her when the baby comes. Grace will be all right, and so are we, okay? No troubles today and good times to come."

"And good turkey," Gabe said as the servers carried in the bird and the fixings. Char recalled that Matt had said Orlando had promised to "talk turkey," whatever that meant, when he and Royce came back, but today, she told herself, Matt was right. Enjoy the day.

Matt had called both of his sisters and their families—one in Florida, one in Illinois—and told them about Char. She herself was with her loved ones. All, that is, but Dad and his young family out West, but they had talked to all of them, too, and they were coming to Kate's wedding. Yes, today was a lovely day.

They said a prayer, and Matt carved the bird perfectly, as if he'd been born to it. He was a wonderful host, but then, that was part of his career here. Watching how adeptly he wielded the big knife, Char forced away the image of the Hear Ye brother with a knife. The cut to her hand could have been so much worse.

"We're going to plan more of Kate and Grant's wedding this evening," Tess told Gabe, who wore civilian clothes instead of his sheriff's uniform. "December's almost here." Tess was finally eating for two to make up for hardly being able to eat anything.

Grant stopped ladling gravy on his potatoes and dressing. "Matt," he said, "I was going to ask you this in private, but a fraternity brother of mine can't be an usher in the wedding, so I'm hoping you could fill in for him. The big day's Saturday, December 17, evening service at the Community Church in old town, reception at the house. If you say yes, I can promise you a very attractive, and as yet unattached, bridesmaid to partner."

"I'm honored," he said. "Count me in."

"Warning! Tuxedo alert, tuxedo alert!" Gabe said in a falsetto voice.

"At least," Grant said, grinning, "I talked Dr. Kate Lockwood out of everyone dressing like the ancient Adena."

"Not true!" she responded. "But I won't embarrass you by tossing a roll at you."

Tess, then Gabe started tapping their goblets with utensils as people did at a wedding to make the wedded pair kiss. Matt and Char, laughing, joined in too until Kate and Grant kissed.

"Mmm," Grant said, "she tastes of tart cranberry sauce, which I skipped. Pass that, would you, Matt?"

"That was my lipstick," Kate said while everyone else laughed again.

"It's like family already," Tess said. "And next year we'll have a baby to take care of between main course and dessert. Maybe Grace and her kids will be back here, too."

Char was so happy she couldn't think of one other thing to say. Yet what if Bright Star was lurking? She hoped Ginger wasn't harboring hatred for Matt, not to mention what he'd said about Orlando telling him off again. And she kept picturing Sam McKitrick out in one of his haunts, as Mandy Lee had put it, laboring over an old pickup truck that didn't run.

Haunted by fears she fought to push aside, she told

herself it was great to be happy, laughing with the others. She only hoped the food baskets that two churches and Lake Azure residents had donated for needy mountain families had blessed them with a good day, too.

Joe Fencer had told Matt that Mandy Lee was going to visit Jemmie and her mountain family tomorrow, and she'd asked if Char wanted to go along. Since Joe and Sara Ann were going along and Adele and Jemmie would be on the mountain, Char and Matt had figured that would be enough people to keep Sam—or even Bright Star—in check or at a distance.

"A toast to future good times together for the six of us," Matt said, and raised his wineglass.

They all lifted theirs, Tess with grapefruit juice in hers. *Oh,* Char thought, *if only that toast could come true.*

They all clinked glasses, and the sound rang in her ears.

Char felt exhausted the next morning. The six of them had stayed up late, just talking after their Thanksgiving meal. Sometimes it was all of them, sometimes the men together, while the women discussed the wedding. Matt had kissed her a quick good-night after midnight just before Kate and Grant scooped her up to take her to their place again. This morning Grant had dropped her at the lodge where Joe Fencer, his wife, Sara Ann and Mandy Lee said they'd pick her up for their jaunt up Pinecrest. Char was grateful to be included and not a bit afraid with Joe along, partly because Matt trusted him.

"It's really somethin'," Mandy Lee said from the backseat next to Char. "I mean, Jemmie just starts school and gets two days off—a four-day weekend. Too much time to spend with his pa."

"We should be grateful they get along. More than I can say for Sam and his dad," Joe said.

"Mandy Lee, will you be moving with Joe and Sara Ann or moving back home?" Char asked.

"To be decided today." She wore her hair down, but kept twisting it around her index finger, yanking it hard. "I owe my kin a lot, but it's my closest family that's needs me. I know that."

Char reached over and patted her arm. The young woman gave her a wan smile.

The truth was, Char was nervous, too. She hoped she could get some answers today about whether Sam was really sick or not. She wanted to trust Henry's observations, yet Sam had seemed off-kilter to her, and her career as a social worker had given her skills for psyching out when someone was lying. Was Sam another version of B.S., "the master," who could con people into believing him?

Char averted her gaze when they passed Coyote Rock. She fought the memory of Matt almost going off the cliff there—and how Brad Mason had said at dinner the other night that everyone was too close to the edge. The edge of what? She should have called him on that. Of danger? Insanity? Death?

The moment they turned into the narrow lane to the McKitrick place, Joe honked. Jemmie ran out onto the porch and into the yard with his dog right behind him. “Ma, Ma,” he cried and hugged Mandy Lee as soon as she got out of the car. “I’m in school now, gonna work real hard!”

His mother hugged him so long that Char blinked back tears. Out West, even working with the darling Navajo kids, she hadn’t yearned for a child herself, but here, lately...

“Miss Charlene told me all ’bout it,” Mandy Lee told her son. “Now you say proper hi to your uncle and aunt.”

The boy hugged them both, then Char, too, before he went back to holding his mother’s hand. His grandmother had come out on the porch, waving and sweeping snow off the crooked boards with a broom. Sam materialized from behind some pines trees and headed slowly toward them with his shoulders hunched and his limp even more pronounced than before.

“A surprise,” he called to them, scanning the area. “But it’s dangerous for civilians to be in enemy territory. Better get inside to cover.”

Char noticed he held a big wrench in one hand. Had he been working on the truck Mandy Lee had mentioned or was it another of his imaginary weapons against terrorists?

“And a visitor who’s not family,” he observed, staring at Char as they walked toward the house. “I hope, ma’am,” he said to her, “you’ve got official clearance because we need to be very watchful for suicide bombers—even women these days."

"No, Pa, she's okay," Jemmie piped up. "I know her, and you met Miss Charlene before. She's gonna tell us kids about Indians out West sometime. I thought I should know 'bout them 'case we visit them."

Sam's narrow gaze slammed into Char's stare. For a moment, neither of them flinched, neither looked away. His eyes were a pale blue, steady but disturbing in a different way from Bright Star's. She tried to read whether Sam was rational or not.

"Still can't be too careful with the enemy around, right, Mandy Lee?" Sam said, looking at his wife.

"Well, course that's right, Sam, but I don't want you takin' our boy on no trips out West."

Adela put her arm around her daughter-in-law. "We sure hope Mandy Lee will see fit to come home, don't we, Sam? For Jemmie, for all of us. We'll keep her safe, welcome her back, give her time to adjust, won't we, Sam?"

"Sure, sure. Come on in. This is a safe house. I checked it out more than once, but Joe—ha, G.I. Joe—keep an eye on the door, okay?"

Adela served them yeast rolls, jam and coffee while they sat on a bench and stools around the low-burning fireplace. When Char got up to help her, Adela gave her a smile and a nod.

"You're pretty close to Matt, right?" the old woman asked in a quiet voice with a glance back into the room as if to be sure no one was listening.

"Yes," Char said, matching her whisper. "I think the world of him. We haven't known each other long but we're getting closer all the time."

Adela nodded as she piled oven-hot rolls on a plate. "You tell him something for me I held back, 'cause I know Mr. Flemming be like a daddy to him. And don't go tell no one else I said it, just pick the right time."

Char's eyes widened. "I promise."

"That Mr. Flemming and his man, Orlando, done come up here to offer my Woody a bundle of money to quit his protesting the fracking down yonder. Woody, he turned them right down, and was they surprised and riled over it, too. That Mr. Orlando come back up. Woody wouldn't talk to him no more so Sam did, talked him into leaving but talked to him a long time first, he sure did. See, I know some folks think Sam mighta hurt his pa 'cause they argued things, didn't see eye to eye about Sam's sickness, all that. I never wanted to make no claims to it, but Mr. Flemming and that Orlando man of his, they were riled at Woody, too, I swear it. You think it's important, you tell Matt. Let him decide whether to tell someone else like the sheriff."

Char held her breath, then let it out slowly. "I'll do that, Adela. I promise." Still, she wished she hadn't been put in that position, but it was something Matt should know—and wouldn't like. She'd have to find the right time to tell him, like tonight when they were alone.

As they ate and sat around the fire, everyone but Sam managed to make small talk. Jemmie sat tight between his mother and Char. Sam mostly stalked the corners

of the room, disappearing
then, still carrying the wr

Finally, Char got up t
"Were you working on s
wrench?"

When Sam didn't answ
fixing his old truck agai
He's gonna give me a ride

"It's a tank," Sam told
mantel. "An M-1 turret A
it's been wrecked going o
a brother to me and he go

Char's thoughts snagge
going off a cliff, but she r
straws again. That really
in the war.

"Sam," Mandy Lee said
you mind about tanks. Y
trip out West, did you?"

"Not taking my boy int
said, frowning. "Fallujah's
dangerous as hell."

Char hated to admit it,
tors must be wrong abou
consistent even if it was c
worrying about him taki
he thought the enemy wa
threatening.

That is, she was done w
saw, through the open do

pacing in and out of, on a small table, a package with a war bonneted Indian chief and the printed crimson words on it, Red Man Chewing Tobacco.

2

Char went straight to Ma
Joe Fencer dropped her o
tell Matt he would be bac
Lee to their old house so sl
he and Sara Ann were rur

Mandy Lee had told th
ing back. "I'm gonna give
tain with the family. But
am I gonna do? Can't take
I miss him something aw
a little laugh, "maybe I ca
army cook at the safe ho
with Sam, I'm scairt it co

"You let me know if y
Char had whispered to her

Mandy Lee nodded ar
just bet you're good with
Jemmie back up. 'Preciate
come by later?"

Now, as Char headed down the business hall of the lodge, she tried to forget the trapped look on Mandy Lee's face. Jen, Matt's secretary, who was standing by the photocopier, called to her. "He's busy right now, Charlene." She lowered her voice as Char walked toward her. "Poor guy. After Ginger threw a fit in there and threatened to quit, now he's got that protestor Lacey Fencer-Ashley on his hands."

"You mean the Green Tree people are back? I didn't see them."

Jen looked up over her reading glasses. "They've made a whole new group of signs and moved to picket the big fracking site on Valley View Road. Before Matt closed his door, she was shouting. I heard her tell him that one sign says 'Hear Ye, Hear Ye: Royce Flemming, Pollution and Corruption.' Sooo," she drawled that word and rolled her eyes, "without Royce here to defend himself and handle things, I'm sure Matt's doing it for him."

Char sighed, thanked Jen and went out into the lobby to wait. With the holiday weekend and the weather, not much was going on today. Her stomach rumbled with hunger. That's what happened when she ate a gargantuan meal one day. The next she felt starved, but she'd wait for Matt's visitor to leave before getting some lunch. At least Green Tree was taking a stand against the dangerous parts of fracking, though she wasn't sure about their tactics. Her mother had always said you catch more flies with honey than vinegar, but who wanted to catch flies?

She dug her phone out of her purse, noting she had an email from the garage that her truck was ready.

Just then, her phone rang.

"Char, it's Gabe."

Her stomach tightened. He hadn't called her with good news lately.

"Is Tess okay?"

"Yes, and don't ask about Grace. She hasn't gone into labor yet, and I haven't heard from her since we all talked to her yesterday. Just wanted you and Matt to know that dead beaver I ordered the necropsy on had toxins in its blood. Of course, it was killed by the arrow, not pollutants."

"Bad news for EEC, though."

"We'll wait, at least, until Matt's friend tests new samples. Listen, I tried to call him first, but his secretary said he's with someone. Just checking to see if it's you."

"No, but he's having a bad day at the office—and it's only a little after noon. He's been yelled at by Ginger, so I hear, and now Lacey from Green Tree is in there, telling him she and her crew are going to picket the big fracking site with posters that attack Royce, and he's not back yet to take her on. But I'm sure Matt's holding his own with her."

"How was the trip up to McKitricks' this morning?"

"It went okay. I think Sam's wife is going to move back, but I can tell she's wavering. Oh—Gabe. Lacey's storming out right now. I'm going to go see Matt. I'll tell him about the dead beaver. And, by the way, I found out Sam either chewed or still chews Red Man tobacco. Saw it there."

"Him and about thirty others in the area Deputy Miller checked on this week. Char, I don't think Sam has any way to get around, and he's too busy hunting the enemy in his own area to be hanging around elsewhere, so I doubt that Red Man you two found in the tree stand was his. Listen, I've got a call. You gonna stay with Kate and Grant again tonight?"

"I don't know. I really have the feeling Bright Star's taken off. Call it women's intuition or just an answer to prayer."

"Tess agrees. Later, then."

Char went down the hall to where Jen was already standing at Matt's open door, seeing if he needed anything.

"What I don't need is another angry woman!" he told her.

Char edged her way next to Jen. "How about a kind and hungry one?" she asked.

"Hey, glad you're back. Come on in and calm me down," he told Char. "Thanks, Jen. Don't know what I'd do without you."

"Or you—in a different way," he whispered to Char as she walked in and he closed the door behind her.

She put her arms around his waist. He pulled her to him. "I'll fill you in on my visitor's histrionics," he told her. "But how did it go up on Pinecrest?"

"Gabe just asked me the same thing on the phone because he couldn't get you."

"Okay, since I see you're in one piece, what's up with him?"

"Matt, that dead beaver did have toxins in its body, but, of course, it died from the arrow."

"Yeah. Which I don't want to admit could have been shot by our own Robin Hood, Ginger Green."

"Jen said Ginger threatened to resign."

"I told her not to if she wanted a good recommendation when all this is over. But I also told her not to target any more human bodies with her charms, to keep it totally professional, not personal, around here."

"One more thing. From where I was sitting in the McKitrick cabin, I could see into the bedroom Sam kept pacing to. According to Mandy Lee on the way back, he used to chew Red Man tobacco, but gave it up because it left a trail of spit for the Taliban to follow—but I saw he has a packet of it in that room."

"Gabe said lots of guys in the area use it, and there's no way to trace who's purchased it. I was tempted to ask Lacey Fencer what her new husband chews, but I didn't need to rile her up more or let her know I've read about the fact they could have tampered with that water in Pennsylvania.

"And," he went on, tipping her back in his arms, which pressed their hips tighter together, "I think you said you're hungry. For me, I hope, as well as a good lunch?"

He didn't wait for an answer, but kissed her so hard and thoroughly, she thought he'd devour her. She gave as good as she got, running her hands over him, too, mussing his hair as he ran hot kisses down her throat and his tongue darted into the little hollow at the base of her throat while one hand cupped her breast.

"Let's go get lunch before I just lock the door and clear my desk to put you on it," he told her, breathing hard.

"You'd better comb your hair."

"Promise me you'll mess it up again tonight?" He held her at arm's length and studied her. She was flushed and felt his touch and look clear down to her belly.

"But that is a huge commitment for me."

"I understand. Anything in life worthwhile needs to be a big commitment. We'll talk about that first, then. If Grant Mason's grandparents can know each other for a week before they make a lifelong commitment, so can we." He went on before she could even gather her senses to nod. "Char, as hard as all this has been on me—on both of us—at least we found each other."

"I know. It carries me through all this, makes anything possible."

"Here's the other thing, something I agonized about last night. I've decided as soon as Royce and Orlando get back, I'm going to tell them what we've found so far, even before the definitive water test results. I can judge where they stand by their reactions to that. Royce has a right to know up front, so he can be proactive, prepare a plan to take care of all this."

"You're the one who knows him best—if that's the best way to go. I think you're right. He should know."

"And it's been worrying me that I'm the one who told

Lacey earlier she should r
big fracking site or to eve
office, just to get her away
just what she's threatenin
Orlando I suggested it. A
to take that fact the wro
I'm on their side, even th
site's poisoning Cold Cre
aquifer. But I'm only on
take care of this mess."

"You've been loyal to
terests. But when one in
threatens the well-being c

"Orlando says I do, th
loyal. He also told me I'm
told me himself."

"What? Which means
ture?"

"Probably potential b
how much he's investing
erties and the fracking. B
me, even turns me out c
controlling, senior partn
know. I keep thinking I r
burying my head in the
Creek."

She hugged him tight.
lose, too. Do you think h
stop paying Henry?"

"I don't know, but it w

and Joe Fencer, since he knows about the possible pollution—that a big storm may be coming, and I don't mean more snow. Come on, sweetheart, let's do lunch before my next appointment hits. It's a banker from Cincinnati, who, I hope, will give us a loan to build the stables and buy some horses. At least it's not another dangerous woman. But then, since you're with me today, the third one's the charm."

"In that case, I'm very glad I came along on the mountain when you were on the edge. Brad Mason says everyone's living on the edge, close to the edge. But I think, if we hang on to each other, like before, we won't go over."

He kissed her again, and she remembered to smooth back his hair—and the worry wrinkles on his forehead—before they went out to the lodge dining room together.

After lunch with Matt, Char called for the gas station courtesy van to pick her up so she could get her truck. Luckily, she hadn't canceled her insurance on the old thing, so she'd be reimbursed for the four new tires and installment fee. It amused her to think of the differences in the two gas stations in town. The new one near the Lake Azure community used email and had a van as well as a small deli on the premises. The old one at the other end of town she recalled from her girlhood days was a good old boys hangout, though the prices were much cheaper.

She was glad to get her truck back and pleased to

see it now had four new snow tires, when hers had been balding. Matt must have ordered those, or was that standard for the winter around here? *A blessing in disguise to get rid of those old ones,* she thought, trying to buck herself up. It would be a good test run on how they were balanced when she made a quick trip to talk to Mandy Lee again. And it wasn't up on the mountain or even in the hills, so surely Matt couldn't argue.

Don't look back, only ahead, she told herself as she paid her bill and headed out to the truck.

She was surprised to see Henry Hanson outside, putting gas in the new Pinecrest school van.

"Oh, afternoon, Miss Charlene," he called to her. He lowered his voice. "I swear, I'd never pay these prices, but Mr. Flemming had his right-hand man, Mr. Orlando, get us a credit card for fill-ups here."

"I didn't know that. He's very kind and thoughtful."

Again, she felt guilty that she and Matt might be hurting their generous donor, but if he was doing wrong with the fracking, he had to be stopped. And then, would this wonderful service to the mountain kids be over, and poor Jemmie's new world—his escape and his future—be crushed again? What should she counsel Mandy Lee, if she asked for advice?

"I'm going over to 'set a spell,' as they say, with Mandy Lee McKitrick," she told Henry.

"What's she say about Sam lately?"

"I saw him yesterday with a wrench in his hand. Jemmie says he has an old pickup—he thinks it's a tank—to work on."

Henry pulled the gas nozzle out of the van and shook his head. "He sure comes up with 'em, don't he? A truck's a tank. Well, maybe he just said that for his boy's benefit if he was there, like make-believe. Or to make the adults think he's off, but I still say he's sane as they come."

"Good luck with the drive on Monday," she called to him. "I'll be visiting a few homes to see if we can get a couple more students. I'm glad it's working out well for your family."

"Real good," he told her, and snatched off his cap as if he were being introduced to her for the first time. "Miss Charlene, you been a blessing."

Char was deeply touched by Henry's words, but she only hoped she could be a blessing to poor Mandy Lee. At least things were looking up for her. She'd fled from a mess she'd made out West, but with finding Matt, getting more mountain kids in school and being with her sisters again, maybe coming here had been for the best.

She drove along Valley View Road, at least the part of it where she'd lived her early years. It made her sad, to see the place Tess had been taken as a child. At least the big tanker trucks for the fracking site didn't come down this far toward town.

As Char pulled into the Fencer place, sadness sat heavy on her heart. It looked so forlorn, and Matt had told her it was scheduled to be torn down. So much for the old house, the barn and a few other outbuildings, not to mention the well-tended yard and fields. At least her childhood home down the road had been sold and would be preserved—unless the tentacles of the fracking monster reached out farther.

Mandy Lee had tea for her again, but the packing boxes were gone and they sat on the floor with their backs to the wall. "I done decided what I'm gonna do," she told Char. "For my boy, I'll go on home through Christmas and New Years, but I'm gonna use that time to get me a job in Cold Creek. Earn me some money, then move down to town, get Sam to agree I can have Jemmie at least half time. When I get all settled, I'll ask Adela if she don't want to come down with me, leave Sam to fight his enemies alone. Cold gets her arthritis goin' somethin' awful up on Pinecrest, anyway."

"I'm glad you've made a decision, Mandy Lee, and I'll help you any way I can, including looking for a job for you. If there's room in the school van, Henry Hanson could get you down the mountain for work until you can move to town, but we're hoping to get more kids to ride, so that probably won't last long. But I will see if there's something for you at Lake Azure. A few of the employees there live on-site."

"Oh, Miss Charlene, that would be so good. Then all I got to worry about is Sam."

They hugged, and Char went out to her truck. It was spitting ice flakes, very pretty but they could make the driving worse. At least, because of the tanker truck traffic and the noise at the fracking site, not many used this road to get into town anymore, so she didn't have to worry about sliding into other cars. Besides, she had new tires that gripped the road. She tried to buck herself up. If a girl who had been mostly raised in Michigan couldn't drive on slippery roads just because she'd lived in the desert for a while, there was something wrong. And, she noted, at least the bad weather had evidently kept the Green Tree protestors from picketing the fracking site, since she didn't see them along the road.

She drove carefully and thought over her plans and her route. She was going to head back to Lake Azure, move back into the Mannings' house, though she knew Matt wanted her to spend the night at his place. She'd feel safer there with him—but at risk, too, since she knew they were combustible together. And that—that would mean, at least to her, they couldn't go back, could only go forward…

The road was icing a bit. She saw a shiny, new-looking black truck was coming at her on the two-lane road, coming too fast. It had huge tires that made the chassis sit higher than usual. Thank heavens, it wasn't the old rattletrap Matt had described that hit him.

She slowed and got way over on the narrow berm, near the forest side of the road about a mile past Fencers' and a half mile before her family's old land.

The truck came at her, slowing, but too far over. *With those big tires, couldn't he control his vehicle?* She braced herself as it hit, not too hard into her front driver's side, pushing her, pinning her back bumper against a big tree.

Damn! She'd just gone through the pain of making an insurance claim. Just when she'd gotten her independence back, just when things were going better, now an accident. Or was it? Had the truck actually slid on the road? At least she wasn't on the edge of a cliff, though there was a drop-off to the valley on the other side of the road.

She started to get out until she saw the driver of the truck was really covered up for the weather. She could see through his windshield that he wore a ski mask, leaving only his eyes visible. He climbed down and started toward her truck, holding up his hands as if to apologize.

Could this be the man who nearly ran Matt off the cliff?

She turned the ignition back on, put the truck in Reverse, yanked the steering wheel and tried to back up to get some maneuvering room, but she was held tight by the tree, and her wheels spun. She laid on her horn, but saw no other vehicle on the road.

The man went back to his truck and returned, holding a metal carjack, the kind needed to change a flat tire. He walked now with swift, strong strides. She knew he was going to use it to smash her window. Was this guy desperate or crazy? They were on a public road in broad daylight.

She waited until he came close and raised the car jack. He hit the glass of the driver's-side window, which only cracked on the first blow. She had to do the unexpected and fast, run for help. She'd seen a car parked at her childhood home if she could make it there. She dug in her big purse for her phone. Too much in here—couldn't feel it. She had to go now or he'd have her!

In an instant, she unlocked her doors, tried to grab her heavy purse, but he reached for it, too, yanked it and tipped her toward him. She slid away from the steering wheel and clambered out the other side, forced to leave the purse, the phone. She had no illusions he just wanted the purse. She slipped to her knees in the ice-crusted snow, then clawed her way up and raced toward the trees.

27

Char's thoughts ran as fast as she did. She knew this woodlot, this land. She had to head for her girlhood home, the closest house. She'd seen a car there.

But she'd have to cross an open field.

If only someone had driven along the road, but most people avoided Valley View now with the trucks, noise and smoke down by the fracking site.

She tried to thrust branches out of her way, but some whipped her. The untouched snow was thick in here—hard going—the icy flakes making it even more slippery. Her pursuer had to be the man who tried to shove Matt off the cliff. Newer truck is all. And he'd wanted to get her out of her truck.

Gasping for breath, she looked back. Unless he was hiding behind a tree, he had not followed her into the woodlot. Could she have mistaken his intent? Maybe he thought she'd hurt herself, and it was his fault, that he had to get her out of her truck to help her. Or did he just want her purse?

But no. That ski mask, that look in his eyes, which was all she could see…and what had happened to Matt.

Still scanning the ground behind her, she sucked in great gulps of cold air that bit far down into her lungs. She couldn't risk stopping or even circling back to see what he was doing. Stealing her truck? And now he had her purse, phone, her ID. She had to get help, have someone call Gabe, call Matt.

Pulling her scarf up over her head, she started out into the windswept cornfield toward her girlhood home. She could see the car still parked over there. Someone had to be home, but it seemed so far away….

Out in the open, the wind buffeted her, but she bent into it and went on. At least the open field had been scoured by the wind so the snow was not deep. It clung to corn stubble and huddled in the furrows. As she trudged across the uneven, frozen ground, she realized this was the very L-shaped cornfield where Tess had been abducted so long ago—the start of her family's nightmare.

But she mustn't think of that, only who that man might be. She realized she should have told Matt exactly where she was going, but Mandy Lee lived so close and it hadn't taken long. No one but Henry Hanson knew she was going to see Mandy Lee, yet it seemed this man knew she'd be heading toward town. Maybe he'd followed her, waiting for his chance. No way she'd been picked at random.

The man was too tall and sturdy to be Bright Star, though it could be one of his robots, even the one who had cut her hand. It couldn't be Orlando, though she knew he didn't like her—he was with Royce in Columbus. Matt had said Orlando was spending the holiday with his widowed sister somewhere. He was probably still there.

Sam? No, they said he never left the mountain. He walked with a limp and had an old pickup he was trying to repair. It had for sure been a man, hadn't it? Ginger was athletic and tall and that getup hid the person's face and gender.

She heard a sound, a roar. Halfway across the field, she turned and screamed. The black truck was coming at her, crushing stubble, its big tires chewing up the distance.

Matt was working midafternoon in his office with the door open, hoping Char's pretty face would appear there soon, when he took a call from Gabe.

"Hey, Matt. Char's not answering her phone, and I can never get Kate when she's working in the tomb. Please let them know that Grace has gone into labor and I'm driving Tess up there to be with her. I didn't even want to ask Vic where she was before, because I worry about phones being hacked. That Wi-Fi you've got there at Lake Azure is vulnerable—you know that."

"We've never had a problem, but yeah, I know. We advise everyone about security. We have a secure system but anything can be hacked."

"Just to be safe, I'm not going to say where we're going. I'll call you later. It's a four-hour drive where

Vic's got her and the kids placed in a really nice foster family situation. No way I want Tess to drive alone. If Grace's baby comes quick, I'll probably wait it out and bring Tess back with me. I'll be in touch. Let Char and Kate know, okay?"

"Will do. Drive carefully and give Grace our love."

When he hung up, he realized the last thing he'd said sounded a little presumptuous, as if he knew Grace well or was part of the family—or as if he spoke for him and Char as a couple. But he wanted it to be that way, and he had no desire to have a long engagement now that he'd found the woman he wanted. He had to convince Char of that tonight.

But why wasn't she answering her phone?

As the black truck roared at her, Char realized it was too far to go back to the woodlot where the truck could not follow. She ran toward her old home, zigzagging, but the truck was gaining on her.

She fell so hard that all the air was knocked out of her. Scrambling up, gasping, she staggered on, but the man was out of the truck now, running. She didn't have the breath to scream. If only someone back on the road or in the house would see her, call for help. Her old house looked so lonely in the scrim of snow starting to fall, hiding all this.

The man grabbed her from behind, spun her. Panting, too, he did not speak.

She fought hard as the man picked her up and half dragged, half carried her to his truck. She tried to claw at his face, his eyes. Kicking, writhing, she fought his strength.

He swore under his breath and hit her so hard on the side of her head that the world went black.

Matt couldn't understand why Char didn't answer her phone, so he kept leaving voice mail. He tried Kate's cell. Same thing, but he knew why she wasn't taking calls. Grant had joked that he'd be better off sending a carrier pigeon than trying to get her on a phone when she was working in the ancient Adena mound.

Matt yanked his coat on and went out into the hall, told Jen to tell Char to use his cell phone number rather than his office number if she called. He went out to his car and drove to the Mannings'. Her truck wasn't there. Still he knocked and called her name. Nothing. Maybe she'd driven to Kate's, was in the mound with her, but he doubted that. She'd been going to take the gas station courtesy van down to pick up her truck, so he could check on that, but why turn off her phone if that's where she was?

He looked up the number of the Lake Azure Gas Station then punched the number that came up.

"Oh, yeah, Mr. Rowan, but she left over an hour ago," Leo, the owner, told him when he explained.

"She didn't say where she was going, did she?"

"No, sir, but she was talking to Henry Hanson, who was here filling up that new school van."

"Thanks, Leo."

He hit his fist on his steering wheel. *That was it,* he

thought. She'd evidently talked Henry into taking her back up on the mountain to talk to more families about their truant kids. He'd made her promise she wouldn't go alone until they learned more about where Bright Star had gone. He'd told her he'd take her up there himself tomorrow, but that they'd have to work around Clint, who was coming at noon to take more water samples. Matt had given Joe Fencer a cell phone, but he'd bet anything Henry didn't have one, and if he did, they worked in very few spots up on the mountain.

He called Jen and told her he had to run an errand, that he was leaving his car and taking the new truck. Too bad school was out until Monday or he'd have a better idea where to find Henry. He'd have to drive clear up to the Hanson place. Not only could that take time and be risky with this ice-snow mix falling, but he'd have to pass Coyote Rock again. Darn that woman. He'd like to chain her to his wrist—his bed.

Despite the ugly weather, he didn't hesitate. He had to find Char and not only to tell her Grace was in labor and that Tess and Gabe were gone. He needed to know she was safe, and that she would agree to be his.

Char swam slowly upward from the cold, black pool. Where was she? Moving, in a car or truck, that much was sure. Her head throbbed, but when she tried to lift a hand to it, she realized she was tied. Her feet, too. Bound tight, she was lying under some kind of cover on the floor of a vehicle. This truck was climbing, turning. Up Pinecrest? Why? And who had taken her?

She tried to shift her position but she was cramped here. Her mouth was dry. She felt sick, then realized she had some sort of gag in her mouth.

This had to have something to do with Bright Star. He'd taken all those cult members' money. He'd hired a hit man, a kidnapper to get even with her. Maybe they were going to meet him right now, wherever he was hiding out. Maybe he was going to try to trade her to get Grace back—or punish her for helping Grace escape. Though she was sweating, she shuddered as she pictured that horrible waterboarding table.

The ride seemed endless, upward, more turns and then a jolt as the vehicle moved onto bumpy ground. She tried to memorize the turns and ruts, but it was useless. She was dizzy. Scared out of her mind.

The truck finally came to a stop, and the driver killed the engine. He got out, slammed his door, opened hers. Cold air and more light rushed in. He yanked the blanket off her, dragged her toward him by the ties around her ankles, lifted and threw her over his shoulder. He slammed the truck door. In the screech of wind, she thought she heard distant dogs, but it could be her blood roaring in her ears, her terror chattering at her.

Ice pellets and snowflakes whipped around. She thought she might throw up, held like this, her belly bouncing into his shoulder. She tried to lift her head, to look around, figure out where she was. Trees, both drooping pine and leafless skeletons. She saw no house where he could be taking her. They were high, because she could glimpse part of the Cold Creek valley far below.

Dear God, please don't let him throw me off a cliff!

It scared Matt that he was in the new Lake Azure truck that had replaced the one that had crashed and burned. But in this storm, he hadn't wanted to go up Pinecrest in his car, didn't want to go up the mountain at all, but the Henry Hanson hint was all he had.

Before he got too high, he pulled over twice to try Char's cell phone again. No dice, as Royce always said. The traffic on the road was sparse. He'd counted just six vehicles, four going up, two down, all pickups, one with big tires on it. He'd stopped at a small old grocery store partway up to get directions to where the Hansons lived.

"Back in the northwest holler," the man told him. "Down by those veins of black gold, been played out long ago."

As if, Matt thought as he got back in the truck and put the windshield wipers on high again, he'd know where the old coal mine shafts were up here, but at least he knew which direction was northwest, even in this mess. He'd have to drive right into the teeth of the storm.

Char could tell she was being carried into an old mine shaft. The tracks the coal cars once ran along glinted in the glow from the big flashlight her captor held. She caught glimpses of support beams and other entrances to the mine. They went a long way in. She tried to memorize the turns but there were too many. He stopped and put her down on a blanket, then tied her wrist bonds to a wooden beam that, with others, appeared to hold up the roof. As he lit two lanterns, her eyes darted around.

This place reminded her of the inside of the ancient tomb Kate had let her glimpse after they had propped up the parts that had caved in. She saw her captor had supplies in here, a sleeping bag, some stacked cans of food, bottles of water.

At least he hadn't thrown her off the cliff—yet. Was she to be his prisoner here? For ransom, but from whom? No one she knew could pay a steep price, except Royce. Could someone think she was important to Royce because she was important to Matt? No, all her thoughts were going in circles, and her head was hurting so bad that bright colors flashed before her eyes.

"Mmmm!" she protested through her gag, hoping he'd take it out of her mouth.

"Mmmm!"

He came at her with a piece of cloth stretched between his hands. A new gag? Or did he mean to strangle her?

She tried to press back against the wall, but he slipped it down over her head. Ready to struggle and kick, she went rigid in panic.

He tied the cloth over her eyes to blindfold her, then yanked the gag out of her mouth. Shaking, she sucked in big breaths, then had a coughing fit as she inhaled cold air and maybe coal dust, too.

He moved away, then came back to thrust what felt like a plastic bottle in her hands. She heard him unscrew the cap. At least he was taking care of her. If he was going to kill her, why would he bother?

She could only lift her arms partway to her mouth, but she slumped down to take a long swallow of water.

"Please," she said, then cleared her raspy voice and coughed again. "Aren't you going to talk? Please tell me why I'm here and how we can solve this situation."

He didn't answer. Had he gone out and left her here alone?

Matt was terrified. He knew he'd found Hanson's holler, not from the directions the guy gave him but from seeing the school van parked in front of a ramshackle house with a crooked roof almost buried in snow. The place had a stovepipe sticking out a window exuding cloudy air, probably from a potbellied stove. The crooked chimney also trailed a finger of smoke, partly beaten back by the wind. And there was an outhouse, for heaven's sake.

It made Lake Azure seem like paradise. Even more than visiting the McKitricks, this place was an eye-opener to him about how some still lived in Appalachia. No wonder Char had been so determined to get Henry a job. No wonder he seemed so elated to have it, though it was just driving a school van twice a day. But then again, Char had mentioned that Royce had given Henry some extra cash, saying it was "to take care of her."

But, for the first time, he really grasped Char's call-

ing, her drive to help the
up here. Yet the ruin of co
funct mines were near he
bone of the people.

He knocked on the door
it, and his daughter Char
was Penny—peeked aro
wore more than one swea

"How do, Mr. Rowan.
in this storm. Good thing
him and invited him in.

Henry was dressed to
there already. His coat wa
and he still had what m
hands. "Something wron

"I hope not, Henry. Hel
woman with a baby in her
Charlene at the gas statior
afternoon. I thought you m
not answering her phone

"Why, she said she wa
McKitrick, over at the F
Valley View."

Matt sighed. That was
place."

"Right 'cross from that
in, obviously concerned
ful. Clearly nervous, he
in his hands.

"Thanks," Matt said, r

knew mountain visitors should do. "I'll check with Mandy Lee. I'm hoping Charlene's truck didn't run off the road in this weather. There are scattered houses along Valley View on one side but the ridge over the river valley on the other."

"And I can see why you'd worry for that, Mr. Rowan, but she's got her those new tires. You know, Mr. Flemming told me the first day I drove the bus to take good care of Miss Charlene, and I done that, so I hope she's okay."

"Thanks," Matt said again. "I appreciate your help."

Now, he thought, as he headed back to the truck, this would be a replay of his almost-fatal drive down the mountain, except this weather was worse. He had to do it, and without Char to help him this time.

It hit him then that he'd seen, hanging on the wall inside Henry's house, next to a hunting rifle, a beat-up leather quiver with some arrows. But then Char had said Henry had admitted he hunted that way and had even taken some of Ginger's arrows out of the trash.

He almost went back to question Henry about that, but he had to find Char.

2

It didn't take Char long
other way out of this old m
came in. Her captor wen
came back in breathing cl
side must not be far. The
the shaft seemed to have a
though no snow swept in
whistled but not now.

Time seemed a big bl
felt she'd been held capt
The next time he went o
drifted in, but it wasn't cl
to place it. Was he singin
Bright Star was in hidin
and he was talking to hin

When he returned ag
back against the hard wall
a skinny space along one
When he came in view, s

saw he had a cell phone. It didn't look like hers, because she had a bright blue case. But he was using a cell phone up here? Nothing like that worked on Pinecrest! She watched him slide it in his sleeping bag. She couldn't let him know she'd been able to peek. It could mean everything to help her identify him, to get to Matt, or escape.

She pretended to be asleep, her head tipped back against the wall, but she knew she needed to establish a relationship with him. That's what a victim was supposed to do, become a person to the abductor, not a thing—an easily disposable thing.

She stirred as if she was just waking up. Her head still hurt. "Please," she said, "I'm cold. I really appreciate your giving me some water, but do you have another blanket?"

She heard him shuffling around. His footsteps scuffed closer through the coal grit on the floor. He tossed another blanket over her.

"Thank you—again. Should I write a ransom note? My family doesn't have money but—"

"Shut up."

There—he'd spoken, though those muttered words gave her no clue who he could be.

"All right. Sorry. I'm just scared, and my ties are so tight I feel like they're shutting off my blood flow. Just a typical woman I guess, talking too much, feeling helpless, but I'm sure you've felt that way, too."

He loosened her wrist ties—slightly. She was making progress. But toward what? And surely she was running out of time. What was his plan or that of whomever he was talking to on a phone nearly at the top of Pinecrest?

Despite the cold, Matt was sweating when he got out of the truck at Joe Fencer's place. He'd called him on the cell phone he'd just given him. Joe said he'd keep an eye out for Char around Lake Azure. He'd tried not to sound panicked, but Joe had picked up on that, asked him if he could do anything else.

"Not right now," Matt had told him. "I hear that Char dropped by to see Mandy Lee, so I'm going to your place to see her. Thanks."

He didn't want to call Gabe quite yet. He must be nearly there, getting Tess to Grace. Why upset them right now, because he just knew he'd find Char, going off on her own for something, being helpful, being stubborn, being Char. But if Mandy Lee didn't provide answers, he'd call Gabe's deputy, Jace Miller, and fill him in, get his help, however busy he was, covering for Gabe.

When the thin, pale woman came to the door, he saw she'd been crying. That upset him even more, but Char had said Mandy Lee had big problems with her husband. He could see the living room behind her was empty of furniture.

"Mrs. McKitrick, we met at your father-in-law's funeral. I'm Matt Rowan, Charlene Lockwood's friend. She hasn't been answering her phone for over two hours, and I wonder if you know where she is."

"Oh. Why no, sorry. She was here 'bout that long

ago. We had us a nice talk, and she's my friend, too, been helpin' my boy, Jemmie, get to school. But it was spittin' ice pellets when she headed back toward town."

"She drove toward town? You saw her drive that direction?" he asked, pointing.

"For sure, I did. Drivin' careful she was, too, not fast. She's been a godsend to me, for sure, so hope she didn't get stuck on the road."

"No—I just came that way. Thanks, Mrs. McKitrick. She's been a godsend to me, too," he said and sprinted back toward his car.

"I work with kids," Char told her captor as he untied her from the beam, though he left her hands bound together. "Do you have kids?" she asked.

"Yeah. Shut up and eat. Baked beans," he muttered and put a soup-sized can between her hands. When he walked away she tipped her head back. A spoon protruded from the open can and the top of it was still attached—and sharp. Maybe he'd made his first mistake.

"One more thing," she told him after she gobbled some down. Her stomach was cramping and she didn't want the beans, but if she got a chance to bolt, she'd need her strength. He should have told her the jagged tin top was still on the can. "Please, sir, I really need to urinate. Please let me do that with some privacy."

"Later. Eat up," he said in a voice so gruff she knew he was disguising it.

"Not tied like this. Please, can't you loosen my bonds? I'm obviously not going anywhere." He didn't respond so she decided to continue with her small talk. "So how many kids do you have?"

She heard him smack what sounded like a can down on the rough, rocky floor. She tipped her head back and saw him shine a flashlight on his watch. He zipped up his jacket, pulled his cell phone out of his sleeping bag and walked in the opposite direction from where they came in.

It had to be an exit. It must be high enough and positioned just right to pick up a cell phone tower in the valley. This had been well planned. But was it by this guy or was he someone's henchman? What was the plan and was she the bait or the prize?

Her eyes skimmed the area where he'd made a nest for himself in here. Behind the bottles of water and the cans of food, she saw what looked like a quiver of arrows and a crossbow! Whoever this was, he must be the one who had shot at her and Matt and left the messages in Matt's burned truck and at his house. *But why?*

She could hear his voice, carried in by the wind. She couldn't place it, too distant, gruff, sporadic. But then she caught some words. "Yeah, I got the goods. What time you gonna get here?"

So there was a mastermind! Bright Star? Ginger? Surely not Royce.

Being certain his voice stayed distant, Char wedged her can of beans next to the support beam and tried to saw through her bonds by pulling them back and forth against the jagged top of the can.

* * *

Matt drove slowly along Valley View Road. He reviewed what he knew aloud, just to hear his own voice, to try to comfort himself. "She left this way, driving carefully. It was icing up—maybe the snow had started, too. But she had those new tires, knows this area from her early days, from coming out here lately, too."

He scanned both sides of the road looking for tire tracks, skid marks—anything. The fresh snow didn't help. In a couple of hundred yards he'd be at the old Lockwood house that Tess had sold. Maybe on a whim, Char had stopped there, wanted to see the old place, meet whoever lived there now.

Suddenly he saw something, not from his lane but on the other side of the road. His stomach twisted. There were tire tracks, partly muted by new snow, but going off toward the ridge over the valley below. No big trees here to stop anything, but some saplings had been snapped off.

Terror slammed into him. He pulled over and ran across the road to look down.

There, below, not in the frozen river, but near it was a truck that looked like Char's, crumpled and overturned.

He almost screamed her name, but he got back in his car. His hands were shaking so hard, he struggled to move the gearshift. He blinked back tears, then sped to the spot where he knew he could get down into the valley. *Please, dear God, don't let her be in that truck.*

He had to get down there, get down fast—if she

was there. Then he'd call 9-1-1. He parked his car, then slipped and slid down the path he'd taken twice before.

Char had not been able to cut through her bonds, but she'd made a start. She stopped when she heard her captor returning. He took the can away from her, then untied the ropes that yoked her bound hands to the support beam and hauled her to her feet.

She stiffened, pulled back, but he yanked her blindfold down around her neck so she could see. "You said you need to go to the can," he said, his voice gruff.

He untied her feet and pulled her around the corner where the shaft went upward toward where he'd been going. There was an empty plastic bucket. He fumbled with her wrist ties, swore under his breath, but loosened and slid them off her wrists. She was grateful he hadn't noticed she'd tried to saw at them.

"I'm turning my back," he said, his voice still unnaturally gruff. "Counting to twenty, then that's it."

Her numb hands were starting to tingle as the blood rushed back into them. "My hands went to sleep," she told him over his slow counting. "I can't be that fast. Don't you know women need some privacy? If I'm here talking to you, I'm not going anywhere."

She lowered her jeans and squatted, with one hand on the wall to steady herself. But she also managed to look past him where a shaft went slightly upward, toward a gray late-afternoon sky as the sun sank behind clouds. At least the snow had stopped. She knew it was going to be a long, hard night. But he hadn't hurt her, hadn't assaulted her—hadn't killed her. Someone wanted her alive, at least for now.

She hurried to put herself back together. "All right. I'm done. Thank you, I appreciate it."

He snorted and turned back to look at her. Blue eyes. Plain, pale blue eyes like so many around here.

"If you're one of Bright Star's men, you know you're not to harm others," she blurted. "'Do unto others.' Please, in God's name—"

He grabbed her arm hard and dragged her upward, over rough rock and the slippery shreds of coal. She almost fell, but he hauled her on. Had she overstepped about Bright Star? Was this man going to kill her after he'd fed her, let her use the bucket?

She gasped. Cold air slammed into them. It was a cliff. *This must be an old air supply shaft for the mine.* There was a ledge, going both ways around the rock. It was wet, icy, slippery. He was going to throw her off.

"Please, I won't talk anymore."

"Good. Especially not about that cheating devil."

He pointed down and pushed her toward the edge. The entire panorama of the mountain and the hazy, white, distant valley below seemed to tilt, then leap at her. She was going to die. Images flashed in her head. The faces of her parents, her sisters. Maria Whitehorse, kids crying, then smiling. And Matt. Matt!

But he did not push her. He held her hard and gave her a little shake, still pointing straight down with his free hand.

Sucking in icy air, she dared to look down.

The sprawled and broken body of Bright Star Monson lay in a crag twenty feet below. And the snow around his head was stained crimson like a bloody halo.

29

Char went limp as the man dragged her away from the ledge and thrust her into the mine shaft ahead of him. She'd detested Brice Monson, but she'd never wanted that. Had he fallen? Been killed by this man? Would that be her fate? Bodies might never be found there.

She realized this man still could be one of Bright Star's followers, maybe one who planned to take over the cult. But how did he dare to kill "the master"? Grace had said they were all afraid of him.

Terrified into silence, she tried to remain calm. She watched carefully as her captor sat her down and retied her hands and feet.

"He tried to fly. The two-timing bastard said he was going to cast himself off the peak of the Temple and angels would catch him. He was evil and nuts," the man said.

She wasn't quite sure why, but a turn of his head, the tone of the falsely gruff voice or maybe his accusing someone of being nuts—suddenly she realized who he was.

"Get some shut-eye," he ordered.

Yes, she knew that voice, though things just didn't fit.

He did not blindfold or gag her, but her bonds were tight, and she was tethered to the support beam on a rope leash, this time with enough slack that she could lie down. She tried not to cry. But she was so scared. Scared to death.

Once he got down to Char's truck, Matt inched his way on his stomach through snow, ice and shattered glass into the smashed wreck. He'd fallen twice on the way, had to cling to trees to keep from sliding. He wasn't sure he could get back up to the road where he'd left the truck. At least there was no fire this time. Thank God, no Char in the truck, either.

When he crawled back out, the afternoon shadows leaned long in the valley. Still panicked, he stood and trudged around the site. On a whim, he made his way down to the hut with the waterboarding table. He saw someone had wrenched the metal rings off the table and carved away the words. Shuddering, he hurried back out. He saw another dead beaver, but at least Char hadn't been thrown free, or wandered off, or he'd see her footsteps—see her body—somewhere down here. Could she have been ejected on the way down and was snagged in the trees? He blinked back tears and walked along the obvious path the truck had taken, scarred by snapped limbs and saplings, even tire marks partway down before it tumbled, taking everything out with its weight.

He had to get back up on the road before it got dark, look for footprints near where her truck went over. Maybe, like him, she had made it out, been picked up by someone. He'd have to ask at the old Lockwood place to see if anyone saw or heard anything, see if she'd been there. But she would have called him. He had to move fast because the early winter twilight was setting in.

He'd call Deputy Miller and Gabe as soon as he made it back up to the road and looked along it. He struggled upward, grabbing at saplings, crawling, clawing his way. Finally, he made it to his truck. If there had been footprints along the road, the snow and wind had obscured them. He fought hard against the fear this wreck was related to his, that it had not been an accident but deliberate. But why and who? He drove toward the old Lockwood place.

Though she was physically and emotionally exhausted, Char only pretended to sleep. Her brain was in overdrive, and the floor was not only bumpy but prickly, evidently from coal being hacked out years ago. She remembered there was a soft kind and a hard kind, so which was this? Maybe she could rub a ridge of it against her wrist ties. Somewhere on the triple-tied ropes, one had already been weakened by the edge of the tin can.

She found a place that seemed sharp. Though he had a lantern near himself, the shaft was dark enough where she was that she could try sawing her bonds under the two blankets he'd thrown over her. Slowly, carefully, she turned her back to him and moved her wrists back and forth against the ridge. He'd see what she'd done if he untied her again, so she knew she had one chance to try this.

Could she be right about her captor's identity? It really made no more sense than if it were Brad Mason, Orlando, Henry Hanson or Matt himself. Still, instinct and observation told her it was Sam McKitrick.

Her captor did not limp or hunch over or act crazy like Sam. If he'd faked all that, he was some actor. If he really had PTSD and thought she was a spy for the Taliban, or a suicide bomber, as he'd implied the other day, he would have said so. What could he possibly want with her and who did he call when he left her alone?

She recalled what she'd learned from Sam's mother earlier today. Royce and Orlando had tried to bribe Woody to stop his picketing. Were they behind this? When he refused, had they used Sam's anger at his father to get him to eliminate Woody by shoving him off the cliff above Lake Azure—just as Bright Star lay sprawled below, as she might soon be disposed of, too?

Or was this all to silence Matt? When Royce saw Matt had fallen for her, maybe he also saw a new way to keep him in line. If Royce paid the ransom for her safe return, Matt would owe him more than he did now—owe him gratitude, loyalty and silence on the pollution, as she would, too. That wild theory made her feel better, that she would at least be returned alive. Unless, that is, her captor had a double cross in mind and wouldn't free her however much was paid.

She had to stop asking questions. She had to break her bonds and get away.

Matt talked to the owner of the old Lockwood house, who knew nothing and hadn't seen anything strange, though he hadn't been home long, and his wife was sleeping while their toddler took a nap.

More frightened than ever, Matt called Jace Miller.

"The way you describe the scene makes it sound like she slid on the ice, but got out in time, because it's doubtful she could have survived the wreck," Jace said. "Possibly bumped her head, got disoriented, and someone came along and picked her up, took her to a doctor or clear to the hospital in Chillicothe. If that doesn't pan out, I'll organize a volunteer search for tomorrow morning, so—"

"Tomorrow morning? It's freezing out there!"

"Matt, calm down. I'll also see if we can get a heat imaging chopper to fly over the rough or forested terrain at first light if she doesn't turn up. Legally, adults have to be missing longer than this before we can get a full force search or even declare them missing, but with all that's gone on, I'll move on things now. I'll call Gabe and have our dispatcher check with the hospital and local doctors."

"I'm calling Gabe. Listen, Jace, the incident was so much like mine it scares me."

Gabe told him Grace was still in labor and Tess was

with her, but he'd come back to Cold Creek right away. "I'm tempted not to leave a note for Tess about exactly why," he admitted. "She still has flashbacks to her childhood abduction, so I hate to drop this on her. See you soon."

Abduction? That possibility had been lurking in the back of Matt's mind. His pulse pounded even harder.

He couldn't reach Royce, so he tried Orlando, explained that Char was missing and he needed to talk to Royce. "He's unreachable right now," Orlando told him. "Said he was turning off his cell for twenty-four hours to be alone with Veronica. Sorry, but he's acting like he's on his honeymoon and he hasn't even proposed to her yet. But listen, I'm on the road, almost to Cold Creek since Royce had a list of things for me to do before he comes back Monday. I'll put them all aside to help you. Hang in there. We'll find her. See you at the sheriff's office instead of the lodge. Ten to one, it's tied to that megalomaniac Bright Star."

Megalomaniac? Hell, that was a big word for Orlando. The guy must be smarter than he thought, but he appreciated the support.

Matt raced back to Lake Azure. He'd have Orlando, Henry Hanson, Joe Fencer and others of his staff meet at the sheriff's office at first light for a search of the area around Valley View Road, then they'd branch out from there. Clint was scheduled to take water samples, but he'd have to put him off, not get him here right now.

But first, he was going back to the Mannings' house and let himself in with the key he had in his office, check the place top to bottom for Char or more clues. Next, he had to call Kate, though he hated to get her upset. Still, Char could have gone there if she'd hit her head or someone had given her a ride.

He only prayed that whoever had picked her up had helped and not hurt her.

The ropes hurt Char's wrists, but she kept sawing, stretching them as she did. One cord had popped free but the others still held. Still, it gave her hope.

When her right wrist came free, she could have cheered. She flexed her fingers, then unwound several coils of rope from her left wrist and untied herself from the tether. Carefully, hoping her captor wouldn't check on her, she pulled her legs up in a fetal position and worked at untying her ankle bonds. It took her numb fingers a while but not as long as sawing the others free.

She lay, breathing as softly as she could, straining to hear his breathing. Was he asleep? When he moved, she froze. He got up with a groan. Was he going to check on her? If so, she was doomed.

She heard him fumble for something and go out. To use the bucket? No, she heard his booted footsteps go farther than that. His voice floated to her again, no doubt out on that narrow cliff. It must be long dark outside.

Now or never!

She got up, stiff and sore, and tiptoed in the opposite direction, wishing she dared to take the lantern with her.

The passage he'd brought her in was pitch-dark, but

she fumbled her way alon
the wall, hoping he kept tal
wouldn't take a wrong tur
her in, she'd seen some bl
cars used to go on tracks d

When she stumbled her
of the snow, even under the
ing. Stars glittered coldly o
tern, he might be able to
snow. If she did the expec
road, following his tire trac
to walk on a stone ridge w
snow away, as it had where
She was determined to lea
confusing ones.

She forced herself to cl
mine, then edge around th
At least her eyes adjusted
and little pebbles as well
pery. Her stomach went i
little farther. Then, if he ra
for her, she'd go into the w
not straight down. If she c
him before he started trac

She was around the edge
against cold rock when she
ting stones. "Get back in
he shouted. His voice ech
mountain.

"You'll freeze or fall! You'll be free tomorrow! Ransom paid! Get back here, you little idiot!"

When he'd yelled, she knew his voice for sure. Sam McKitrick was hardly the veteran with PTSD. It was such a shameful thing to lie about that. The man would honor nothing, including his own promises about the ransom. She'd be an idiot for going back. She's gotten Grace and her kids out of captivity, and she was going to do the same for herself.

From what she heard, Sam evidently climbed into his truck, started it. Balancing carefully, she edged back around the curve of rock. She saw him turn on his headlights and slowly head down the road.

She inched around to the mine entrance, went to the fringe of trees, making tracks in the snow that resembled playing fox and geese. Then, following one of her own trails, she ran for those trees. She was tempted to go back inside for a blanket, some food, but no. It would take time and he could come back. When he didn't find her on the road, he'd return and look around here. Sam, more than most mountain men, especially since he'd been in the army, was a tracker, hunter and a good shot—even with a bow and arrow. No matter what he said, he might have thrown Bright Star off that ledge and his own father off a cliff.

And she'd just made herself his prey.

30

By nine that night Gabe was at the sheriff's office organizing the volunteer search for Char for the morning. After checking everywhere he thought she could be, including the cabin on the ridge, Matt was relieved to see Gabe had turned the office into a command post. Joe Fencer had come in. Kate and Grant arrived after looking every place they could think of uptown. There was a domestic situation just outside of town that took Jace away, but Gabe manned the phones to pastors, even the new mayor, to activate their contact lists to call in people for the search.

Orlando showed up and pitched right in, suggesting a complete search of the Hear Ye compound. "From what you tell me, Matt, they're the ones who have a beef against her. Maybe they're even hiding Bright Star there, too."

Matt nodded, but that idea really scared him. He kept seeing the waterboarding table in the hut near the wreck of Char's truck. He was losing control, but he couldn't bear to lose Char. If—when—he got her back in one piece, he was going to propose to her right away. No more putting his job first, playing the field the way Royce always had. Not even a fake honeymoon like Royce was evidently on. He wanted Char; he loved Char.

"Listen," Orlando said, squatting beside Matt's chair in the noisy conference room, "I've talked to the Green Tree picketers a couple of times, so how about I go chat up Lacey what's-her-name just to see if they'll help with the search tomorrow. I hear they're at the B and B on the west side of town. But I'm actually going to indirectly question that new husband of hers about where he's been."

"Thanks, fine," Matt told him. "Good thinking." He was grateful for any help and was fast revising his opinion of Orlando. Of course, since Royce trusted the man so completely, he had to have a lot going for him.

Across the room where Gabe had tacked up a contour map of the area, Matt overheard Kate whispering to Grant. "This is the horror of Tess being taken all over again."

Though the moon's sharp smile had appeared through the clotted clouds overhead, it was horribly dark in the heavily treed area as Char started downhill, following the road but staying just off it, unless a ledge or cleft impeded her. The moon was swallowed up again. If only she could find a place to hide out of the wind, go on in the daylight, but she knew that would be risky, too.

Would he find her trail by then? If she fell into a chasm or broke a leg on this uneven ground in the dark, she was doomed anyway, and it was so cold. She wore her coat and boots but had no hat or gloves. She wasn't sure how far or which way she'd have to get down the mountain to get help, maybe at Hanson Hollow or from someone else who lived far up.

As if it was an answer to prayer, a small cave loomed ahead of her, only about twenty feet above and off the road. It looked like a good shelter, but she hadn't walked far enough yet. She should press on, but it was so tempting to rest here until it was light. How long and hard would he look for her, or would he just leave?

She edged in for a moment where it was warmer. But she jolted when she heard breathing. *Snoring?* She put her hand out to grope her way and touched something soft and furry—and warm. She instantly pictured a bear rug her dad once had on their floor.

She heard a snort and a shuffling noise. She gasped and rushed out, her heart beating so hard she heard it pounding in her head. A hibernating bear? Did they ever wake up? If it smelled human flesh or danger, would it wake up? Should she run?

She waited for a few minutes but heard no other sounds so she made her way carefully back to the edge of the road. She continued to follow it until she heard snow crunching under a large vehicle. Headlights slashed across the tree trunks just below her. Sam must be driving back up, since he hadn't found her on the road. The vehicle stopped but left its lights on. She froze.

Afraid to make noise by running, she bent down and watched to see who got out. It was Sam in his new truck, this time without his ski mask on. She could see him clearly in his own headlights, then in the crisscross of another set of headlights, this one from a car that pulled up just behind him. This meeting on the dark, desolate road below was too strange to be coincidence.

The two men, sharply outlined, met between their vehicles. She nearly fell to her knees in shock. Orlando!

Despite the lambent light, she edged closer to the two men, leaning behind another tree trunk. Both motors were running and with the wind, it was hard to hear.

Sam was speaking, lifting his hands, shaking his head.

Orlando's voice floated to her, strident, angry. "Find her… Return her…"

They kept arguing, gesturing. "Find her," Orlando said again. The wind suddenly died down and she could hear more clearly. "His body's still there?" Orlando demanded. "She won't believe he fell just like your dad. You could fry for that—worse than 'You're fired.'"

"I need the rest of what you promised now. Get my kid and head out."

"It's all screwed up, without my part to rescue her," Orlando shouted. "Here's half of what I said, but clean up your mess and get out! It's enough I got you that new truck!"

Char watched wide-eyed, mouth agape, trembling.

Orlando handed Sam a thick envelope, pulled some money back out of it and gestured him away. Standing farther apart, they were shouting louder now.

"Clear stuff out of that mine shaft, too, before she's found and brings someone back here," Orlando ordered. "No ties to you and me and that body down there."

"She doesn't know it's me. He fell, I swear it. God help me, I didn't mean to push my dad, but Bright Star fell after I told him to keep his mouth shut on the bad water. He said he would blackmail Mr. Flemming."

"Get permanently lost, and I mean it!"

"Anyone who stands in the way of you worming into Flemming's fortune, right?"

"Get back to chasing Taliban somewhere out West! That act may save you, because I'll deny anything you say!"

Sam swore at Orlando, stalked back to his truck, bent over to get something from inside, then, standing behind his car door, pulled out a crossbow and arrow. He rested the bow on the top of the open door. Char's first impulse was to shout a warning, but she watched, transfixed as Sam jammed in an arrow and let fly. The arrow struck Orlando's windshield with a *crack,* right in the center, though the glass didn't shatter.

Sam laughed, got in his truck and roared away, uphill, back toward the mine.

Orlando stalked to his car, retrieved the arrow stuck in the glass, then got out a flashlight and examined his windshield.

Two thoughts hit her hard. She had to stop Sam from

taking Jemmie from his mother and grandmother, which meant she had to get back to town fast. And, if Orlando wanted to rescue her to play the hero with Matt and Royce, she'd let him help her. It was a risk but she must get down on the road ahead of where he would drive back. He'd deliver her, if he didn't guess what she'd seen. She'd escaped Sam and a sleeping bear, so maybe things were going her way.

Trying to be careful she didn't trip or make a sound, she went from tree to tree, hoping to get ahead of him on the road—and hoping he could drive them safely down with that crackled, cobwebbed windshield.

Char didn't make it far before she heard a car on that narrow width of road. She tried to make it look as if she was surprised, fleeing, terrified. Only when the car stopped with her pinned in its headlights, did she realize Orlando would have a hard time explaining how he knew to drive up here to find her. He was out of his car, walking toward her. Had she made a mistake? All she knew was she was so cold, so tired, and he was the quickest way back to Matt and her family.

"Char? Char Lockwood? It's Gordon Orlando, Royce and Matt's friend. I'm working with Matt and the sheriff to find you! I got lost somehow on this road up, thinking you could have come up to see one of your students or their families below here, then I went way too far up. How did you get way up here? Come on, I'll take you home. Lucky, Royce sent me back early to work on some things. Are you all right?"

How quickly he'd come up with that story. She realized she'd underestimated him again. Time for her lies now, laced with emotion.

"Oh, thank God! Orlando! Someone kidnapped me. I don't know who or why. I got away, but it's so far down and slippery."

He took off his leather jacket, swung it around her shoulders, took her hand and led her back to his car. "Wish I had a four-wheeler up here, but I'll get you home."

"Oh, your windshield," she said as they approached his car.

"A rock flew up and hit it. It makes the visibility poor, even with the snow stopped. I can use another pair of eyes on the way down. Did—he or they hurt you?"

"I'd better save it all to tell the sheriff. The man stayed masked and disguised his voice, so I don't know who it was," she repeated to assure him. She desperately wanted to ask him to let her off at Hanson Hollow so she could warn Adela to hide Jemmie, but she'd have to give everything away then.

So Orlando became her supposed savior, when all he wanted was to endear himself to Matt and Royce, maybe even demand Matt back off from the pollution probe.

It was torment to be near this man, to pretend to be grateful to him. The driving was hard since the road was narrow and twisting and he had to lean away to peer out where the windshield was not all crazed glass. Squinting through the windshield on her side, she told him about turns if he wavered. Their progress was slow, but her mind was still going a mile a minute. Imagine, working with Orlando when he hated Matt and had risked her life, was probably behind Matt's near death, too. They crawled along with the heater blasting warm air at her, not that she'd stopped shaking.

The moment they came off the mountain, she told him to call Gabe for help. "I'm so grateful you saved me," she added, though the words turned to ashes in her mouth.

He pulled over and made the call, telling Gabe he'd found Char and where they were. She could hear Gabe's voice, repeating that to someone. *Matt? Kate?* Then cheering. "When I was there, others were, too," he said, and dared to smile, evidently thinking he'd salvaged his plan.

Unable to bear his presence anymore, she opened the car door. "After being tied in a cave somewhere, I've got to get out, just feel free." She got out of the car despite the bitter cold, but leaned against it on the far side from him to steady her shaking legs. She did feel free and hoped Orlando was going to remember her words because when she told everyone what really happened he was going to be locked up for years to come.

At the police station, Char hugged Kate, then ran right for Matt, threw herself into his arms and held on hard. Deputy Miller was there, Joe Fencer, too. Over Matt's shoulder, she saw Gabe clapping Orlando on the back. Everyone talked at once, which helped when she whispered to Matt, "I have some things to tell you and Gabe right now. But not here. Now!"

"But you're safe, Char, that's what matters. Thank God for Orlando. Seems we'll have to make him a blood brother in all th—"

"Now, please. A child's life is at stake."

He sobered instantly and motioned to Gabe, but he was taking a phone call. "Quiet, everybody. It's Tess. Yes, Char's fine. Okay. Yes, tell me," he said into the phone, walking toward his office with it. Kate, Char and Matt went, too.

Gabe turned back to everyone. "Grace Lockwood has had a girl she named Lee after the baby's father. And Tess says she has his eyes."

There were more smiles and cheers. But Matt hustled Char and Gabe into his office and closed the door.

Gabe held the phone out. "Char, Tess wants to talk to you."

"Tell her, later. I need to tell you I do know who's behind all this, possibly Matt's accident, for sure Woody's death, Bright Star's—"

Gabe spoke into the phone. "Call you back when I can, sweetheart. Yes, she's fine. Good work with Grace. Glad you can stay in her room." He punched the phone off. "Char, in the squad car on the way back, Orlando said you didn't know who took you, and you agreed."

"Sam McKitrick kidnapped me. His PTSD is fake. And he was working for Orlando all this time, not Royce, I think, but I'm not sure about that. Orlando bought Sam a new truck and paid him off, and I think

Sam's going to take Jemmie with him to head out West. Bright Star's dead at the bottom of a cliff way up on Pinecrest where Sam took him because I think Bright Star was going to try to blackmail Royce or even Orlando over what they called 'bad water.'"

She was suddenly out of breath and strength. She burst into sobs and collapsed against Matt, who held her tight. Both men looked shell-shocked. Gabe swore, opened his office door, went out in the hall and called out. "Jace! Sorry to pull you out of this celebration, but I need to send you to check on another domestic."

The minute Jace came in, Gabe told him he'd have to go up to bring Adela and Jemmie McKitrick down to stay with Mandy Lee at Joe's new house. "I'll explain it all later," Gabe told him. "Watch the bad roads and watch out for Sam McKitrick, who may be armed and is dangerous and will try to take his son, Jemmie, if he hasn't already."

"Wait!" Char said, still pressed to Matt's side with his arms around her as Jace headed out. "I didn't see a gun, but Sam has a crossbow."

Jace nodded grimly and left.

"Matt, Char looks like she needs to go home, wherever that is lately," Gabe said.

"I'll take care of it—of her."

"Go out the back way. Now," Gabe said. "I am going to go out into that celebration, bring Gordon Orlando in here and arrest him as an accessory to kidnapping, and that might just be for starters. I'm sure you'll be hearing from Royce Flemming soon or a brilliant lawyer."

"Maybe not when he hears what Char has to say. I trust Royce, Gabe. I swear he wasn't in on any of this. Sweetheart, let's go home," Matt said.

"I'll need a complete statement early tomorrow morning," Gabe told her. "Let's just pray we get Sam before he gets Jemmie. I'll call you."

Char was amazed how warm she felt just because she was with Matt. It was still cold outside as they hurried around the back and side of the building toward his car.

"Is my truck here, too?" she asked as he put her in the passenger seat and closed her door.

He came around and got in. "It didn't burn, but Sam evidently pushed it off the ravine into the river valley, which I'm sure he was very familiar with from shooting and burying sick beavers for Orlando, who must have known about the toxic water. I'll bet Bright Star had disobedient cult members waterboarded with that water, too, including Lee."

Her fingers shook as she fastened her seat belt, so he helped her. They kissed, holding hands, lingering despite their rush. It had been a bumpy ride so far but she was expecting better. Her truck, new tires and all, didn't matter. Jemmie mattered, Grace and her new baby mattered, Matt mattered. And she was alive and free. A surge of joy coursed through her. She felt almost dizzy with it.

Char told him, "I hope there wasn't a note left behind that said 'Your Fired.'"

"I guess that was Orlando's wishful thinking about me for not backing Royce on the fracking."

"At first, he wanted to get rid of you so he could take your place with Royce, and when that didn't work, maybe he didn't dare to try it a second time. So he decided to become your partner by saving me—after he had me taken."

"We'll explain everything to Royce as soon as we can so he can clean up the toxic water mess."

"At the very least," she said, as a great wave of relief surged through her, "Orlando's going to get a note that says, 'You're Fired!'"

31

"Feeling any better?" Matt asked Char as she came into his kitchen, wrapped in his big terry-cloth robe that came almost down to her ankles. She'd soaked in his tub for almost an hour.

"Achy, exhausted—but happy. And hungry."

"I want to put something on that big bruise on your temple, but your wish is my command. That is, if you like grilled cheese sandwiches. That, and grilling outside in decent weather is about all I'm good at—for food." He put his arm out as if to formally escort her while she scuffed along in his huge slippers. "Your table is waiting this way, *mademoiselle*."

He guided her into the living room and pulled out a folding chair for her where he'd set up a card table for them before the fire. He'd fixed them hot cider toddies and added chips and pickles next to the grilled cheese sandwiches on what appeared to be good china plates.

"I do have some things to recommend me," he said as he seated her. "Even if your life has been in chaos since we met. Char, I'm so sorry you've been through this terrible kidnap ordeal."

She nodded, unable to speak for a moment. Her eyes welled up, but she didn't want to cry. He sat, too, so they were kitty-corner, touching arms.

She'd told him about her ordeal. He'd said he could kill Sam with his bare hands if they found him. But now, she forced all that from her mind.

"This looks wonderful," she told him. "By the way, you do, too. Can't say the same for myself with this blooming black-and-blue eye."

He turned her face toward him, lifting her chin with a gentle hand. He leaned over and kissed her thoroughly, expertly, then pulled back a few inches. "Sweetheart, this has all been so quick and crazy. And it won't get better for a while with Gabe taking your statement in the morning, so you have to relive it all. Later you'll have to testify against Orlando and Sam."

"Royce won't want all the bad publicity for Lake Azure or the fracking. I know you value his judgment."

"He won't change my mind. Not about cleaning up the pollution. And no one will change my mind about you. Remember, I told you he was talking about a wedding, visiting our kids someday when he visited here. And that wasn't a smoke screen. He wasn't in with Orlando and Sam—I just know it."

She nodded but she still wasn't sure. Of course, she'd like to believe Matt was a good judge of character, because he loved her. Right now, he looked so nervous that she almost wanted to comfort him. She bowed her head and said a silent prayer of thanks for her safety—and a plea for Jemmie's, too. Gabe had phoned to say that Sam had taken Jemmie by force from Adela, but Gabe had the Highway Patrol looking for him and Amber Alerts were out in a tristate area.

Matt covered her clasped hands with his big one. A cut hand, a sore head—both felt instantly better when he touched her.

"I'm not finished," he said. "I'd like to think we're only beginning, you and I. If we wouldn't horn in on Grant and Kate's big day next month, I'd ask you to marry me right away and we could celebrate with others later."

Wide-eyed, she stopped with her sandwich halfway to her mouth. "Kate and Tess would kill me if they couldn't fuss over our wedding and help with the reception," she whispered. She rolled her bloodshot eyes. They hurt, too, but once again, she felt suddenly better than she'd felt in days, weeks—ever. This man was serious, and she was so in love.

"Well, you know," she went on, "they say the middle child is always a problem, and that's me." She was surprised she wasn't hungry for food now, just for him. She put the sandwich down. "We could elope, then have a ceremony or a renewal of vows, or at least a party later. But—but you haven't exactly asked yet, so I shouldn't—"

"You should. I like the way you think, Ms. Lockwood. So let me buy you an engagement and a wedding ring to seal our deal, and we can drive to the big city—Chillicothe or even Columbus—to find a judge who marries people who just can't wait. Like you said, we'll do things our own way."

Holding both her hands, he went down on one knee. "Charlene Lockwood, I love you and always will. So, will you have me for your husband, to have and to hold, from this time forth, through good times and bad—"

"We've already had the bad," she said as she pushed her chair back to stand and he rose to meet her. "To have and to hold, yes. Yes!"

He laughed, lifted her in his arms and spun her. Their reflection whirled by in the windows, the happiest, craziest-looking couple with their whole lives ahead of them—together.

At nine the next morning, Gabe borrowed Matt's office at the lodge for Char's deposition. Matt had finally got through to Royce, who told Matt he had proposed to Veronica last night. Matt told Char that he'd wanted to share the same news with Royce, but he'd kept that quiet. He knew Royce would try to take over, throw money at them for a wedding planner and a big shindig. They had vowed to tell no one until after Kate and Grant's wedding.

However, Matt had explained to Royce about Sam and Orlando's partnership. Royce had claimed he was shocked. He was now on his way to Cold Creek, driving himself, no less. But he'd said it was not to help Orlando lawyer up, but to see if Char was really all right.

The better phone call, Char thought, was the one

from Gabe
arrested by
chase near
Jemmie wa
he'd driven
they were b
play the PT
testimony,
yet, Gabe
away that i
Jemmie's r

When C
Gabe, Mat
"Can you
Gabe?"

"Mr. Ro
escape fro

"And ca
steel in her
workaholic
elor willin
see Royce.

After th
walked dov
with a big
all that—a
read Orlan
I could ha
I'll do wh
you—to b

a quick one-armed hug before going back to sit behind his desk, facing the two of them. He gripped his hands so tightly together on the polished wooden surface his fingers went white.

"There's more, Royce," Matt said, sitting in the chair beside hers. "There is proof, though final tests are yet to be made, that the old Hear Ye fracking site is leaking toxins into Cold Creek in the valley below."

Royce clenched his hands into fists. "My foreman or Orlando never said so. You—you've called someone in? Has it gone public? I—I can't believe it. That's all I need around here with the hard feelings about Lake Azure you've worked so hard on smoothing over."

"I put off having the water formally tested when Char was taken. I'd like to know if you want to be part of the testing and recovery effort, take responsibility and charge of that. So far, we have one test and dead beavers with toxins in their systems. Green Tree's only guessing so far, and we can buy more time with them, make them back off while you fix things, because in Pennsylvania, they were accused of polluting water themselves before demanding it be tested. I don't think that's the case here. My guess is that Bright Star knew there was a problem and planned to blackmail you—but made the mistake of telling Orlando, who sicced Sam on him in a phony setup of a meeting. Then Bright Star either fell or was pushed. But that's all the past now. If you—we—work on cleaning it up completely and quickly..."

"I like that 'we' there. Could you be my local liai-

son to work on tl
into the fracking i
though I think it's
country needs to
hostage with forei
Charlene. You se
I'm sorry Orland
replace Matt or ge
admit, Matt, it hu
McKitrick, an em
he insisted, holdi
with his fall off tl
Tears in his e
always knew. Bu
liaising the pollu
the near future—
you see."
"I do see. Hell
so I may just buy
wedding present.
"Maybe," Ch
summers if we c
tain kids here at
for all of them, o
They all stoo
hugged her again
on Matt's. "This
If you don't hire
might. Camp Az
it down at the we

we don't rile our owners, though I bet you could convince some of them to chip right in, Char—if I can call you that. And we'll be sure the mountain kids can swim safe in Cold Creek soon as possible, too."

Char kissed Royce on the cheek. Matt had been right about him all along, not a bad man, just one who needed help and love, like any human being, no matter how rich or poor. Orlando had betrayed him. But surely better times were ahead for him and Cold Creek, too.

One month later

"Oh, this wedding photo of all of us is my favorite," Tess cried, thrusting it in front of Char's face. "What do you think?"

"Love it, but there's another one here I like better," she said, and started sifting through the pile of pictures from Grant and Kate's wedding on the coffee table.

The six of them were drinking leftover champagne from the wedding in front of the low-burning fireplace at Grant and Kate's, who had returned from their honeymoon earlier in the week.

"Wow," Tess said, looking up from a photo to Kate and Grant. "One look at this and you seem even more tan now. That Caribbean sun must be something, even in the winter."

"Oh, these tans are out of a bottle," Grant said with a grin. "I just didn't want flak from Gabe and Matt if we came back lily-white, like we never got out of bed."

Everyone laughed at that, but Matt's narrowed gaze

snagged Char's. S
in Columbus, the
on the hearth rug

"You've got a
interrupting her f
given you good co
of students. Then
you, you blush, s

Tess leaned in
what's that on thi
asked, giving it a
engagement ring
on the slender ch

Kate sucked i
men riveted their
then lifted his ch

"Well," Char s
and pulling it up
my love."

"And the ring
"When? You did

"It was just be
didn't want to up

"As if anythi
his eyes. "We hav
gifts we haven't
gifts from long-
the entrance to t

But Tess and
suaded. As Char

rings off, she explained. "We're holding a special announcement dinner at the lodge soon, and I hope both of you will help plan a reception later."

"Wait. Wait," Matt insisted, and scooted closer on the couch to her. While her sisters leaned forward to watch, he slid both rings on her finger, then took out his wallet and, from behind his driver's license, pulled out a gold wedding band, which Char put on his finger.

Grant and Gabe clapped while Kate and Tess cried.

"So," Gabe said. "How was *your* honeymoon?"

"We do plan one—a formal one, I mean," Char stammered.

"It's continual. And more to come," Matt said.

"So will the reception be at the lodge, too?" Tess asked.

"I think we'll combine a renewing of vows with an outdoor reception at the far end of Lake Azure, where Royce is going to help us build a summer camp for mountain kids," Char told them.

"If we have it outside," Matt said, "we think folks like the Hansons, Fencers and McKitricks might feel comfortable enough to come, too. Casual all the way. I hope to have a couple of horses in our new stables by then, so maybe we can have some gentle rides for the kids, balloons..."

"Well, you always did do things your way, Char," Kate said, getting up to come over and lean down to hug her. "I used to despair you'd ever mind me when Mom went out to work, and, as the oldest of us, speaking for

her, I know she'd
chosen. Will you c
"I did last week
working hard to
Flemming, turn C
Kate disappeare
came back in with
she put in Char's
rice over Matt anc
Everyone laugl
Kate said.
"I knew the si
ter what," Tess sa
hind you when yo
Sam McKitrick. A
phony, Bright Sta
says she thinks th
to move back her
"They're going
left behind," Gabe
Flemming to dem
and Orlando had
"Well—" Tess
"—when Grace g
quite a bit—I stil
day care for free.
two best friends
Tess, Kate anc
entwined arms. C
looked so happy

stood behind their women, arms around their waists in a group hug that Char wished she had a picture of, but she'd keep this treasured moment always in her heart.

The Lockwood sisters had finally all come home.

* * * * *

Autho

I have greatly enjoyed w
Lockwood sisters and the
in life and the men to lo
combine suspense with
ways a lot of suspense in
trials of life.

Fracking worked wel
in this book, since it is a
and literally fractures th
oil. Other kinds of frac
lives—broken marriage
the community that forc
the surface. Fracking is
ting on shale, but there is
and bad results. I have a
fracking in the Midwest

As for the edge-of-Ap
dergrad work (as an Eng
University in Athens, Oh
step of Appalachia. The t
the students/professors/
times deeply felt. When
High School (they have
school), my classes were
thing from deans' and p

As for my inspiration

Cold Creek: Athens, Ohio, was the site for such a community, dating from 1868, now called The Ridges. Some of the once fine, old buildings have become university facilities; however, there are continued problems with trespassing and vandalism. Of course, the rumors are that the old buildings are haunted.

Although there are government and charitable programs to help children and families in Appalachia, simply searching online for "Childhood Hunger in Appalachia" reveals that much still needs to be done. Ninety-one of the four hundred and ten counties are "economically distressed." Illiteracy rates are high, and much housing, as described in this novel, is substandard. In many places there, the past is still the present.

I appreciate the help I received at Cabela's sporting store in Columbus, Ohio, concerning crossbows. I was able to learn to shoot one—just for background information. The only hunting I do is for a good topic for my next novel.

Special thanks to Nicole Brebner, my editor for this trilogy of *Shattered Secret, Forbidden Ground* and *Broken Bonds.* And to my agent, Annelise Robey, and everyone on my support team at my literary agency. I appreciate the help from Dr. Roy and Mary Ann Manning, who live in Chillicothe. And, as ever, to my husband, travel companion, business manager and proofreader.

Karen Harper
March 2014

[illegible] the ore for [illegible]
[illegible] called The Kaiser. Some
[illegible] have become very
[illegible] and producers with
[illegible] the names, we
[illegible]
[illegible] and incredibly pro-
[illegible] as dependent,
[illegible] Childhood [illegible] in
[illegible]
[illegible] ten countries are
[illegible]
[illegible]
[illegible] with the present,
[illegible] regarding
[illegible]
[illegible]
[illegible] for a good table for

[illegible] my editor [illegible]
[illegible]
[illegible] and
[illegible] library many
[illegible] Roy and Mary [illegible]
[illegible] And, as ever, to
[illegible] manager and